T0117038

B. J. Sharp

Early American Migration

Norman Spears

iUniverse, Inc.
New York   Bloomington

B. J. Sharp
Early American Migration

THIS BOOK IS A WORK OF FICTION.
Names, characters places, and incidents either are products of the author's imagination or are used fictitiously. Any resemblance to actual events or locales or persons, living or dead, is entirely coincidental.

iUniverse books may be ordered through booksellers or by contacting:

iUniverse
1663 Liberty Drive
Bloomington, IN 47403
www.iuniverse.com
1-800-Authors (1-800-288-4677)

Because of the dynamic nature of the Internet, any Web addresses or links contained in this book may have changed since publication and may no longer be valid. The views expressed in this work are solely those of the author and do not necessarily reflect the views of the publisher, and the publisher hereby disclaims any responsibility for them.

ISBN: 978-1-4401-8958-6 (pbk)
ISBN: 978-1-4401-8960-9 (cloth)
ISBN: 978-1-4401-8959-3 (ebook)

Printed in the United States of America

iUniverse rev. date: 2/12/10

I would like to thank E.C. for editing my punctuation, spelling, and country English. Without her help the book would have never gone to press. I would also like to say a special thanks to Mr. Robert Naha of Writer Services for pushing and believing in me when everyone else said I was wasting my time. Thanks, Robert; you are one of a kind. A great deal of gratitude goes to my wife Elisabeth who never thought I could do it, but never turned the lights out on me. I hope I have not let you down.

1:

Benjamin Joseph Sharp was the third son of Joseph Benjamin Sharp and is called B.J. Sharp in this novel.

B. J. Sharp's father was born and raised in the territory known today as Vermont. His birth name was Joseph Benjamin Sharp, known to his friends and family as Joe Sharp. He was raised in a very religious family and lived with the word of God all his life. His father, Luther Sharp, was a high ranking member of a religious group calling themselves the Disciples of God. Joe was required to attend church weekly and as he grew to become a young man, he took up duty as a church deacon. His belief in God and the rules he had been taught was strong in all the deeds of his life.

As a young man he met and married Margaret Phiffer. Joe met Margaret in school but as a young boy did not pay much attain to her. As he grew older he began working with a silversmith in Jonesburg, Vermont. One afternoon he was asked to take the buckboard to town to have a wheel repaired. He had a little time on his hands, as the blacksmith told him it would take two hours or more to finish the work. As he was walking down the street, he noticed a woman having a great deal of trouble trying to get her horse to back up a buckboard so she could go forward.

The horse did not like what she was trying to do and was dancing around and rearing up. Joseph watched the scene for a minute and decided to see if he could help. He spoke to the woman and asked if she needed help.

She replied, "Oh please! She does not like the way I drive and wants to do things her way."

With that, Joseph got up into the buckboard and took the reins. With a few quick pulls to the left and right he had the mare backing up. He then guided the horse and buckboard to the street where he stopped and jumped down. As he gave the reins back to the young woman, he thought her face looked very familiar. "Ma'am, may I ask you your name?"

She said, "Thank you, sir! My name is Margaret Phiffer."

"Margaret Phiffer!" exclaimed Joe. "I went to school with a Margaret Phiffer in Greenville."

"Yes, I went to school there."

"My God, Margaret, my name is Joseph Sharp."

"Oh! Yes, I remember you now. What are you doing in town?"

"I'm working for Jake Hathaway over in Jonesburg as a silversmith. Do you still live in Greenville?" asked Joe.

"Yes, I do," said Margaret.

"How would you like to go to church with me next Sunday?" asked Joe.

"Yes, I would like that very much. It would be the least I could do for your kind help."

"Well, in that case, I will see you next Sunday at 10.30 AM," said Joe as he tipped his hat.

He hopped up onto the walkway as she headed down the street. He was very happy he had met a nice looking lady. How she had changed since school days.

Joe kept his word. When Sunday came he was at Margaret's front door at 10.30 sharp. He tied the horse off at the hitching rail just outside the gate and made his way to the front porch. He knocked on the door. As the door opened a woman said, "You must be Mr. Sharp.

Joe said, "Yes, ma'am; I'm here to pick up Margaret for church."

The lady replied, "She is ready, and with that Margaret appeared in the doorway. She looked so young and beautiful. She was wearing a white hat and white dress, carrying a Bible and umbrella. Joe could not believe what he was seeing. There stood a fully grown woman that had taken the place of a giggling young girl on the school ground. He took her hand and cowered slightly as he led her off the porch.

The church was just a short drive from their home and took maybe 30 to 40 minutes to get there. On the way they talked about the old days and some of the kids they could remember. Joe liked her a lot. She was quick to respond to his conversation and seemed to have a gentle, caring nature. Joe was very pleased with her and wanted to know if he could see her again.

She said, "Yes". She would like to go to church with him on Sundays. They arrived at the church, where everyone was pleased to see that he and Margaret had come together. Joe found her a seat down front next to Mr. Miller and his wife. He then sat about his duties as deacon. During services he sat beside the minister and stared at her most of the time. He kept thinking how beautiful she was and how lucky he had been to find such a woman like this in the small town of Grenville. Joe was 25 at that time and guessed her age to be 23 or maybe 24.

After church everyone stood around outside the door and talked for a few minutes. Most of the people had known both of them all their lives and rejoiced in the fact they were now seeing one another. Time went by quickly and the next thing he knew, they had been seeing one another for almost a year. Joe wanted to get married; working for the silversmith, he was making good money. He thought there was no better time than now to ask her to marry him he said to Margaret, "Why don't we pack a basket and go for a picnic next Sunday after church if the weather is good?

"Joe, that sounds like a wonderful idea! You bring something to drink and I will fix the basket."

On Sunday Joe picked a gallon of apple cider from the cellar and cleaned it up. He wrapped it and placed it in a box under the buggy seat. As he left the barn he thought he would through a fork or two of clover in the back of the buckboard for the mare as they enjoyed the day. After church, he knew of a place west of town on a nice hill overlooking a creek and a nice green meadow on the other side. There were some large oak trees at the crest of the hill that would make fine shade for a picnic.

When he went to pick up Margaret, she had a nice basket ready to go. Joe loaded it in the buckboard and helped her up. She looked so nice in a new dress her mother had made. Church did not last long, as it never did in the summer; people had to get back home to tend to their livestock and things around the house. They stayed long enough to speak to everyone. The place Joe had picked was a good mile and half from the church; they could drive that in 15 short minutes.

Margaret was very happy and said to Joe, "What a beautiful place you have picked! I could not have done better myself."

With that they unloaded the buckboard and found a nice shade tree for the mare. After tying her to a small bush nearby, Joe put down some of the clover he had brought along. By that time Margaret had a blanket spread out and the lunch box ready to unpack. Joe had great plans for the day and was going to ask her to marry him. He was a little nervous as he found his place on the blanket across from her. He didn't know if he should blurt it out or wait for just the right moment. They sat for a while and talked about the people at church. Then the subject got around to the English Guard that ruled that part of the territory. Joe had no use for them and spoke up about their arrogant and overbearing ways. He just did not like them trying to take over as if they were back in England; after all, people had left England to get away from their telling everyone what church to go to and how to run their lives. Now here they were back in the middle of a new country and new life with their rules and ways, and Americans did not like it. He did not want to spoil the day with his dislike for them; besides, it was Sunday. However, he did get enough in to find out that Margaret had much the same feeling.

After they had eaten their lunch Joe was so nervous that he could hardly hold his drink without her seeing his hand shake. Looking across the blanket Joe said, "Margaret, I have an important question to ask."

"Joe, we have been friends for a long time and close friends for over a year--what could be so important that I do not already know about it?"

"Margaret, this is important: would you marry me?"

"Joe! Oh! Joe! Yes! I will marry you. You are a good man, you work hard, and I would be very happy to help you make a home and raise our children."

With that Joe got up from the blanket and jumped straight up yelling, "Hallelujah!" He then reached down and took Margaret's hand, pulling her to her feet. He kissed her cheek and then her lips. He moved his hands from around her back and placed them on her shoulders, looking her straight in the eyes. He said, "Margaret I love you very much and I will do all I can to make you a good husband."

"I know you will Joe, or I would not have said yes! Oh, Joe I have to tell my mother!" exclaimed Margaret.

"When do you want to have the ceremony? Let's do it next October. I like the fall colors so much," said Joe.

"Fine with me. I will see what mother thinks about it, and Margaret, we do not have to worry about a house right away. I will ask Father to use the house he built for the farm worker some years ago, if that is all right with you. It's back next to the creek and may need some repairs since it has not been used for a few years."

Joe said that would be fine. "I can fix it up while you girls plan the wedding."

"Oh Joe, I'm so happy! What a day this has been! Let's go tell everyone."

It was mid-June and Joe had a little over a year to fix up the house and get it ready. He worked every day at the silversmith's workshop and every night and Saturday on the house. They were married October 17, 1765. Eleven months later Margaret gave birth to their first son, Joseph Grant. One year later their second son was born, Jimmy Adam Sharp. They were very happy.

Mr. Hathaway had started to repair some pistols for their customers. Joe found out he was good at the work and Mr. Hathaway used him a great deal to finish most of the orders. The English Guard was one of their best customers, but Joe just did not like their manners and the way they would strut around in their uniforms. They thought they were so smart, yet they would overload the breach of their pistols with too much powder and swell the barrel when it was fired.

Joe could make the repairs by heating the breach and hammering it back into place. Sometimes they had loaded the pistol so heavily that the breach would start to crack. When this was found Joe would place a band around the breach to reinforce the damaged area. This one day a Captain Schneider came into the shop to drop off his pistol. The breach was at a point the next round fired from the pistol could blow up the entire breach. The gun was repaired and placed on the shelf with the Captain's name on it. A week or so later the Captain returned for the gun. Joe found the pistol and explained to the Captain it had cost $5.00 to make the repairs and explained to him what was wrong with the gun.

With that the Captain exploded, saying in a deep Irish brogue, "You damn Americans charge too much for your work; besides, you make too much money for the work you do. Besides, I don't like the damn band you put around the breach."

Joe replied, "I'm sorry Sir! It was that or destroy the gun. It was a lot of work to make the repairs; I did it the best that could be done."

"Well, I don't like it and it will disrupt my sighting of the pistol and the balance."

"We have made many repairs that way and never had any of them go bad or complain."

"Well, I don't like it and I don't like you either; I should take the pistol and give you a good shelling with it."

"Well, that would be your choice, sir. You see, I have one also."

With that Joe took the $5.00 dollars and the Captain stormed out the door.

Joe was mad. His whole day was messed up from this smart know-it-all Englishman. He went home that night still mad as he could be. He told Margaret about the problem and how his dislike for the Englishman had grown. "I would like to take my family and move out of this mess before there is a war and I have to kill some of them."

Margaret said, "I don't know, Joe. Moving would be hard on us with two little ones."

"Yeah, I know," replied Joe", but if we stay it could mean death for one or all of us."

Margaret said, "Let me think about it and talk it over with Mom and Dad".

"Good! I will speak to some of the church people and see what Mr. Hathaway has to say about the idea."

A week or so later the subject came up again after supper. Joe said he had spoken to Mr. Hathaway and some of his friends from church about the move. Joe said they had heard a lot of people were moving into the central part of the country, far away from the English control. That there was plenty of land to be had and it was good farming.

"What did you learn from your dad and mother?" Joe asked.

"They said they did not like it and did not want us to leave; they said if something were to happen to one of us they would never forgive themselves. However, whatever you and Joe decide will have to do. It's your life and you both are still very young."

After a few weeks it was decided that they would make the move. They would take a wagon, four mules, one saddle horse, some chickens, and two ducks. With help of some friends and Margaret's dad and mom, everything was made ready in the winter of 1772 to be ready to go in the spring of 1773. Joe figured it would take three months for the journey if they left on the first of April. They hoped to arrive sometime in June or July, with still enough time to get some shelter before winter.

They did not have a lot of household items to take with them, so they had planned to load the wagon with as much food for them and the animals as they could carry, bed clothing, a few tools and personal belongings.

April 10 was the day they would leave. Joe did not like it because it had been raining a lot and he knew trails and the ground would be soft, but if he waited much longer winter would overtake them before they were settled. It was a bright spring morning as they climbed aboard the wagon. The boys were fighting about which side of the wagon each was going to ride on. Margaret was crying as they pulled away from their parents and friends they had known all their lives. It was hard to leave your loved ones and go somewhere you knew nothing about. They were saying goodbye to people they most likely would never see again.

After four days on the trail they had not covered a lot of distance. The wagon had been stuck twice and Joe had to unload some feed barrows to make the wagon light enough to pull out of the deep mud. Thank God, after five days on the trail one drum of corn was low enough that he could transfer the full drums around to allow him to lift the drums back and forth. However, all of this took time and a lot of work, and Margaret was worried that maybe they were not going to make it.

After 14 days on the trail Paul, the oldest mule of the four, came down with a bad foot. Joe had been using him as the lead mule on the right side of the team, but he was limping so badly he had to pull him out and put the saddle horse in his place. Two days later they had stopped for a midday rest and to see how the mule was doing. He was not limping as much since he could now rest the foot a little more. As they were enjoying their food a man and his family pulled up behind them. He had two wagons and two older kids, a girl and a boy. They introduced themselves as Adam Higgins, his wife Grace their son Peter and daughter Sue Ann, on their way to Ohio. Joe asked, "Why are you moving to Ohio?"

Adam said, "We have heard there are a lot of people moving to Ohio and to tell the truth, we didn't like the way England has taken over everything."

Joe said, "Believe it or not, that is the same reason we left. I had to leave before I killed one of them or they killed me."

Adam said, "I'm a blacksmith and I figure there should be just as many horses to shoe in Ohio as there were in Vermont. Therefore, we packed up and left."

Joe said, "I'm sure glad to hear you're a blacksmith; I have got a lame mule tied to the back of the wagon. Maybe you could have a look at him."

Adam said, "Yes! I would be glad to do that." They walked over to the back of Joe's wagon and Adam picked up Paul's front foot. He pulled a knife from his belt and picked a big stone out of the center of the mule's foot. Adam put the foot back down and said to Joe, "I don't think the hoof is spit. I think it is just tender. If you don't have to work him too soon I think he will be fine. Joe said, "Thank God! No, I can leave the horse on the team for a few more days.

"How far west had you planed ongoing, Mr. Sharp?" asked Adam.

"I don't really know", answered Joe. "You see, I'm a silver-smith and do some work on guns now and then. I would stop anywhere I can find people land, and water."

"Well, since we are going the same way do you mind if we trail along?"

Joe said, "Not at all! It will be nice to have the company. I think Margaret is getting tired of talking to me, anyway."

After they finished the meal it was back on the trail. The road, if you could call it that, had dried up some; however, the creeks and rivers were still running high and were hard to cross.

Seventeen more days found them in middle of the Ohio territory. On the 23rd day of June they had just crossed a shallow creek with lots of nice wood for the nightly fire. The next morning Joe planned to saddle his horse and take a ride down the creek see what lay south of them. After a half hour in the saddle he began to see signs of more wagon tracks; another fifteen minutes, and some buildings came into view. He continued on down the trail and found himself in a small town. My God, this was more buildings and people than he had seen in two months. Looking around he spotted a barber shop pole. He turned his horse toward the hitching rail, reined in and stepped down. After all, it had been a few months since he had a good hair cut and a shave. Why not now?

As he walked in, he nodded and said, "How much for a haircut and a shave?"

The man said, "Two bits".

Joe said, "Thank you", and sat down.

It wasn't long until he had finished the shave and said to Joe, "I guess you are next."

As he sat down in the chair the man said, "You are new in town."

Joe said, "Yes, we are just passing through. Another fellow and I camped up river last night and I thought I would look around before we move on this morning."

"Where are you headed?" asked the man.

"Well, I don't really know", answered Joe, "just about any place where they don't have Englishman running the place".

"Well, we sure don't have any around here, and you are sure welcome. We need new people to help us grow."

"What is the name of this town, sir?"

"Old Town," replied the man.

With that Joe held out his hand and said, "My name is Joe Sharp."

"It's good to meet you, Mr. Sharp. I'm Leo Smith and I'm the barber here in Old Town."

"It looks pretty new to me," said Joe.

"It is the oldest town west of the Ohio River", answered Mr. Smith.

"You mean that river I spent three days getting across is the Ohio River?"

"Yes sir, it sure is," replied the barber.

"Well bless my soul; I guess I'm farther west than I thought."

"Well, sir, you are just a little bit over halfway through Ohio territory."

It looked like a pretty good size town as Joe untied his horse and pulled himself up into the saddle. He thought he might as well take a ride down the street to see what he could see. As he traveled south his eyes caught a church and a stable not far from a sign that read Mary's rooming house. A jail, two trading posts, and a saloon also lined the street. It was getting close to mid-day and he thought he had better ride back to camp before they sent out a search party for him.

When he arrived everyone was glad to hear what he had found. Joe said to Adam, "Why don't we stick around and see what else this part of the country has to offer? We have a good campsite here, with plenty of everything we need, and there are two trading posts in town that if we run low we can buy things."

"I do not see anything wrong with that," replied Adam. "Let's have a bit to eat and we both will go have a look at things before it gets dark."

"Fine with me", said Joe as he seated himself on an old log lying next to the fire.

After a mid-day meal they turned everything over to Adam's son and the women. Joe said as he rode off, "We will do everything we can to be back by sundown."

The ride took them a half hour to reach the city. There was not a whole lot to see, so it did not take long to ride up and down the street. As they came back up the street Adam said he would like to talk to the stable operator. A tall, slim man came from behind some buggies parked in an overhang just to the right of the main building. He said as he drew near, "Can I help you gents?"

Joe spoke up, saying, "We hope you could tell us a little bit about your town. My name is Joe Sharp and this here is Adam Higgins. We are new around here and thought we would stop and ask you a few questions. We are camped a few miles up the creek from here."

"Glad to meet you fellows. You say you are just passing through?"

"Well we don't know; we looking for a new home. We are from up East and are trying to get away from the English," Joe said.

Adam spoke up saying, "I didn't see a blacksmith around here. Do you think you could use one?"

You betcha! I have to take my horses all the way out to Wily Owens' farm, about five miles west of here, to get them shoed."

"Who would I see to be able to buy some land here in town?"

"Well, sir, that would be Huck La Chance. He runs the Huck trading post just down the street. Huck was one of the first settlers in Old Town so he claims most of the land around here."

"If a fellow wanted to build a house or shop where would you get lumber?" asked Joe.

"You would have to see Mr. La Chance. I think he brings a load or two in from Dayton every month or so."

"Well, I sure enough want to thank you, sir. I think we will ride over to the trading post and speak with Mr. La Chance. Buy the way, sir, what did you say your name was?" Joe asked.

"I'm sorry, sir, my name is Phil Casey and if I can help you fellows in any way, stop by any time.

There was a man leaning over the counter with paper and pencil in hand when Joe and Adam walked in. As he turned to meet them, he heard the door open. "Howdy gents, what can I do for you?" he asked, speaking with a French accent.

Joe walked up on the right side of the man and Adam went to the left. "Well sir, Mr. Casey over at the stable said you might know something about some land for sale around here," Joe said.

"Well, could be. How much land are you looking for?"

"Oh, I don't know," Joe said", maybe an acre or two, depending on the price."

Adam spoke up, saying, "Yes sir, I'm looking for about acre myself".

"Well, you fellows have come to the right place. I have got one acre, more or less, between the stable and the jail that I would sell off. Then there is two and half acres just south of me, about three hundred yards, that I could let go."

"How much do you want per acre?" asked Adam? I will take 50 cents per acre said Mr. La Chance.

"Do you have anything outside of town?' asked Joe.

"Yes, I do! I have 400 or more acres five miles up creek."

"I will bet you that is where we are camped," Joe said.

"Could be, sir. You see, the trail going west goes right through the middle of my land."

"Well, would you sell any of that land?" asked Joe.

"Sure would," said Mr. La Chance.

"How much would you take for 100 acres of that up north land? Asked Joe.

"I would have to get 20 cent an acre for it," replied Huck.

"I'll tell you what, you keep all this under your hat and we will talk to our wives and speak with you again in a day or so."

"Fine gentlemen, but don't wait too long. I have to sell to the first fellow that has the money. Thanks for stopping by."

As they turned to leave Joe spotted the hard candy bowl. He said to Adam, "I think we had better take the boys back some candy and maybe a bar of that sweet smelling soap over there. The girls might like that."

"That is a good idea," replied Adam.

It was getting close to dark as they got close to camp. Joe said, "I think I smell supper cooking."

"Well, I sure could use it," replied Adam. I'm as hungry as a bear."

As they pulled up next to the tool wagon the kids came running out to greet them. "What have you got in that bag?" asked Jim.

"Oh! I don't know something Adam bought for his wagon wheel that has been squeaking."

They unsaddled the horses, rubbed them down and gave them some hay. Joe had left the bag tied to his saddle as he threw it up over the back end of the wagon. The boys were slapping and grabbing at the bag to see if it was what their father had said it was. Joe Jr., being the tallest, said, "It sure doesn't smell like anything to fix the wagon with."

"You boys leave that bag alone; we can talk about it after supper. Now go wash up!"

The girls were glad to see them and wanted to know how they had found things in town.

"Well, let us get washed up and we will sit down, enjoy this nice supper you girls have cooked, and tell you all about it." With that they were off with the kids to wash up. The girls had fixed a big pot of beans, corn bread, and potatoes. As they sat there Adam spoke up saying, "Girls, I think Joe and I have found our new home. The town name is Old Town. It is not a big town but it is growing and it has about everything we need. There is a man that runs the trading post by the name of Huck La Chance. He was one of the first men to settle Old Town and owns most of the land around here. He has agreed to sell me a lot next to the stable to build a blacksmith shop and Joe some land south of town to build a silversmith shop. He said he owned the land where we are camping. Joe wants to buy a hundred acres somewhere around here to build his home and farm on."

Grace spoke up saying, "It's all right with me, but where will we live until we get a house built?"

Joe said, "I have thought about that. If I can buy the land right Adam, and I can build a pretty nice log house by the time winter sets in. We can live in the wagons until then. In the spring we will build a house and blacksmith shop in town for Adam. Mr. La Chance said they are bringing in lumber from Dayton and with all of that we should be able to build a pretty house and shop. Margaret what do you think about all of this? You have been sitting there not saying a word. What do you think?"

"It sounds great to me and whatever Joe wants to do, I will be there to help. We have to live somewhere."

"Well, it is settled then. We will ride around tomorrow and find the best place to build a house and mark off 100 acres of land with good timber. We will then go back to town and inform Mr. La Chance we will take it."

The next morning the two men rode north for five minutes or so, and then turned west. As they traveled west the land began to rise, not hilly, but you could see the earth had a climb to it, the further they got away from the creek area. After a half hour of viewing the landscape they came upon a hill--not a high hill, but a nice big change upward from where they stood.

Joe said, "Let me get down and look around here for a bit. I kind of like the way that sits. What do you think about a house next to that timber line up there?" Joe asked.

"Not bad," replied Adam. "It's got a nice view of this meadow we are standing in, and it wouldn't be far to bring logs to build with."

Joe said, "You are right. I think we should take it. Let's ride up to the crest and see what lies back of the timber line. This should be far enough," Joe said. As he dismounted he pulled an ax from his rifle holder to cut an X into the side of a big tree. He said to Adam, "If you will take my horse I will walk off 4034 yards and then cut back toward the creek. I will mark that spot. If La Chance agrees to sell this section to me I will mark the other two corners." Joe was pleased with what he had found and thought he would bring Margaret by to look it over before any building was started.

It was mid-day by the time they rode into camp. It was too late for business in town today, so they would save that until to-morrow. Joe told Margaret all about what they had found. As she listened she said to Joe, "It sounds a lot like the place where you asked me to marry you."

"Margaret, you are right! The only difference is the creek runs on the left side of us and the place where I asked you to marry me the creek ran in front of us. I never thought of that. Then you think it will be all right if I ride into town tomorrow and buy the land?"

"Joe, I think it will be just fine. I'm sure we can find a place on a hundred acres we can agree to build a home."

As they rode up in front of the Huck Trading Post Mr. La Chance was just coming out to load some supplies in a wagon for a man and his wife. Adam spoke up, saying, Sir, we have come back to talk to you about buying those lots here in town."

"Well, I'm glad you fellows want to settle here in Old Town with us. I'm sure you are going to make good citizens."

With that they dismounted and went inside to finish writing up the Quit Deeds. Mr. La Chance said, "I will write you fellows a bill of sale and a Quit Deed here at the post, but you will have to take them over to Howard Palmer, who lives next to the last house as you come into town. He will have to record the sales."

Joe spoke up. "Sir, we rode up yesterday and marked off what we believe to be 100 acres of that land north of town. I would like to buy that land also."

"Very well! Did you run into Old Skinner Joe up there?"

"No, we did not see any one," explained Adam.

"Well, I thought I would let you know. He has been trapping and hunting up there along the creek for years. He does not own any land but I think he has built a cabin somewhere along the creek. If he gives you any problems just let me know."

"No, I don't plan to give the old hunter any problems."

"Well, I want to welcome you to Old Town and wish you well. By the way when do you plan to build a blacksmith shop on that lot?" Huck asked.

"Well, I don't really know right now," said Adam. "We have to build Joe and me a house this summer so we have someplace to spend the winter."

"Well, whatever you need just let me know. I can get lumber in here in about three weeks. So put your orders in early and I will take care of it."

With that they thanked him and walked outside. They sat down on the edge of the porch and Joe said to Adam, "What do you think?"

"I think we had better work our tails off and try to get in out of the cold for the winter.

"What about money, Adam, can you hold out until you get the shop up and running"

"Oh yes, I planned on two years before I would have a new shop up and going. What about you?" Adam asked.

"Well it will be close but I think we will be all right. Maybe I can get a gun or two to fix and help out a little bit. Well, we can't get any of this done sitting here on this porch."

On the way back to camp they talked about moving camp up where they would be building Joe's new home. Adam spoke up saying, "I think we had better find out if we can build a spring or dig a well so we will have water before we move away from the creek. Without water we have nothing for the livestock or ourselves. Well, let's deal with that tomorrow."

The next day the two of them spent the best part of the day looking for a spring. Joe thought the best place to look would be east of the spot he wanted to build the house. It was rocky and hilly in that direction and he thought the creek had to have something feeding it. They walked east toward the creek for a mile or less when Adam spotted a waterfall coming from some rocks running southeast toward the creek. It was just what they were looking for. They could dig out a hole that would fill with fresh water for a spring house. Later they could dig out below and build a pool for the stock. Yes, they could now move the camp north and start to build.

On July 20, 1775 Adam Higgins and Joseph Sharp started a new life three miles north of Old Town, Ohio. The two men had a need to leave the crowded east coast area and help settle the great country west of them. They were young, strong men, ready to face anything life had to offer. Both of them were early American business men with a chance to build a better life for their families.

In 1776 Joe Sharp sat by the fire place with his pipe and a cup of warm tea the midwife had made for him. Margaret lay in a bedroom down the hall, waiting to give birth to a new baby. Joe stared at the flickering flames in the fire place as his mind took him back to the trip west and the two years it had taken him to build a new home and business. The war between the English and Americans had gone well. The country was in a state of happiness and was still celebrating the great victory. The country was now a free nation with no ties to England. God had blessed it with the rights to stand alone. People were moving west in great wagon trains and business for Adam Higgins and he was all they could take care of.

October 25, 1776 Joseph Benjamin Sharp came into this world crying hard enough to be heard all the way to Old Town. Joe jumped from his chair and headed for the bedroom, but was stopped at the door. Someone said, "Not yet, Mr. Sharp; we have a little more work to do before you can see your new son."

As Joe walked back and forth in front of the warm fire Grace Higgins came in and said, "Joe, you are a lucky man. You now have three sons to help you through life."

"Thank you, Grace! I hope they grow up to be fine men."

As Joe walked into the bedroom Margaret was smiling as he knelt down beside their bed. Tears ran down his face, and she knew he was going to give thanks to God, so she reached out with her left hand and took his hand. *Oh God! I thank you with all my strength, with all my love for this wonderful gift you have given us. Bless him, Oh God, with wisdom and strength. Thank you for caring for my wife during this trying time. Amen."*

With that he rose and walked to the other side of the bed where he could see his new son in the arms of his mother. He said, "Margaret, I love you and I thank you. I will leave you so that the two young men outside the door can see their new brother."

With that he took one long look and walked out the door. Joe and Jim walked past their father and asked, "Is he big yet? Can we play with him?"

"No. Not yet," their father replied, somewhat in surprise.

Life had been good for Joe Sharp; his business was finished, at least for the time being. He was pouring shots, selling gun powder, repairing guns, and now and then he would repair a sliver cup or bowl for someone. He had been making a lot of gun stocks and planning to make barrels for the cap and ball gun. He had added on to the gun shop twice and built a stable out back for his buckboard and mare he drove to work every day with.

He and Adam, along with a few of the townspeople, had gotten together and built on to the church just east of town. They went to church every Sunday and while the boys were in school

Margaret and some of the other women would help out the old and sick at the boarding house. It was a church thing and she could leave young Ben with his father over at the gun shop every day. There was just too much to do at home with washing, ironing, and her garden work.

A few days before Thanksgiving 1780, Margaret became sick. Joe had the doctor come out to see her. He spent almost an hour checking her out. When he came out of the room he sat with Joe for a few minutes around the fire place. He said, "Joe, I think she has got scarlet fever. With you and the kids here in the house, I think we should move her to the boarding house and let the girls there take care for her. It would be the best thing we could do until we know for sure. The girls can put her in a room by herself and I can stop by every day and check on her. If she does not have the fever we can have her back home in a week. In the meantime you and the boys will be safe."

"What in the world am I going to do with three growing boys and work every day?"

Doc said, "Do you know Millie Ward?"

"I have heard of her."

"Why don't you ask if she could help out for a few days? Her husband was killed a couple years back somewhere up in Dayton. I think she could use the work. I will stop by and ask her if she would stop by the gun shop and talk with you."

"My God, yes!" replied Joe. I will be glad to pay her if she can help."

"Well, in that case, I will stop by on my way into town and speak with her. In the meantime, I do not want the boys in her room, and do not eat or drank anything that she has used. If I can get her moved tomorrow to the boarding house, I would like for you to have the bed stripped and wash everything down. I want the boys outside in fresh air as much as you can. Don't let the boys go to school until next Monday. We just have to pray she is going to be all right.

The next morning Millie showed up at 10 am to speak with Joe. She said she would be happy to help out and that Joe did not have to pay her. Joe said, "No, I will not stand for that. Doc said we should strip all the beds and wash everything down real good. Air the house out every day from first light to dark."

Millie said, "I can do that, and I will take good care of the boys, Mr. Sharp".

"I know you will, and if they get out of hand just let me know."

"Well, it is settled I will see you tomorrow bright and early."

It was Thursday morning and Millie showed up at the house at 7 am. They got Margaret out of bed and sat her up in a chair on the porch. It felt good to get a breath of cold air. Joe brought the buckboard around where they made her a bed using most of the bed clothing she had been lying on for the past two days. Joe waved goodbye to Millie and the boys and headed to town. He drove like he had a buckboard load of eggs, watching every rock and bump in the road.

They soon arrived in town where three people, along with Joe, carried the bed Millie and Joe had made into the boarding house. Margaret was placed in a room where she could look outside. The ladies who had helped carry Margent in said to Joe, "It would be best if you changed your clothes as soon as you can and wash your hands and face with soap and water. Joe agreed and said he would change into work clothes as soon as he arrived at the gun shop.

Joe did as he was told and spent the day with work he had planned. He was uneasy and was sick worrying about Margaret. He closed the shop at 5 pm and saddled a horse. He thought it would be best to let the buckboard sit outside for a day or two. He arrived at the boarding house in a few minutes, tied up the horse and went in. Someone told him that Margaret was not doing well but thought the trip to town had made her nervous. They were hoping she would improve with rest. Joe asked if he could see his wife.

"Well, I don't advise it, but if you must, I will get you some clothes. In a few minutes she was back with pajama and top and a pair of socks. She said to Joe, "Go into that room and change your clothes".

Joe returned in a few minutes wearing what she had provided, along with his boots. She said, "No! Mr. Sharp, you will have to take off the boots and just wear the socks."

Joe began to know things were not right with his wife. The ladies said the Doctor had just left and that he had given her some more medicine and they were to try and get her to rest.

Joe went back and removed his boots. As he came back into the room, the lady took him to Margaret's room. As he entered the room she whispered, "Please do not get her excited and try not to stay too long. We are trying to get her to rest."

Joe thanked her and made his way across the room to Margaret's bed. She looked to be in a daze and her neck and face were covered with a reddish rash. She turn to face him and the first words from her mouth were, "How are the boys?"

Joe replied, "They are fine. I have asked Millie Ward to help me take care of them until you get better." He stayed a few more minutes and told her to get some rest; that he would stop by tomorrow and see how she was doing.

Joe was worried as he left town. He stopped by the church to pray. As he knelt before the pew and clasped his hands tears ran down both sides of his cheeks. *"Oh God! I have come to you this day to ask forgiveness for anything that I might have done to bring this sickness on my wife Margaret. I ask you, Oh God, do forgive me. I ask you, Oh God, to take away her pain and give her life. I know she belongs to you and that you have loaned her to our home to bring forth new life and care for us. Please spare her life and allow us to love and care for her. I praise your love and ask that you hear my prayer. Amen."*

He allowed his horse to walk as he headed north for home. He was a beaten man. Without Margaret he had no drive. It just seemed he had no will to go on. He also knew the boys needed him and that in case God took her, he would have to go on. He also needed to stop by the blacksmith shop and talk to their old friends Adam and Grace Higgins. "God, I pray that no one else gets sick."

It was dark as he rode into the barn yard and put his horse away. He could see the light through the kitchen window as he made his way to the house. Millie and the boys had waited dinner so they could hear what was going on. He didn't know if he should tell Millie in front of the boys or wait until he could speak with her alone. He said to himself, "No! The boys are old enough to understand about their mother, and Ben will figure it out with the help of the other two boys."

Millie had prepared a good meal with the help of the boys, showing her where everything was. Joe washed up and sat down to eat. Jim spoke first, asking, "Why did you leave mother in town?"

Joe said, "Your mother is very sick and we had to leave her there to get some rest. She will be there for a few days until she gets better."

Joe asked, "What if she does not get better?"

"We cannot say that," replied his father. "She is in God's hands."

"Can we go see her?" asked Jim.

"No, she is in quarantine and must remain there until she is better."

Ben got up from the table and went to bed. He closed the door and took off his shoes; he lay there crying until he went to sleep.

The next day Joe stopped by the blacksmith shop to give Adam the news and to see what he had to say about everything.

"Joe I don't need to tell you this because you have heard enough about this sickness. All we can do is pray. She is in God's hands."

Joe left the blacksmith shop and rode over to the church. He prayed for almost an hour. His mind took him back to the first time he met Margaret--how young and pretty she was. How happy they both were the day at the picnic and how he felt to ask her to marry him. Sixteen years had passed since that day, and they were the best part of his life.

Sixteen years--where did they go? Life had been on a fast pace. It seemed only yesterday since his marriage, yet he had started a home in Vermont, had three sons, traveled 700 miles across the Ohio River, and built a new home and business. Margaret had been the start of his life; Margaret had been the reason for his life. Full of life beauty and strength, she brought the day to life and ended it with love and laughter. Why would God take such a wonderful gift?

Joe untied his horse and pulled himself to the saddle. He felt tired and drained, and the day was just beginning. He rode on through town and out to his shop, where he put the horse in the stable and went to work. Just before noon the doctor came by to speak with him. He said, "Joe I was just over there to see her and I'm afraid I do not have good news. I'm afraid she is not going to make it."

Joe thanked him and asked if he could see her one more time.

"Joe, I don't like it! You have three boys and a housekeeper at home. If you go see her you must take a bath before you leave the boarding house." Joe agreed and finished the day.

He rode over to the boarding house, tied the horse up, and went in. The caretaker met him and said, "Mr. Sharp, if you must see her you must change your clothes."

Joe agreed and was led down the hall to a room. Here he found clothing the caretaker had provided. He quickly changed and stepped outside. He was taken to Margaret's room where he found her in a deep sleep. The room was well lit and what was left of the day's sunlight came through the window in a golden ray. Joe looked at her and said, "Margaret I love you very much; please don't go". He knew his words could not be heard and clasped his hands and began to cry. Big tears dripped to the floor as he stared at her face, swollen with a reddest rash. Some of the rash looked as if it had begun to form scabs. He turned and made his way back to the room to find a big tub of hot water, soap, and towels. He removed all his clothing and took a bath as he had been told. When done he dressed himself and sat on the box at the foot of the bed, placing his head in his hands, and cried. There was no one to see or hear him. He was alone. He didn't know how long he had sat there when he heard a knock on the door. "Mr. Sharp, are you all right?"

Joe said, "Yes, I will be right out".

He untied the horse and pulled himself into the saddle. He was confused for a moment and did not know which way to direct the mare. He didn't want to go home. He had no home without Margaret. He knew he had to tell the boys and Millie.

It was dark when he got home. He put the mare in her stall and went to the house. Millie was sitting at the table when he walked in. She could tell by the look on his face; there was no need to ask. However, she could not keep from asking. "Is she any better?"

"No!" Joe replied. "She is worse. I don't think she will make it through the night."

"Do you want anything to eat?" Millie asked.

"No, I have no place for food." He then washed his face and hands and went to bed.

Next morning was Friday and he did not have the heart to go to work so he thought he would take a walk down by the spring house. When they built the farm the first building to be built was the spring house. It sat in a little bit of a valley. The water came out of the rocks behind the house. They had dug a hole in the ground, making a pool, and filled it with large rocks. The spring house was then built over the pool. Water running down the hill toward the creek made a nice relaxing sound. Just above the stream was a knoll with some big flat rocks along the edge. As you came down the path the large tree provided shade for the rocky knoll. It made a wonderful place to just sit and have a cold drink of water. This morning Joe thought it would be a good place to talk to God and be with the blue jays as they went about their life. He sat there for a long time when he heard footsteps from behind. He turned to see the doctor coming down the path. Joe knew he would not come this far with good news and braced himself to hear his words.

The doctor spoke. "Joe, I do not have good news. We lost her early this morning. I did all I could do. I knew she was gone last night when I went by to see her."

"Will you go with me to tell the boys?"

Doc said, "Yes, I will; I don't want to but I know it needs to be done".

They walked in silence back up the path past the house to the barn where the boys were cleaning out a stall. Their father said, "Boys, the doctor has bad news. Your mother passed away this morning at 6 am."

Ben cried out, "No! Dad, he does not tell the truth." With that he turned and ran back into the barn with Jim close behind him. Joe ran to his father, grabbing his leg, and began to cry. After a few pats on the head Joe turned and ran to the house.

Joe said to the doctor, "What do we do next?"

The doctor said, "Joe it is Friday and I don't want to keep her until Sunday. I think because of the disease we should bury her tomorrow. I will go back to town and take care of the gravesite."

Joe said, "Fine, what time do you need me tomorrow?"

The doctor said, "Joe, around eight meet me at my office."

"Fine, I will see you then. Would you be kind enough to stop by Adam and Grace Higgins' place and give them the news?"

Doc said, "I will be glad to do that; it's on my way to the office".

Saturday morning Joe got dressed in his best clothing and headed for town. He stopped by Adam and Grace to speak with them. They were just finishing their breakfast and offered Joe coffee. He took them up on it and talked for a while. As he got up to leave he told them he and Doc was going to bury Margaret at 10 am. They both said they would be there.

Joe said, "No!"

Grace said, "We will not hear it. She was our friend and we will be there to say goodbye."

With that Joe headed over to the doctor's office. The doctor had made arrangements on Friday afternoon and the early morning to finish the burial arrangement. There were not many people there: Joe, the doctor, preacher Williams, Adam, and Grace. As they sang and prayer was offered, Joe could hardly stand alone. Adam stood just a little closer than normal just in case his legs gave way. When the service was over Joe returned back to Adam and Grace's home where they talked about Margaret and made plans for the boys.

It was decided that if Millie wanted to stay on he would allow her to take care of the boys and the house. He would bring the two older boys to school every day and allow Ben to remain home with Millie until he was old enough to attend school.

Jim and Joe took the loss of their mother very hard. Joe could hear them crying at night. Millie reported to Joe that the boys spent a lot more time down at the barn or someplace else. Millie tried to see that they had little jobs to do around the farm but knew there was not much she could do to lessen their grief.

Time passed by and the two older boys went back to school with their father each day. After school they worked over at the gun shop. This kept them busy from early morning until late at night. Ben worked the garden and helped around the house. When they had time to play, it was riding their stick horses and playing marbles. It seemed Ben would win most of the games they played, and Joe and Jim would pick on him. Ben was smart, quick, and taller than the other two boys, so since they were outmatched they always tried to get even with him. Ben soon started to school with his brothers and would work at the gun shop. Since he had done most of the farm work, Joe and Jim would see that he got the dirty jobs like cleaning the barn and cleaning up around the shop.

They were all growing up and turning into young men. The gun shop was now a factory making gun parts and making guns and gun stocks. Joe had also added to the building. It was no longer a little store selling balls and powder but a well-run business known in the whole state as the place to order your gun supplies. Since Joe Sharp was a very religious man, every Sunday was spent in church. It was his belief to give one day a week back to God. He would have to be very sick not to load his family up in the wagon and head off to church each Sunday.

2:

It was September 15, 1802, and Benjamin Sharp had just left his gun shop for the day. He was feeling a little guilty for leaving early, but he knew his wife of 7 years was very near the time she would go into labor and give birth to their third child. Ben was very anxious and wanted to be on Doc Henson's doorstep at the first sign of life.

Mary Sue arrived at 6:30 p.m. that very evening, kicking and screaming. You could tell by the sound of her cry that she was ready to push the world aside and do things on her own.

Ben had waited nearly all day, and could not stand it any longer. He told Doc Henson he would like to see his wife and new baby! The Doctor said, "Yes, but let's give the midwife, Mrs. Johnson, a few more minutes to clean things up."

Ben walked back and forth on the front porch, thinking how grateful he was to God to now have a daughter. It seemed like a lifetime before the doctor came outside and stated, "Ok, you can see them now!"

Ben entered the bedroom to find his wife Elisabeth, cuddling his new daughter like a small doll in her arms. He felt mixed emotions as he stared briefly at his wife and child. He felt proud to have been a part of this wonderful God-given event, but he also felt ashamed that as a man he could not bear more of the pain. Elisabeth looked a little pale and weak, but her normal wonderful smile was the same. Ben leaned over and kissed her, saying, "God bless you and thank you for such a beautiful daughter!" He wanted to hold the new baby but knew now was not the time. "I love you!" he said. "Please get well. I will run down the hill and tell the Owens' the great news, and leave you in the hands of the midwife. Please get some rest."

Ben was so happy he had married Elisabeth. He had met her at a church picnic twelve years ago, and more or less fell in love with her on sight. The Sharp family did not want him to marry, feeling Elisabeth was not good enough for him. Her mother had died in childbirth, and her father turned her over to his sister and went west. Neither the sister nor Elisabeth had heard from him since. Ben did not care about her past. She was pretty, kind, and caring. When they were going together, they would walk down by the spring house on his dad's farm, and listen to the water running over the rocks. On the warm summer nights they would talk and dream about how life would be for the two of them. Ben told her how he would like to go west some day. She, too, liked the idea and thought that maybe she could find her father if they did.

Elisabeth was a good wife; she was easy to talk to. She always came to Ben and got his views on things she could not understand. Thomas Joseph was born two years after they married, and Elisabeth had proven to be a good mother. Two and a half years later Benjamin Joseph Jr. came along. Elisabeth and Ben wanted a girl but were grateful to God that Ben Jr. was healthy and full of life.

A few years after Ben and Elisabeth were married; Ben's father had died and turned his business over to Ben and his two brothers as equal partners. Joe was the oldest and took charge of the shop. Ben, being the youngest, was given most of the hard jobs. He did not like it but did as he was told. As he grew older and learned more about the business, they found he was very good with his hands and could do things quickly, with excellent quality. He was smart and had good ideas. His brothers began to show jealousy knowing that he had been blessed with talent they did not have. They were afraid he might take the business from them.

The brothers belittled Ben, and bad-mouthed him to try and keep him down. They had fought against his marriage to Elisabeth, but Ben kept her at his side and their love for one another grew even stronger. The two of them belonged together, and Ben and Elisabeth knew it. Ben was a strong man and would not let anyone come between him and his family.

He was a tall man and could pick Elisabeth up in his arms like a doll. She loved him dearly, and wanted to make him happy and give him many children. The pain of childbirth was nothing if it gave him a son or daughter to call his own.

Today, Ben was so happy he did not bother to use the steps to get off the porch, but instead jumped to the ground in a run down the hill to see Nate and Helen Owens. They were his good friends and neighbors, and he needed to let them know the good news. Nate and Helen lived two miles down the hill in a beautiful green valley. He covered that two miles in record time, only to find them enjoying their supper. Ben jumped to the porch and grabbed the door in a run.

As he entered the room, Helen knew by the look on his face that something was wrong. "Ben! Ben, what is the matter?" she exclaimed.

Somewhat out of breath, he responded, "We have a baby girl!"

"My God Ben, why didn't you tell me sooner? Is she all right?" inquired Helen.

"Yes! The midwife, Mrs. Johnson, is with her at this time and she is doing fine," replied Ben.

"Well, I'm going to see if I can help. I'm sure the boys need something to eat!" said Helen. With that, she pushed her chair back from the table and left the room. With Helen gone, her girls began to pick up and clean off the table, while Ben and Nate retired to the front porch with a pot of coffee. Ben was beginning to return to normal but was still somewhat out of breath.

Nate and Helen enjoyed a good life. Nate's father had been a blacksmith for 50 years, and had built a nice business shoeing horses, along with building and repairing wagons. He was known for miles in any direction as one of the best metal men in the state. His father had passed on three years ago from a heart attack, and had left Nate and Helen a 100-acre farm and the blacksmith business. Nate had grown up in the business and was very good at it. He had learned well and began to grow his business as more people moved into Ohio.

The two men sat on the porch, not saying much. This had been one of the best days of Ben's life. About the only thing that was troubling were his brothers, with whom he had had words with that very afternoon about a gun project he wanted to build. Why not tell Nate about the project and see what he thought? He sat there for a long time before words came to him how he should talk to Nate about the project.

"I have had a great day, except for my brother. Joe and I had words this afternoon," said Ben.

"What about?" asked Nate.

With that, Ben opened up and stated, "Nate, I want to build a long rifle that will fire more than one round. I want the gun to reach out 800 to 1,000 yards. Joe thinks I'm crazy, and won't let me use shop equipment or my time to build it. So we fight a lot."

"Well, what are you going to do?" inquired Nate.

"I don't know! I have been meaning to ask you if you would rent me a small space in the blacksmith shop where I could work when I have time." replied Ben.

"No," exclaimed! Nate, "I will not rent you anything, but you can have the space you need, and there does not have to be anyone who knows what you are doing. It will not cost you one penny!"

Ben could hardly sit still. Nate continued, "I have got some space in the back I do not use very much. It's kind of dark, but I guess you can hang a couple of lanterns up for light."

"Thank you! Thank you! It is wonderful to have a friend like you. I don't need much: a work bench, a stool, a lathe, and a vise. I will bring my tools and lock them away each night in a box. I thank you, and I will never forget this!" said Ben.

"You do whatever you need to do, and come and go when you get ready," responded Nate.

"Ok! I may come down this weekend, and build a work bench, and tool box," replied Ben. With that, Ben thought he had better get back to the house, and see how his girls were doing.

He thanked Nate one more time and quickly, headed back up the hill to the girls. It was dark as Ben arrived at the house. He found everyone doing fine. Helen had fed the boys, and they were in bed. Elisabeth and the baby were asleep, and Mrs. Johnson and Helen were enjoying some coffee. Ben said he would walk Helen back down the hill, and thanked her for taking care of the boys. He made it back up the hill feeling good about the day, and blowing a little steam from his mouth in the September night. Mrs. Johnson was going to spend the night, and a bed had been set up in their bedroom so she could be close by.

Next morning, Mrs. Johnson had eggs and bacon on the table, and the boys were off to school. Ben went in to see Elisabeth and the baby before he left for the gun shop. He found her with more color than the night before, and she was so happy that Mrs. Johnson had to almost tie her down to keep her in bed one more day.

Ben reported to the gun shop and told everyone about the new baby. His brothers, Joe and Jim, were very happy with the news, and couldn't wait to tell their wives. The shop was busy building the new single shot Sharp long rifle they had patented last year. They had over 200 orders for the gun. It was a big improvement over the Kentucky long rifle, which was the old cap and ball gun. This new gun was a bolt action 44/40 with a large lead bullet. The bolt action meant you could fire the rifle twice as fast as the Kentucky long rifle, but you had to reload it every time it was fired.

Ben did not like the rifle. He thought the round was large, and the powder charge was not big enough to give that large bullet the range he felt the gun should have. It was not a lot better than the Kentucky gun as far as range, only faster, but it was Jim and Joe's idea, and it had been patented under the name of the Sharp Gun Company. This meant he was entitled to one third of the profit. Business was good, but it did not make it right in Ben's eyes. He was making triggers as the day wore on, and was very fast and good at hand finishing. He spent the day at his work bench, but in the back of his mind he was planning how he would build and work at the blacksmith shop.

It was Saturday when he got up the next morning, a bright, sunny day. Elisabeth and the baby had rested well. Mrs. Johnson would try and get her up to walk around a little bit today. Ben thought he would take the boys out behind the barn and cut a walnut tree that had fallen last spring. It would make beautiful gun stocks, and he could store them in the blacksmith shop to let them dry out.

He told his son, Tom, to harness the mules to the small wagon while he got the tools together. He had some 2x6's and 4x4's left over in the loft which he had from some repairs last year, and he thought he could make a work bench and tool box out of them. Some of the things he needed were a plane, a hammer, nails, a wood chisel, and wood vises. He also needed a saw and an ax to cut the tree. By this time, Tom had the mules ready, and they loaded the wagon. It was just a short distance to the back of the field where the tree had fallen.

Ben propped the tree up and placed a limb under it so it would not pinch the saw. Then he and the boys cut off four logs, 30 inches long. The tree was 18 inches in diameter, and each log could make four gun stocks if it split clean. They worked at their task for two hours or so, loaded the wagon, and headed for the house. Ben thought he would stop by the house to see how Elisabeth and Mrs. Johnson were doing. They were doing just fine. Elisabeth could now walk around the table a few times and then sit down for a while. He stayed a few minutes, and told Mrs. Johnson she could go home Sunday or Monday--whichever she felt best.

Ben and the boys pulled up in back of the shop to unload the wagon. As they arrived at the shop they found Nate with three horses to shoe and a wagon bed to repair. It was already 10 o'clock. After they had put everything away, Ben told the boys to take the wagon back to the barn and let the mules out to pasture. "I'm going to give Nate a hand for a few hours and don't give your mother and the new baby any problems."

He then set about seeing what the wagon needed in repairs, and found three boards in the bed that needed to be replaced, and the side board stakes were broken. Nate had lumber storage in the loft above the shop, so Ben picked out what he needed, and went to work. It was not long before the wagon was ready for service.

Since Ben was not that good at shoeing a horse, he started to build his work bench. The two men worked together most of the day. When he packed up his tools and got ready to go home, Ben had been thinking most of the day about a lathe. He knew his brother Jim would never consent to him taking one from the shop, so he had to find one somewhere else.

He had heard that there was a man over in Clearwater that had a lathe for sale, and it was driven by a windmill. He said to Nate, "I think I will ride over to Clearwater next Saturday, and see a man about this lathe I heard he had for sale. Is it all right with you?"

"Well, for God's sake, man, yes! You do what you have to do to get your project started," replied Nate.

"Well, I was just thinking, the darn thing is wind-driven, and I have not figured out how to mount the fan and shaft so they cause you the least amount of trouble," said Ben.

"Ben, don't worry about it. You go check on the lathe. If you like it, we will get it mounted!" responded Nate.

With that, Ben said, "Good day" and headed up the hill to the house.

Saturday was a pretty day, and Elisabeth was up and about. The baby was beginning to move about a little more when she was awake. The boys were busy cleaning out the barn, so Ben thought it would be safe to leave them for a few hours. Clearwater was 15 miles downriver, and he could make the ride in three hours on his mare. He had heard the man's name was Joe Morris, and he had been using the lathe to build wagon spokes. He saddled the mare, and gave the boys last-minute instructions, before heading downriver.

He arrived in Clearwater and set about finding out where Mr. Morris lived. He thought since Mr. Morris had been in the wagon business most of his life, a good place to start would be the blacksmith shop. The man said yes, he had known Joe Morris for more than 40 years, and that he lived just west of town on High Street. Ben thanked him and headed west.

It was just a short ride to the west end of town, and he didn't have any problem finding Mr. Morris' house. You could see the windmill fan sticking up next to his work shop out back. Ben tied the mare at the hitching rail and went to the front gate and yelled, "Is there anyone home?"

In a minute or so, a lady stepped onto the porch and asked if she could help. Ben inquired if this was the Morris home, and the lady said, "Yes". He then asked if her husband was home, and she replied, "Yes, I think he is out back somewhere. I'll see if I can find him."

A few minutes later, a man in his late 60s, well built, and wearing a striped blacksmith cap, stepped onto the porch. Ben identified himself, and asked if he still had the lathe for sale. The man said yes and asked Ben if he would come in and sit a spell. He slipped the ring off the gate post and went up on the porch and sat down. Ben asked what kind of condition the lathe was in. Joe replied, "It's in fine shape. I just quit making spokes last year, because there is a fellow over in Big Town that had set up an operation that was turning them out by the hundreds and selling them for a lot less than I could make them."

Ben further inquired, "Tell me about this windmill operation--does it have enough power to turn the lathe when working?"

Joe responded, "Yes, if you have good wind, it has more power than you need. However, I put some counterweights on the main drive, and once it is turning, if you step on the counterweight peddle it will keep turning for a minute or so."

Ben asked, "Can I see it?"

Joe replied, "My wife is fixing something to eat, and we would like for you to stay and have a bite"

"Yes sir, I could do that, and I'm much obliged. It was a long ride down here this morning", answered Ben.

"After we eat, I will take you out to the workshop, and we will have a look," said Joe.

Mrs. Morris had set the table for three. She had fixed fried chicken, mashed potatoes, green beans, and hot coffee. How could a fellow that had just spent three hours in the saddle turn that down? Mrs. Morris wanted to know if he was married. Ben said yes, and that they had three kids with the new baby last week. "Oh! That is great, and is your wife doing well?" asked Mrs. Morris.

"Very well, thank you," replied Ben.

Then Mrs. Morris stated that they had two boys, both gone. "One lives here in town, and the other one lives in Dayton, Ohio."

After eating and some small talk, Joe and Ben went out back to check out the lathe. The old man kept a nice clean shop, and the lathe was mounted on a work bench. The windmill shaft came down through the roof and mounted on the end of the lathe shaft. A series of step belts that would allow him to change the speed of the lathe were mounted between the drive and cutting head. It was a 48 inch lathe, which was more than enough for what Ben wanted.

"How much do you want for it?" Ben asked.

Joe replied, "I would like to get fifty dollars for everything. That includes the cutting tools and the windmill."

Ben exclaimed, "That's a deal! I will come next Saturday and take the mill down and load it up."

"There is no need to do all that. I will have it ready for you when you get here!" said Joe. With that, Ben said goodbye and rode off.

It was a long ride home, and it was starting to get dark. Ben was happy that he had found the one tool that would allow him to work on the project and not involve his brother. Besides, Jim did not know he would now have a lathe all his own. He stopped by the blacksmith shop and watered his horse. He pushed the mare hard and got home a little sooner than planned. The lights were still burning as he pulled up in the barnyard. He led the mare to her stall and brushed her down, throwing a blanket over her back for the cool night air; then he headed for the house.

Elisabeth was beginning to be her old self and had prepared something to eat for the boys. They were glad to see their father and wanted to know how the day had gone. He told them the whole story, and that he and the boys would take the wagon next Saturday and pick up the lathe. He helped clear the table while the boys went off to do homework.

It was a good time for him and Elisabeth to just sit and talk. After all, he had not had her to himself for two weeks, and he missed talking to her. Elisabeth fixed some hot milk, and they retired to the bedroom, where they would be close to the baby. Ben told her all about the problems he had been having with Jim, and how Nate had let him have some space in his blacksmith shop to build his gun. He explained how discontented he was with Jim and the shop and wanted to know what she thought about moving west after he was done with the gun project. She said, "Ben Sharp, I love you, and when I married you I gave my life to you and our family. Whatever you want to do, I will be by your side. I like it here, and the boys have school, but I feel you know best for us all. If I was to stand in your way, it would be unfair to you and cause us more problems. No, I will not do that."

"The boys will have to be home schooled, Elisabeth, and it's going to be hard on us for the first winter, and maybe the next. What are we to do about a doctor if someone was to get hurt or sick?" inquired Ben.

"We will do the same thing we do now: doctor ourselves. I will pick up some books from school, and don't worry about me; we will be fine! Just tell me what you want and need, and I will try to get it together," stated Elisabeth.

"Well," continued Ben, "It's like this - I do not want us to go by ourselves. So if I can talk Nate and Helen into going with us, we will plan the trip, okay?"

The next day was Sunday, and being the Christian man Ben was, he felt the needed to thank the Lord for the new baby and his wife's health. Elisabeth did not want to go. She still felt a little weak to ride the wagon to town and it was too early to take the baby out just yet. When he got back Elisabeth had fixed a nice dinner for them. She had even found some canned apples and made a pie. After dinner Ben built a fire in the fireplace; the September nights were beginning to get a little chilly. They had some pie and a glass of warm milk and talked about the trip at great length. They decided why not take a walk down the hill to see the Owens? Elisabeth said, "We cannot stay long because I do not want the baby out to long in the night air." It would be Elisabeth's first time out of the house, and Helen would be glad to see the baby. So they wrapped up Mary Sue, put her in a two wheel cart Ben had made, and off they went.

Nate and Helen had just finished dinner and were glad to see them. Helen was all excited about the baby, and could not get over how she had filled out in the two weeks since she had seen her. The men walked out to the shop, and Ben told Nate about his trip to Clearwater and his finding the lathe. He explained the size and the shaft coming through the roof. Nate said, "Ben, I don't care. I told you to do as you wished, and a hole in the roof is not a place to make a fuss."

"Well, in that case, I will take the boys and the wagon next weekend and pick it up. I don't think I will be back in time to unload the wagon, so can I leave it parked out back until Sunday afternoon?" asked Ben. Nate said that would be fine, and he would give a hand when he got back.

Nate had a bench where the fellows could sit while he shod their horses, so they sat down and had a talk. Ben told Nate his conversation with Elisabeth last night and again this morning, about going west. Nate said, "Ben, it's strange you would bring something like that up, because I have been thinking about it for years. Ohio has been talking about statehood now for two years. Yes, I think it would be good to go west. When do you want to go?"

"Well, I would like for the baby to be at least a year old before we put her through such a trip. So let me do some thinking about all this, and I will get back to you," replied Ben.

Nate said that was fine, and that would give him some time to talk to Mr. Adams about buying the farm and shop. He had been after Nat for years, ever since his dad died, to buy the place.

"What about Helen--would she go along with a trip like this?" asked Ben.

Nate replied, "Yes sir! We have talked about it ever since Dad passed, so she will be delighted to hear we have talked."

"Well, let's stop at the Government Land Office and see what they think about land in the Midwest. I don't want to go too far west, because it is too dry for farming. What about this Saturday?" inquired Nate?

"No, I cannot go this weekend because I have to go get the lathe."

"Sounds good to me," responded Nate. "We will go next Saturday. I will close the shop for a half day, and we will check it out. I will meet you at your house around 9 am."

"See you then", said Ben.

Just a little before 9 am Nate rode up to the gate. Ben was ready; his mare was tied at the rail outside the fence. It was just a short ride over to Old Town. By going to town every day Ben knew right where the land office was. It was a small place next door to the post office.

They tied the horses off at the rail and went in. A man was sitting behind a table in the center of the room. He got up and extended his hand, saying, "My name is Joe Bray. I'm with the U.S. Government Land Grant office. You are Mr. Sharp and Mr. Owens?"

"Sir, we are! We would like to speak to you about a land grant west of the Mississippi."

"Fine, please sit down." With that he motioned Ben and Nate to a couple of chairs next to the table. "I'm glad you fellow stopped by to talk to us. The Government is very interested in getting people to move west. You say you are interested in land west of the Mississippi."

"Yes sir! That is what we have been thinking about."

"How far west of the Mississippi were you thinking about?"

"Let's say 100 to 200 miles."

"Mr. Sharp, that is fine. However, we have a problem. You see, sir, most of the land west of the Mississippi does not belong to the government. Therefore we do not have the authority to grant you a land grant. However, we have received letters from the government where they may be trying to buy the land. Now they have said that in the event that a party or parties come along that would like to take a chance on the government getting that land, we can issue a preliminary grant. That means that if you stake the land off and farm it for five years, if the Government buys the land after the five years you can have title."

Nate asked, "What happens if the Government does not get the land?"

"In that case you would have to work with the French Government."

"What do you think Ben?"

"I don't care if we get it from the French or the U.S. Government. For all we know the French could provide the same kind of grant."

"You are right. I know the U.S. Government wants to get people into that part of the country as soon as possible and is willing to make a good deal. I don't see why the French would not want the same thing."

"In that case we will take it. How much land are we talking about, sir?"

"That would be 640 acres per homesteader. Now this does not mean that after five years if land is available next to yours that you can't buy it. You can buy all the land you want."

"Mr. Bray, do you have any maps of the area?"

"No sir, we do not. As you should know, this is new territory and we have never mapped the area. I have been told by scouts and people that have come from that region that if you follow the wagon trail just south of Chicago it will take you to Saratoga, where the ferry crosses the Mississippi. From there on I have no idea."

"What do we need from you to make this official?"

"Well, not much. If you will stop by the office next week I will provide you papers that pretty much say what we have talked about."

"We thank you very much, and you just got yourself two settlers." With that they rode back to the shop where Nate opened up for business. Ben stayed around the rest of the day and gave Nate a hand while they went over small talk about the trip. After that he said he thought they had better get the boys to bed so they would be ready for church tomorrow morning.

The week went by quickly, and it looked like Saturday was going to be a nice day. Ben loaded the wagon with two bales of hay and a couple of ropes. He got the boys out of bed, and they headed down to Clearwater to pick up the lathe. The boys were all excited about the long wagon ride and wanted to know if they could drive. Tom was 11 years old and could do a pretty good job driving a two-mule team so he needed all the time he could get looking at the tail of a mule if he was going to drive a four-mule team west. Ben Jr., on the other hand, was 8 years old and could drive but soon got tired. Ben thought this was a good idea and would give them a little training for when they got ready for the long trip west. They left at 7 a.m., thinking that should get them down to Clearwater about midmorning.

Mr. Morris was sitting on the front porch when they pulled up. "I thought you would be coming this way today. Why don't you pull around back? We will water and feed the team while we have some dinner! Is that all right with you boys?" asked Mr. Morris.

Ben said to Mr. Morris, "This is my oldest son, Tom, and this is the man of the house, Ben Jr."

Mr. Morris responded, "I'm glad to meet you fellows!" Mrs. Morris had a nice lunch prepared, and they set about some small talk. Mrs. Morris wanted to know how the boys liked having a little sister. They said they liked it a lot and thought she was pretty.

After lunch, they went out to the shop to prepare to load the lathe. Ben got up in the wagon and broke open one of the hay bales. He spread the hay on the wagon bed, so the lathe would have something soft to ride on. They loaded it between the other two hay bales. The mill and fan were slid in long side, and Tom tied it all down. It was now loaded and ready to go. As they pulled around front, Mrs. Morris appeared on the porch with a bag of cookies and wanted to know if the boys would like them for the trip home. Ben Jr. went up to thank her and thought he would be in charge of how many everyone got.

The trip took a little longer than planned, so it was dark when they pulled into the barn. They unhitched the team and brushed the mules down. They would unload tomorrow, after church. Mom had a big pot of beans and cornbread for supper and was glad to see them.

Sunday after church, Ben hitched the team up and headed down to the shop. Nate figured he got back too late last night to unload and headed out to the shop when he saw the wagon coming down the hill. The lathe was not that heavy, and two men could manage it well. They sat it down on the bench Ben had built to find out if it would fit. It looked like the mill shaft would go through the roof in the right place. After cutting a hole in the roof where the shaft would go, Nate got up on the roof and with a rope, pulled the fan and shaft up, while Ben pushed. They lowered the unit through the roof, while Ben went down to the lathe to line it up. Within a few minutes, they had it in place. Ben disengaged the clutch before Nate untied the fan. Ben Sharp now had his own lathe! It had been agreed that Nate could use the lathe anytime he needed to work on a wagon spoke. The shop was now complete!

Ben thanked Nate for the help, and took the team back to the barn. Monday would come soon enough, so he thought he would spend the rest of the day with Elisabeth and the kids. He told Elisabeth about how much the boys had enjoyed the chance to drive the wagon, and what fun they had enjoying the cookies on the way home. Elisabeth told Ben she would like to go into Dayton just as soon as she felt the baby was old enough to leave with the midwife. She needed to order two or three bolts of sheep skins or whatever they had. She wanted to make sleeping bags for everyone. "I think we should have one for each of us, including one for Mary Sue. I also need to get material to make a few more quilts. I don't think we have enough for the cold weather out there. Helen will go with me; she needs a lot of things for her people, also."

Ben said that was fine and asked if she could pick up a few things for him when she made the trip. She said yes, if he would give her a list and explain what he needed. They spent the afternoon in small talk and just enjoying one another presence.

Monday morning as he headed out the door for work, Ben was feeling good. After all, he had found a lathe, spent some time with his wife, and talked about a lifelong dream, only to find out his best friend wanted the same thing! He did not know what he would talk about at work. He did not want anyone to know about his second life. That really is what it was. He was now building the gun of his dreams and planning a trip that would put him in a whole new world, but he couldn't tell anyone--at least, not just yet.

Therefore, his day was spent talking about the new Sharp single shot rifle. It was a major improvement over the old cap and ball, and orders were coming in by mail every day. Joe and Jim were thinking their profits should be good for the next two years and were talking about some new lathes and equipment. Ben was just glad to bring the day to a close and get home to his other life.

After supper Ben helped Elisabeth clean up and said he thought he would go down to the shop and work on the gunstocks for a while. Elisabeth said that was fine, she had things to do, but to please try and not stay later than 10 p.m.

Nate had closed the shop and was at his house. Ben found a couple of lanterns and lit them. The wood they had cut last week was beginning to dry out in the warm shop air. He found a piece of paper and made a small sketch of what he wanted the gunstock to look like. He wanted a high cheek rest, and long goose neck for the hand rest. He thought he would leave the breach mount long, just in case he wanted to make the stock and hand rest all one piece. He mounted the wood in a vise, and located his drawing knife. The knife had not been used in a while, so he needed to file and whet the blade a little bit. It was not long before he heard the door open and knew Nate had seen the lights.

"Looks like you are working a little late," said Nate.

"Yes, I can't seem to get my mind off this gun, so I thought I'd see if the wood was ready to do a little work on," responded Ben.

"Ben, I have been thinking about this trip you brought up the other day. How far west do you want to go?" asked Nate?

"I was thinking about South Dakota. There should be some good farm land out there, and the Homestead Act will allow us to claim all we want. The growing season is a little short and the winters a little cold, but other than that it should make a fine place to build a home," said Ben.

"How far do you think it would be?" questioned Nate.

"I would say about 700 to 800 miles," replied Ben.

"How long do you think it would take to make a trip like that?" Nat further inquired.

"I don't know maybe a month, maybe two, depending on the weather. I think we should leave sometime in February. That way, we would get there in early spring so we can get some crops in the ground and build shelter for next winter," replied Ben.

"Good idea, but Ben, it's going to be bad to leave here in February. You know how cold it is here. It should really be cold out there!" stated Nat.

"Yes, but the farther we go, the warmer it will get."

"How many wagons would we take?" Nat asked.

"I was thinking three each, if we can get all our equipment in three."

"You mean three for each of us--that sounds about right! If we take any more we would have to take another driver with us, and that is just more animal feed we would need," said Nate.

"Well, you have given me something to think about, and I think I'll go to bed and sleep on it," said Nate.

Ben had dressed the wood down to where it began to look like the drawing, so he thought he should pick up and get home also.

Elisabeth was feeding the baby and getting ready for bed. He went to wash up and join her. As he came back into the bedroom, she asked, "Did you get anything done?"

"Oh yes, I made a drawing and cut the stock out. Yes, I did well for the night. I talked to Nate a bit about the trip, and we have agreed on three wagons apiece," replied Ben.

"Three wagons each? My God, Ben! We only have one, and it is not big enough for a trip like that! Where are we going to get six wagons?" asked Elisabeth.

"We will make them. After all, we have the finest blacksmith in the state just two miles down the road!" responded Ben.

"Well, if you think you can do it, that is good enough for me," said Elisabeth.

Monday, it was back to the Sharp gun shop and then back home. He had everything he needed now to build the gun, except for some gun barrel stock and a 33 inch Boeing bit. He would have to order them from Philadelphia. It would take about a month for them to get here. It was mid-October, and the weather was beginning to get cold at night. He thought he would make sure he and Nate had plenty of firewood for the stoves in the shop. He would take the boys next weekend and start to cut and haul wood for everyone. In the meantime, while he waited on the barrel stock, he would work on the breach and other parts. A lot of the hand work he could sit by the fire at home and work and not have to leave Elisabeth and the baby so much. Ben was happy Nate didn't have a lot of work in the shop and had begun to make room to work on the wagons when the weather got cold.

Saturday was here before he knew it. He got the boys up early, loaded the wagon with tools, and headed up on the west side of Nate's farm where the woods were full of fallen trees and new stuff they could cut. He and Tom started cutting logs about 24 inches long, and Ben Jr. put them in the wagon and stacked the brush. They worked until noon and decided to take a load down to the house and get some lunch. Nate was busy in the shop, so they unloaded the wagon and started up the hill to see if Elisabeth had some lunch. Nate said, "No, you can have lunch with us today!"

Therefore, Ben said to Ben Jr., "Why don't you go up the hill to tell your mother?"

Ben said okay. Just as he was about to leave Helen asked, "Would you like to have a biscuit and some ham for the trip?"

"Oh, yes ma'am!" exclaimed Ben.

"I guess after stacking all that brush this morning a young man like you could be hungry," said Helen.

Ben took the biscuit and ham, taking a big bite out of it as he ran out the door. He was skipping along, thinking about school and the fun he was having with his dad and Tom today, when he heard snoring noises in back of him. He turned to see where the sound was coming from. Much to his surprise there was a black bear running along the roadside, trying to catch up with him. Ben gave out a yell that could be heard into the next county and broke into a fast run. Just for a second he turned and threw what was left of the biscuit and ham at the bear. This was just what the bear wanted; as he stopped to find the pieces, it gave Ben a chance to gain some distance. He ran with all the strength and speed he could muster. Once the bear had finished looking for what he could find of the ham he was back into the chase. Ben did not know what to do: he was running as fast as he could and the bear was gaining on him. Just as he thought all was lost he spotted a white oak tree about thirty feet to his right. Ben was young and had been climbing trees ever since he was old enough to walk. On the run, he leaped for the first branch he thought he could reach. Like a monkey, he threw his legs around the trunk of the tree and pulled himself up. He grabbed another branch and was a good ten feet up the tree before the bear reached the tree. Ben watched the bear with great fright as he walked around the tree snorting and trying to make up his mind as to what to do next. After the third trip are so around the tree, the bear made a leap for the side of the tree, landing about two feet off the ground and climbing fast. Ben was now yelling at the top of his lungs, "HELP! HELP! BEAR! Please, someone help me."

As the bear got closer, Ben raised his heavy booted foot and kicked the bear on the nose. This seemed to change the bear's mind for a second. Ben was still yelling for help and kicking every time the bear made a move.

Helen spoke up and said, "Nate would you please get me a bucket of water from the well?"

Nate said yes he would and stepped out onto the back porch. On his way to the well he thought he heard someone yelling for help. Sure enough, someone was in trouble, and it sounded like Ben. He dropped the bucket and ran back into the house. He bolted through the house, scaring every one half to death as he ran straight for the front door. He grabbed his rifle from above the door and yelled, "Ben is in trouble."

With that he jumped off the porch and hit the ground running. Ben and Tom were not far behind. The girls, seeing all of this excitement, began to join in. Nate ran with all his strength as he thought to himself, *did I cap that rifle the last time I used it or not?* After he had covered three hundred yards he spotted Ben in the tree, kicking and yelling for help. He could see the bear trying to reach Ben's foot. After another fifty yards he stopped and went to one knee, placing the rifle in a position that allowed him a steady shot. He cocked the gun and fired. He had only one round and he had to make it good. Watching the bear as Ben kept kicking, he saw it begin to lose its grip on tree and begin to slide down. He knew the shot had been good. He rose up and started once more to Ben's rescue. As he approached the tree he could see the bear was on his last leg. Ben Jr. asked, "Is he dead? I'm not coming down from this tree until you tell me he is dead."

By this time his father had arrived on the scene and picked the bear up by one leg and dragged him off a short distance from the tree. With this Ben climbed down, shaken and as white as a sheet.

Helen came up and gave Ben a big hug saying, "I guess I should have fixed a biscuit for the bear."

Ben started laughing and said, "It would not have made any difference because I gave him mine and he still wanted to eat me."

They all had a big laugh. His father said, "You go on down to the house with the others and I will go tell your mother you are fine."

Nate picked the bear up by the back leg and said, "I will skin this fellow out and feed him to the dogs".

Ben arrived at the house just a little out of breath to find Elisabeth had lunch already finished. "God, Ben, I wish you had told me sooner."

"Well, dear, I would have, but we had a little trouble on the way here."

"Oh yeah, and what might that have been?" asked Elisabeth.

"Well, a bear tried to eat Ben Jr. on the way up here to tell you.

"OH GOD--OH MY GOD! What happened? Is he all right?"

"Yes, he is fine. Nate shot the bear and he is fine. Why don't you cover the food up and we can have it tonight. I will help you wrap the baby up and you come with me and visit with Helen while we cut wood this afternoon."

"Since I need to see if my son is in one piece I will take you up on it," Elisabeth stated. "You go wash your hands and put the food away for tonight and I will take care of the baby." In a few minutes she had the baby ready to go and they were off to have lunch with the Owens; Helen was glad to see her and the baby and set about preparing another place at the table.

After lunch, Nate loaded the rifle and told Ben he had better take it with him. Since the one bear had been killed his brother might come looking for him. It was back to the wood project. After all, he needed three loads for Nate's house, three loads for himself, and four loads for the shop. There was still a lot of work left. He sent Ben Jr. and Tom down with two more loads, while he split the bigger logs. They worked at it all day, until it got too dark to see. They had finished Nate's supply and the last load they would take home with them, and quit for the day. The boys were getting tired. Elisabeth had a nice meal for her working men and was glad to see them. They wanted to get to bed early.

Tomorrow was Sunday, and Mary Sue was to be baptized. It was going to be a special day! While the boys were cutting wood Elisabeth and Helen planned Mary Sue's baptism. They had all planned to go to church together, then come home and have dinner at Ben and Elisabeth's house. They had plans to let the kids play; the men talk about the trip while they put together a nice meal for all of them.

Pastor Walker was waiting for them when they arrived. The church was located in Old Town, Ohio, and was three miles or more from the house. Ben hitched up the team and threw a bale of hay up in the wagon. Elisabeth got the boys and a couple of blankets, and they were off. They made a quick stop at Nate's place and picked up his family. There seemed to be a few more people at church today than normal, but maybe it was Elisabeth's imagination.

Old Town was not a big town and had been settled sometime around 1650. Ben knew most of the people since he was born in the area. Most of the people were farmers, but they did have a few shops like the Sharp Gun Company and a new Canvas Mill. They had three general stores and a good leather saddle shop, a telegraph office soon to become the post office, a barber shop, and the old boarding house. The blacksmith shop had now become the buggy shop, where Ben had spent a lot of his time as a boy growing up. Yes, Old Town was the only town he had known.

Pastor Walker did a good job, and there was now a brand new Christian in the family. Elisabeth was doing the driving, and Helen was enjoying holding the baby. The kids were playing in the wagon bed, and Ben and Nate were making small talk in the back of the wagon. Elisabeth said, "Look, you fed the boys yesterday, why not come home and we will all have something to eat at our place and celebrate Mary Sue's baptizing?"

"That sounds good to me," replied Helen. She hollered back to Nate, "Elisabeth wants us to have dinner with them; is it all right with you?" He yelled back - it was fine with him!

Elisabeth had done her baking Saturday, while the boys were cutting wood. She had fresh bread and a big cake. It did not take too long before the two women had put together a real nice Sunday meal. Everyone joined around the table while Nate offered a prayer. It was good enjoying one another's company. After dinner, they retired to the front porch for some warm tea and cake. It was a beautiful fall day, with the leaves turning the colors of the rainbow. They talked for several hours and Ben said he would drive them home.

The next three weeks went by fast, and it was time for Ben to stop by the post office to see if his barrel stock had arrived. He thought he might as well stop in at the land office to see what Mr. Bray had found out. As he went through the door of the land office he found Mr. Bray sitting at his desk. As Ben came through the door he rose up from the chair and said, "Mr. Sharp, it's nice to see you. I was hoping you would drop by."

Ben said, "I was in town to pick up some supplies and thought I would check on those papers while I was here".

"Glad you did, sir. I have them finished. Mr. Sharp, I'm sorry we don't have a map of the land, but I was able to find a section plot diagram and I have marked off sections 12, 14 and 15. You and Mr. Owens have 1,300 acres anywhere in those sections you wish. Now if you will sign these papers that you have filed a claim with the government for this land if it becomes available. Remember, you must live and farm the land for five years."

Ben said, "Yes sir, I understand."

"I also will need Mr. Owens to sign for his sections."

"If it is all right, sir, I will take them to him, as I will see him this afternoon. I will bring them back when I go to work tomorrow."

"That will be fine, sir. That will close the deal."

Ben said, "We thank you for the quick service."

"Mr. Sharp, the government thanks you for helping bring a new land into production. We wish you all the luck in the world. When do you plan to leave asked?" Mr. Bray.

Ben said, "On the first of February if all goes well".

"Have a safe trip, sir, and may God be with you."

Much to his surprise, the barrels had arrived two days before. It was COD, so he paid for it and headed home. He still needed casing and primers and 50 pounds of black powder, but he could pick them up next week. He thought 2,000 casings and 3,000 primers would be a good start. He would show the boys how to load the primers into the casing. It would keep them busy for a few days. In the meantime, he would work on the trigger and bolt. The gun shop had a big stock of breaches, so he would bring one home and rework it to fit his new gun. Besides, the Sharp breach had a double thick front wall, which would make it nice for the heavy load he was planning on. He now felt he had everything he needed to build the gun.

Ben worked on the stocks and barrel on Saturday and on the trigger and breach at night, at home. He had showed the boys how to load the primers into the casing, and he could watch them while they worked. The primers were a small, center-fire cap, one fourth inch in diameter and open on one end, so that when the hammer struck the cap, the shell would fire. All they had to do was place the primer into the hole of the casing, and by placing a small block of hard wood on top of the cap and tapping the block, the primer was forced into the casing. This was a lot of fun for a little while, but the small boys tired soon and wanted to play. Ben understood this, and allowed them to work when they wanted to. After all, he only needed a few rounds to test fire the gun, and the rest could be done any time.

The boring bit he had ordered went from a 22 caliber to a 44/40. He set the barrel stock up in the lathe and made sure it was running true. He then set the bit at the smallest setting he could, which was 20 thousands. He started his first pass. He wanted to run the lathe at a very slow speed and did not want to get the bit hot. By setting up an oil drip line, he could lubricate the bit as it made its cut. It would take close to two hours to cut all the way through 30 inches of barrel stock. He would work on the stocks while keeping an eye on things. It took two and one-half hours for the first run, and he liked everything he saw. He did not want to remove the barrel, because he had three or four more passes to make before the barrel was done, and he wanted all runs to be the same.

It was now mid-November, and Thanksgiving was coming up soon. It would be nice if he could get the first unit done by Christmas. He had planned to present it to Nate for a Christmas present. When he got home, he told Elisabeth about the barrel, and how happy he was with the work. She was just as happy and thought it was a wonderful idea to give the first unit to Nate.

He had finished the stock down to the finishing surface, but needed a piece of glass to hone the wood just the way he wanted it. Elisabeth provided that from a broken dish. Ben wanted to complete the stock with the long handheld support that rested under the gun barrel but couldn't finish that part until he knew the size of the ammunition feed tube. The gun was beginning to fall into place. All that needed to be done was two more passes down the barrel, and then set the lathe up to cut rifling down the barrel. This was one of the most important parts of the gun if it was to do what Ben wanted. Ben wanted that bullet to come out of the barrel with a high twist. He felt high twist, along with the speed, would carry the round far beyond the 175 yard mark, which would make it far better than the Sharp long rifle. Besides, his round was half the weight of the 44/40 round. These three points: higher twist, more speed, and a smaller round - should give him the distance he wanted. Tomorrow night, he would make another pass down the barrel and see where he stood.

After measuring the bore, he found the mike reading at .2218. That was a little tight, but would be all right until the rifling was done. Then he would make a final pass. The barrel was now ready to cut threads in the end, so it could be screwed into the breach head. With this done, he could now plan the ammo feed tube, but first he needed to know how long the shell would be. He had an adjustable bullet mold at the shop. He would bring it home, and pour a few rounds. The mold could be set for 223, but the point was too blunt, so he would have to shave it to suit his needs. When done, he filled the casing with black powder and crimped the casing tightly around the bullet after setting it deep into the casing. The round measured three inches from end to end. Not a bad looking round. This meant that if the gun was to have five rounds, the feed tube would now have to be 17 inches long. This would allow for the spring and lock. If all worked out, he would make the feed tube tomorrow night.

Ben brought the stock with him as he started his nightly work. His first order of business was the feed tube spring and lock. If he could get that done tonight, a lot of the other work was file work, and he could do that at home. He found some stock, and sat it up in the lathe. He needed to cut the feed tube thin, but thick enough to cut threads in the end to screw into the breach. The locking end had a bayonet type lock, and the spring was strong enough to feed the ammo to the breach and bolt. Ben fastened the barrel and feed tube to the stock and hand rest. The remainder could be finished at home.

He came into the house carrying the gun for the first time, and Elisabeth was amazed at how beautiful the stock was, and he had not yet finished it or applied any linseed oil. For the next week, work was done to complete the bolt and tongue. As the bolt pushed the round into the barrel, the bolt was pulled down and locked. This action compressed the tongue and allowed the feed tube to place another round on the tongue, ready to be picked up by the bolt and loaded after firing. When the bolt was lifted and pulled back to eject the spent casing, the tongue raised the next round to the barrel, and the bolt reloaded the gun. It was very nice and had a quick action. Ben was so happy, he could not wait to show Nate, but he was not going to do it until after Christmas. By then, he should be done with the stock and hand rest. He wanted to give Nate a complete package - ammunition and all. Now, if it really did work, Mr. Nathan Owens would own the first semiautomatic rifle in the world, designed and built by Benjamin Joseph Sharp! Elisabeth was very proud of her husband and prayed the gun would work when tested.

It was now December 15, and ten more days before they could test the unit. Ben wanted to polish the stock just a little more. He had Elisabeth wrap the gun in some oil cloth, and they waited until Christmas. With the first unit done, it felt like a big weight had been taken off his shoulders. He knew his gun was far better than the Sharp long rifle, and he couldn't wait to show his brothers, but it was Christmas time, and he had to get a tree and help Elisabeth put it up.

Come Sunday, Ben and the boys hitched up the team and stopped by Nate's, and told him what they were going to do. Nate said, "Wait for me, and I will go with you. We need one, also." It was about all he could do to keep from telling Nate that he had finished the gun. They made small talk and looked for Christmas trees. It had snowed the night before, so all the trees looked very pretty. They selected two and loaded them onto the wagon. Ben helped carry one into Nate's house, and Nate and Helen would set it up.

Next week, Elisabeth got information to Mrs. Johnson asking if she would look after Mary Sue for a day, while she and Helen went to town to do some shopping. She had Ben hitch the team before he left for work. With everyone off to school, the women were off to town, something they did not do very much. Elisabeth told Helen about the sleeping bags, and she thought that was the right thing to do and said she would do the same thing.

The store did not have as much as they wanted and inquired as to what in the world they were going to do with all that sheep skin. Their mouths were closed, and they changed the subject. They picked up some crocks and a lot of jars for canning. Food had to be canned in order to have plenty to eat on the trip, and when they got there. The men folk thought they had lots of things to do, but so did the women.

There were a lot of people to feed and keep warm. Medicine had to be bought, along with coats and underwear. The day was spent buying out the stores. It was three o'clock when they got back, so they left the wagon loaded until Ben and the boys came home. Elisabeth dropped off Helen, and said she would have the boys bring down her stuff when they got home. It had been a full day, and she still had to get something to eat together.

Ben arrived home a little bit later and helped the boys unload the wagon. They placed the stuff on the back porch, out of the weather. Ben remarked, "Did you women leave anything in the stores for other people, or did you get it all?"

"We will have to go back before we are done," replied Elisabeth.

"Well, don't forget we are only taking three schooner wagons on this trip!" said Ben.

Ben Jr. spoke up, saying, "Daddy, can I drive a schooner wagon?"

"That is a big wagon, son; it is almost as big as a house! That is why they call it a schooner. It is named after a ship", answered Ben. "We will have to see if you can drive it. It will be quite a handful for a nine year old boy. It is not only big, but you will have to have four mules, instead of two. That means you will have four reins, two in each hand. That will be quite a handful for a nine year old boy. We will see! Do you think you can drive four mules?" inquired his dad.

"I don't know. I will have to try," replied Ben Jr.

"Well, you are not the only one, and your mother will have to be trained as well. You are going to have to grow up, Ben Jr.;

you are not going to have much of a chance to be a boy. We have some time, and we will think about that later. Let's get this wagon unloaded and get down to Helen and Nate's," said Ben.

The Owens was just finishing their nightly meal when they pulled up. Ben Jr. jumped off the wagon and ran into the house to ask Mrs. Owens where she wanted the stuff. "Let's put it over there, in the corner of the living room. I will have to find a place for it later," she replied. Ben Jr. had to tell her that maybe he was going to drive a schooner. Nate spoke up and inquired, "By the way, Ben, how large do you think I should make those wheels? I would like to give the wagon two feet or more clearance off the ground to get over rocks and ditches. What do you think?"

"That sounds good to me. That will give us a four and one-half foot wheel. I think we should also make a 3 inch band, instead of the 2 inch; that way, it won't cut into the mud that deep," replied Ben.

"Good idea, my friend. I will have to go to Dayton and get materials. You know, Ben, it is going to take me a month to build one wagon, and that is if the shop is slow. It could take longer," remarked Nate.

"I will help, and give me half of the bill for the materials when you order," Ben said."

"Ben, it will take us six or seven months just to build wagons," stated Nate.

"I know, and then we have to find mules and harnesses," replied Ben.

"Well, we are not going right away, and nobody says we have to be in a hurry," declared Nate.

"Well, let me know when you want to go to Dayton, and I will try to go with you. If you cannot close the shop for a Saturday, then give me a list of what we need, and the people to see. Then I will take the boys and go for us."

"Ben, that sounds good to me," agreed Nate. By now, the boys had the wagon unloaded, and it was time to go home.

It was now the 20th of December, and snow was beginning to fall. That was good; at least they might have a white Christmas. Ben thought he should have started to cut wood much sooner, even though he had some wood left from last year, along with the one load he and the boys brought home last week, but he knew if the weather got bad, he would be out soon. He would just hope for a break and go cut some more.

The nights were spent working on triggers and bolts. "I will have to order some breaches. I don't want to take five more from the shop," remarked Ben.

Elisabeth said, "Why not? One third of everything at the Sharp Gun Company is yours, anyway."

"I know, but if I do that, then they will know I'm working on guns," stated Ben.

"Do what you want to do. I'm sure you know best," acknowledged Elisabeth.

Next morning, the snow was close to a foot deep, and Ben thought that he would take the mare to work. They had a small barn next to the shop where they could leave their horses, so it would not be a problem. Friday was Christmas, and if the snow got too deep he would stay close to home until after the holiday.

Thursday came, and the snow was still coming down, not as bad as before but every now and then, it would let loose. Halfway through the day, Helen showed up at the door. She had ridden her black mare up the hill. She came to talk to Elisabeth about Christmas. "Why don't we have Christmas dinner together at our house?" asked Helen. "After we get our presents open let's spend the day with one another and let the kids play," she continued.

Elisabeth thought that would be a good idea. They sat down and planned what they would cook, and who would bring what.

Ben came home a little early and said he was done for the week. The boys had shut the shop down until the Monday after Christmas, so he was available for whatever they needed. "But since you don't need me here, I think I will ride down the hill and see what Nate is doing."

Nate was working on a wagon he had moved inside the shop. Ben said, "I think I will work on some gun stocks. I've got five more to hew out." He fired up the other stove and went to work. A little bit later, he heard Helen at the door saying she would put the horse in the barn, if Nat would unsaddle hers and rub the mare down. The men worked until six pm. They let the fire burn down and went home. The next day was Christmas.

Last week, Ben had stopped off at the general store and done his Christmas shopping. He had put his items in the barn and had to tread through the snow to get them. The boys wanted to get up before the sun came up, but their mother said, "No!"

Elisabeth needed some new dresses. Since the baby came, nothing she had fit. Ben picked out three, two for the week and one for Sunday, which he thought she would like. Elisabeth rang a bell she had, which indicated that the children should get up and enjoy her eggs and bacon, hot coffee, and milk. Everyone wanted to see what was under the tree and did not want to eat. The rule was: eating first, and then open Christmas presents. They finished eating and ran to the tree. Even Mary Sue had been made to get up and was propped in a chair so she could take in the whole event. This was her very first Christmas and everyone had a present for her.

Ben got socks, underwear, and some new boots, the boys got new school clothes and a new wagon to haul wood from the barn area to the house. Elisabeth opened up her presents one by one, and each time had to get up and give Ben a big hug and a kiss. After finishing their presents, they had to clear a little snow so they could get to the barn, chicken house, and springhouse. Ben had a bucket scoop that would hold one yard of snow, and was pulled by one mule. It did not take him long to clear a path everywhere they needed to go. When done, the boys had the team ready to go to the Owens, and Elisabeth had the table cleaned off and things picked up.

It was ten o'clock when Ben and the boys came in and asked Elisabeth if she was ready to go. She said, "Yes, just as soon as I get Mary Sue wrapped up. You can put Nate and Helen's Christmas gifts in the wagon while I do that." The boys took their presents with them, all except their new clothes. After all, the Owens girls would want to know what they had gotten.

They pulled up in front of the house and unloaded everything. The kids were so excited, and the house smelled like Christmas! Nate took the wagon down to the barn, and unhitched them. God, they were glad to spend the day together.

Everyone was playing and talking when Ben slipped out of the house and made his way to the shop. He had hidden the gun up in the loft under some lumber. It looked like no one had moved it since he brought it down last Sunday. He came into the house and got Nat's attention. Nat looked at him, wondering what he had in his hand. Ben handed him the gun and said, "Merry Christmas!"

As Nate unwrapped the gun, his eyes got bigger with each fold of the oil cloth. "My God, Ben!" exclaimed as he continued, "What have you got here?" By now, everyone had crowded around the table to see what all the commotion was about.

Helen spoke up, saying, "What a beautiful stock! Ben, did you make this?"

"Yes! It's the world's first semiautomatic rifle. It holds five shots, and can be fired as fast as you can pull the bolt back and reload," replied Ben. "Nate, please hold it down because it is loaded," cautioned Ben.

"Have you fired it yet?" asked Nate.

"No, I have saved that for you," replied Ben.

Nate said, "Let's go see what it does!"

"Nate, there is two feet of snow out there! What in God's name are you going to shoot at?" Ben asked.

"I don't know, but I have to shoot it!" stated Nate.

The men got their coats and headed for the door. The boys were right behind them. They made their way over to the wood pile and spotted an old barrel up next to the woods about 250 yards away. Ben asked, "Can you see that?"

Nat replied, "Yes, I can see it."

"What part of it are you going to shoot at?"

"I don't know just yet."

"Ok, all you have to do is pull the hammer back to you, and you are ready."

Nate laid the gun up on some wood to steady it against his cheek and followed Ben's instructions. He took a long time in sighting the target before he pulled the trigger. The gun gave off a large bang and went silent. Nothing could be seen from where they were at to indicate if the round went that far or not. Tom, the oldest boy said, "I will go see if you hit it."

"Tom, that snow is too deep, and it is 250 yards up there. I'll tell you what let's do. Let's ride the mules up there. That way we can all go," suggested Nate.

"Ok!" agreed everyone, "Let's do it!"

The snow was deep and it was slow going, but within a few minutes they were there. At first, Ben could not see anything and was feeling badly the gun did not go the distance. However, after a closer examination, Nat noticed the splintered wood on the inside of the barrel, and a larger hole on the other side of the drum.

"My God, Ben!" exclaimed Nat. "I had aimed just a few inches from the top of the barrel. I do not believe it had any drop in 250 yards! I don't know what to say; it looks good," continued Nat. "I'll tell you what, let's take my red handkerchief and put it over the hole, and go back down and fire the other four rounds," suggested Nat.

"Good idea," replied Ben.

After securing the handkerchief over the hole and holding it in place with some sticks, they went back to the wood pile to test fire the other rounds. Nate took up his position on the wood pile, and loaded and cocked the gun one more time. This time he felt a little more secure after firing the one round and took his time.

He fired the second round, and the gun sounded the same. He took about five seconds between each of the next three rounds.

"Well, let's go look," said Nate. Going was not so slow this time, since a trail had been broken. Nat hopped down from his mule and found a black hole in the handkerchief about the size of a coffee cup where the lead rounds had passed through. "My God, Ben!" exclaimed Nate. "This is unreal to fire five rounds, and get that close of a pattern at that distance; I cannot believe it! What have you done here? I could not be happier! I will keep this weapon for the rest of my life! Thank you! Thank you, Ben Sharp! You could not have given me a better present!" declared Nate. He put the handkerchief in his back pocket, and they headed for the barn.

The girls wanted to know all about the test. Nate was so excited he couldn't keep all the facts together. Ben spoke up and said, "I still need to do some more work on the gun before it is done."

"Ok, but don't do anything with the way it shoots," insisted Nate.

"I won't!" responded Ben. "And make sure you save all the casings after you shoot. I will reload them. We cannot buy the rounds anywhere just yet," declared Ben.

After all that excitement, dinner was ready and the boys were ready to eat. Nat gave the blessing, and thanked God for giving Ben the wisdom he possessed. "I would like to talk about something else since we are all here. If we are still planning on going west next February, we need to talk a little bit about all the things that will have to be done by then. That is only fourteen months away, and there is much to be done, both by the girls, and us. I need all the help I can get," said Ben. "I normally quit working around 10 pm, but I will keep the lathe running until midnight," continued Ben.

Elisabeth said that was fine with her; she had quilts to make and lots of other things to do. Helen said, "Me, too!" So it was agreed; they would work a little harder and longer, in order to be ready.

The New Year came and went. The winter was in full swing, but they didn't mind. Nate did not have to fight the snow to go to work. Ben and the boys used the wagon to go back and forth to town. Nate had all he could do to work on the six wagons. The twenty-four wheels had eight spokes each. The wheels, spokes, and wheel hubs would tie him up most of the winter. Ben would help when he was not working on the other five guns he had planned to make. There was still more wood to be cut as soon as the snow melted.

As Nate finished the spokes, he dropped them in a tub of linseed oil. This would help keep the water out, and let the spokes fit tighter in the wheel for a longer time. The wheel rims were also dropped into the tub when finished. By March, he had enough wheel rims, spokes, and hubs to put a wheel together. He fitted all the pieces, and made the steel band that would hold the rim and spokes together. When done, he coated the wheel one more time with linseed oil, and rolled it over next to a wall to await the inner hub rings. Not a bad job, he thought, but one wheel was a long ways from twenty four, so he would spend every day putting them together.

The snow had begun to clear off, and you could see the ground for the first time since Christmas. Nate asked Ben if he would take a weekend and cut logs for the wagon axles. "I need six each: 18 inch wide oak logs seven feet long for the rear, and 12 inch wide for the front axles."

Ben replied, "Not a problem. I will get on it this weekend - weather permitting. It will be a good time for me to finish the wood cutting." Ben was there every night and every weekend to help. The lathe really was getting a workout between Nat making hubs and spokes and Ben making guns at night. The winter winds were a big help.

Ben had told Nat at Christmas time that he had more work to do on the gun. His thoughts were that because the gun had such a long range, the shooter needed to see farther than just the plain eye could see. He had seen an ad where a company in New York made spyglasses for sale. Therefore, Ben wrote and asked if he could buy twenty-four lenses, each 1¼ inches in diameter, and if so, pleases ship them COD at once to the address below. He did not know if they would do such a thing, so he waited. Within a month, the postman told Ben he had a COD package for him. He had been so busy that the lenses had slipped his mind. He was excited to pick them up and see what he had. Much to his surprise, they were just what he needed!

That night he ran the lathe to make a tube to fit the lenses. After cutting two small holes in the top, the two lenses were placed 1½ inches into the front and back. After fitting the magnifying lenses, he locked them into the tube, three inches apart, leaving plenty of space in the middle point of the tube. Next, he coated the inside space with some light oil.

Ben had picked up a small package of phosphate powder from town the other day. With this, he coated the inside of the tube space. Next he took an old felt hat and cut two strips three inches long and 1½ inches wide. By placing them into the tube, one on each side, and attaching one end of the strips to the top of the tube using the two holes, the other end of the strip was affixed to the inside of the three inch space. Now he would let this all dry, and tomorrow he would see if he had changed the world.

It was all he could do to get to sleep, even though he had worked until midnight. The next day at work, it was the same thing. He managed to get the day finished and rushed home to Elisabeth and the kids. He ate his supper in gulps and ran down the hill to see how his project had turned out. It was better than he had planned! He turned the scope over in his hand two or three times, trying to see how he could fix the scope to the gun barrel. He decided on two clamps around the scope; the end of the clamps would lock into the top of barrel, one facing to the left and one facing right. This would keep the scope tight while allowing it to be quickly removable.

While getting the scope mounted, he looked through the thing and could not believe what he saw! The magnifying glass made the object he was looking at so large he could no longer recognize it! He then took the scope to the door and looked outside. He could not see well. By rubbing the felt pad he had placed on the top of the scope, the most amazing thing happened. The space between the two lenses came to life. The felt pad, when rubbed, produced static electricity. This caused the phosphate powder to produce light. He now could see hundreds of yards - in the dark of night!

"My God! My God, what have I done?" He ran to the front door of the house, and banged on it until Nate opened the door. "Nate, you have to come out here now, and see what is going on!" exclaimed Ben.

Nate put his coat on and walked over to the shop with him. Ben handed him the scope and said, "I think I have just finished your gun. I want you to rub the felt pad on top of the scope, and then look through it."

Nate did as he was told. As he placed the scope to his eye to look, he jumped back, almost dropping the gun. The light soon faded, but Ben said, "That is ok; rub it again".

Again light was made, and Nat could see far into the night. "My! My! My, what have you done?" stuttered Nate.

"I don't know," replied Ben", but I think we have a night scope that will allow us to fire your gun in the dark of night, and hit a target 300 or more yards away! If this works, we have got the world's first semiautomatic weapon that will shoot just as well at night as it does in daylight!"

Much to his surprise he was right. Not only did the gun see at night; it reached out much farther than they had planned. The nice thing about it was that you could see things far into the night you could not see with the naked eye. The bad thing was that if the felt on top of the scope got wet or damp, it would not produce electricity. Ben had to make a cover that went over the felt and made it hard for moisture to get to. The gun was done!

Ben walked up the hill, tired and happy with what he had just done. He told Elisabeth about the scope. "What are you going to do? Are you going to tell your brothers?" she asked.

"No! Not just yet. I have to wait until I have finished the other five guns," replied Ben. With that they went to bed, and Ben went back to work in the morning.

By May, Ben had the other guns finished by working on them every minute he had time. With the guns done and test-fired, he could now give Nate more of his time. They worked on the wagons, Nate during the day and Ben at night.

Bill Adams had stopped by the shop to get some plows fixed for the spring. While talking to Nate, he saw the wagon wheels and the work being done. He wanted to know what Nate was up to. Nate would not tell him too much. He said a man had come in from the west of town and asked to have the schooners made. Nate would not tell him anymore. "I have to have them done by fall." He did not lie, because Ben lived north and west.

Well, it was not long before Mr. Adams told someone he knew that worked at the gun shop that Nate was working on schooners. It was only a matter of time before Joe and Jim wanted to hear the story about what Nate was doing. Ben wouldn't tell them much and let the subject die, but talk would start again, and the whole story would come out soon.

All the guns had been fired, but not sighted. Ben and Nat would take a weekend with the boys and do that later. Right now, it was wagon time. They were working hard together to hew out the axles, the tongues, and finish the wheels. The wagon beds would not be a lot of trouble. All they had to do was nail and bolt the bed boards to the axle plates and then came the sideboards and canvas rails.

The first wagon was about to be pulled outside the shop, where the world would get a firsthand look at what was going on. Nate was not in a hurry for this first one. He had rings on the side of the wagon where they could tie water barrels. He then built a chicken coop under one of the wagons. Many things had to be thought about, and he was sure he would forget something. On every tongue, he mounted a cap with a large ring through it. This would allow more mules to pull a wagon out of a hole or ditch.

It was now the end of June, and they had made better time than they thought they would. The wagons were almost done. If they could finish by August, there would be more time to get their equipment loaded and tied down. "Why don't we use next weekend to sight the rifles and teach the boys how to shoot?" asked Ben.

"That sounds good to me," replied Nate.

"After that part of the plans are finished, we can see what the girls need help on," added Ben.

Bright and early Saturday morning the boys were gotten out of bed and Nat's wood pile was the gathering place. "We know, or we think we know, the guns will shoot 300 yards. So let's make a target out of some old canvas I have in the barn. We will paint a large circle in the middle, and a small dot in the center. We can then step off 500 yards and place the target."

Everyone agreed that was a good idea. All the guns had been fitted with the new scope, so Ben said, "Nate, since you are the experienced shooter here, we will let you go first".

"Fine with me!" replied Nate. He got up on the wood pile and found a place to sit. Each rifle had been loaded with five rounds.

Nate stated, "I'm going sight the first shot at the very bottom of the small dot".

"Ok, let's see what you have", agreed Ben.

Nat looked through the scope for the first time since he and Ben had worked with it that night in the barn. In the daytime, he did not need to use the nightlight. As he looked at the target for the first time, it looked like the target was stuck on the end of the barrel. He pulled away for a minute and told Ben what he saw. After a long pause he fired the first round, then in quick order the other four rounds. The men had saddled two horses so they could ride up to check the pattern. As they got down, Ben could not believe what he saw. The pattern was tight and well-grouped. It was placed in a group the size of a coffee cup, and right in the center of the target.

Ben asked, "Where did you place the front sight?"

"Right on the bottom of the small dot," Nate replied.

"Then we have got a problem. Our target is too close. Let's go out to 800 yards," suggested Ben.

The target was picked up and moved another 300 yards down range, the hole was repaired, and it was back to the wood pile. This time, it was Ben's chance to shoot. He had sighted a lot of guns in his time and really knew what he was doing. He got up on the wood pile, and without the scope he could hardly see the target. Once he looked in the scope, he was as surprised as Nate had been to find the target in clear view. My God, what a gift this scope was to the shooting world!

He placed the sight on the bottom of the dot as Nate had done, and squeezed the first round off. He noted the trigger was a little rough, and needed some work, but the round fired nicely. He shot the other four rounds, and it was go, look, and see time. What they found was the pattern was still tight and well grouped. This time, the group had fallen just below the dot. Ben knew the rounds were beginning to lose their power, but to shoot 800 yards and get only a 5 or 6 inch drop was more than had ever been done.

It was hard to believe what they had just accomplished. They spent the rest of the afternoon teaching the boys how to shoot the guns, and Ben gave each of them one of their own. Ben Jr. had a little trouble with the kick but was able to get a pretty good grouping for such a young lad. Tom did very well, and was right in the pattern with his dad. The boys could not stand it any longer and ran off to show their mother what Dad had just given them.

3:

Ben said to Nate, "I guess I will have to spring the news on my brothers, but if I do, I'm going to tell them we are planning to leave the state."

"It's all right with me, it will get out sooner or later," Nate remarked. He spent Sunday afternoon working on the wagons, while Ben and the boys loaded more ammunition. After all, they now had six guns that would shoot five rounds and needed a lot more for the trip.

Monday Ben went to work as always, but this morning he carried with him the rifle and a few rounds of ammunition. Joe and Jim were in the shop working when he arrived. He made a gesture for them to meet him in a room off the shop floor. Jim asked, "What is going on? What have you got in the package?"

Ben laid the package on the table and turned his back to it, facing them. He began, "I have got a lot of information to share with you this morning, and I would like to do it now. Is it ok?"

They both said, "Yes!"

Ben continued, "You know, I have been leaving the shop pretty much at quitting time each day, and I thought I should tell you why."

"Ben, we just thought it was the new baby and helping out at home. We did not mind," stated Joe.

"Well, that is not the reason. Nate Owens and I have been planning a trip. We want to leave Ohio, and go west.

"So that is what the schooners are all about!" exclaimed Jim.

"Yes sir that is it. We have built six of them, and we are getting ready to leave next February. I wanted to wait until the baby was at least one year old. She will be a year and a half in February, and Elisabeth and I think she can make it."

"Ben! What are you going to do out there?" asked Jim.

"And I have more questions when we have time", added Joe.

"Yes, I know, and I will answer each of them as we go forward. That is only half of the story," stated Ben.

"There is more?" Jim asked.

Ben answered, "Yes! Do you remember how I have tried to get you to see that the single shot weapon we are making is not the right gun?"

"Ben, we have been through this a dozen times", interrupted Joe.

"Yes, we have, and on the table behind me is the proof we are wrong!" continued Ben. With that, Ben turned to the gun wrapped in oil cloth, and began to unwrap it. Jim and Joe watched in amazement as the beautiful stock and hand finished barrel came into view.

"What in the world is that big thing on top?" inquired Joe.

"Brothers, here is a five shot semiautomatic rifle that can shoot 800 yards. Not only will it shoot 800 yards - it only has a 5 to 6 inch drop," explained Ben.

"Hell! And what have you been drinking?" questioned Jim.

"Nat and I have tested this gun at 200, 500, and 800 yards, and what I have just told you is true!" declared Ben. "Here is how it works. The gun holds five rounds at one time. It will shoot the five rounds as fast as you can pull the bolt back, reload, and aim. I want both of you to shoot the gun to see for yourself. You can shoot it here in the shop range, but you will have to take it to the farm range to get the 800 yards. I would like for you to lock the gun up until we are ready to go."

"That needs to be right now," stated Joe.

"Let's put Peter in charge, and we will all three use my buckboard and leave right now," suggested Jim.

Ben said, "You boys go on with the buckboard, and I will ride my mare".

It was only a ten minute ride out of town to Jim's farm. Joe had put some targets, nails, and a hammer in the buckboard as they left. Ben told them, "Do not bother to put up targets at anything under 800 yards".

They looked at one other and said, "You are crazy! I can't even see 800 yards out there!"

"Don't worry about it," Ben said.

Joe was the best shot and said he would go first. He sat down on the grass and loaded the gun. He then placed his elbow on his knee and got ready to shoot. As he looked down the scope, he almost dropped the gun. "My God, I cannot believe what I see through this thing!" exclaimed Joe. He fired off one round and said, "Not bad".

"Now try the other four, and try to place them in the same spot," urged Ben. Before the last round was gone, Ben and Jim were on the mare and halfway down range. They rode up and Jim slid off the mare. Ben followed. Jim looked at the target and said, "There is no way this can be true". Yet there were five bullet holes in that target - and they were not there before! "Ben, what have you done? You are crazy! Only a crazy man would make such a gun!" exclaimed Jim.

Ben explained the nightlight and how it worked.

"Well, we will see about that tonight. Let's take the target back and show Joe," said Jim. Joe was sitting on the back of the buckboard when they rode up. "Joe, where did you put the front sight?" inquired Jim.

He answered, "On the very bottom of the small black circle".

"Well, you got a five inch drop in 800 yards!" said Jim.

Joe looked at the target and said, "That is where I shot."

Jim said, "I'm going to try it from the back of the mare" He pulled the mare around so he could shoot from her side instead of over her head. He thought she may not jump around as much from this angle. She did not move very much, and he fired the remaining four shots. He handed the gun to Ben and rode off to check his skill. He pulled the target off and rode back. "Let me tell you! We have got ourselves a shoot in' machine here!" exclaimed Jim.

"Here is what we need to do. How many of these have you made?" inquired Joe.

"Six at this time; that one belongs to you," replied Ben.

"Well, for God's sake! Protect them with your life until I get the patent filed," demanded Joe.

Ben spoke up and said, "I have only one request - that you patent it under the Sharp name, but list me as the inventor".

"We can do that," agreed the brothers.

"Ben, never again will you hear me say you are crazy. Maybe a little bit out of step with the rest of us - but not crazy! I will lock this up in the gun safe today, and tomorrow I will make a drawing and get ready to file. What do you want to call it?" asked Joe.

"Let's name it the Sharp Semiautomatic Five Shot Long Rifle. Let's sell it for $35.00 without the scope, and $55.00 with the scope," replied Ben.

"Do you think anyone will buy it for that money?" asked Joe.

"They will once the word gets out. They will come from far and wide. Besides, we sell the single shot for $25.00, and orders are coming in every day," stated Ben.

"Are you sure you still want to go west, Ben?" asked Joe.

"Yes, our minds are made up, and we are too far along to change our minds now," said Ben.

"We will deposit your profits in the bank as we have been doing, and you can look at the numbers any time you wish," stated Joe.

"That is fine with me," agreed Ben.

He spent the rest of the day at his work bench, glad his brothers liked the new gun. He told Elisabeth that night and she, too, was very happy. She did not like it when everyone was mad at one another. After supper, it was back to the wagons and making sure they were ready.

It was now July, and they put the order out for mules. Ben's vote would be for 24 mules between two and three years old, and around fifteen hands high. Nate said, "That sounds about right. We want big mules for those big wagons." Where in the heck were they going to find 24 mules that age and size? Besides, what about feed?

They had been too busy to put crops in the ground and they needed a lot of corn to feed 24 mules, four cows, and a bull - to say nothing about the chickens and pigs and themselves. They would have to buy. How much should they buy, and could they take enough to last until next fall? Ben would try and figure how much each animal would eat per day and figure out what was needed. Nate heard from someone that had stopped by his shop that a man in Low Berry, Ohio had mules for sale. He said he thought the man raised them. Low Berry was 25 miles to the east. Ben said, "I will ride up there and talk to the man this weekend".

"Well, the sooner the better," agreed Nat.

When he got home he thought he would spend some time talking to Elisabeth, only to find out she was dog tired. She and the boys had spent the day working the garden. They had planted three times as many beans as normal. There was a lot of weeding and working the soil. She had planted cabbage, potatoes, beets, and cucumbers. She wanted to can as many beans as she could. The others, she would let dry on the vine and shell out to be put in bags. She would make pickles out of the cucumbers. As fall arrived, she would can apples and make jelly. She did not want to overload the wagon with food, but she wanted to have what they needed.

While she was talking, Ben was trying to figure out how much corn to take and whether it would overload the wagon. Nate had said he thought the schooner could haul a little over 4,000 pounds or more and that a good mule should pull twice his weight. That should be around 3,600 pounds each, or 21, 600 pounds for six wagons. He could load each wagon with all he could get on it without damaging the wagon. He just did not know. They would have to load a wagon and test run it uphill to see how hard it would be on the four mules.

With these numbers, Ben thought they could take 36 drums of corn; six on the side of each wagon, at 300 lbs. each. That would be 1,800 lbs of corn per wagon. That would leave room for tools, and all the other things they would need. He wanted to load one wagon each with hay, and let the animals eat pasture wherever they could. He needed four water barrels; three for the animals, and one for drinking water. They would have to be re-filled each day, providing fresh water could be found. One wagon would be loaded with household items and some food. The heavy food could go in the hay wagon; like beans, potatoes, and meat. He thought they could get everything they needed loaded. He would share this information with Nate tomorrow, when he got back from Low Berry.

It was six am. Elisabeth called Ben for breakfast. He ate, drank some coffee, and put some jerky in a bag - just in case there was nothing to eat for lunch. He said goodbye to Elisabeth, and said he would try to be back by dark. He saddled his mare and headed toward town.

Low Berry was a good 25 miles the other side of town. There was a wagon road all the way, so he should make good time. It was a small town and it shouldn't be hard to find a mule breeder. The best place to get information was the blacksmith shop. He reined up and asked the man if there was a man around that raised mules. The man said that would be Pete Wilson, about 5 miles west of town. Ben asked if he could water his mare and said, "Thanks"

It took him 30 minutes to cover the 5 miles. He found Mr. Wilson's farm off the road a mile or so. He opened the gate and rode down to the house. A man came outside as he pulled up and asked if he could help him.

"Are you Pete Wilson?" asked Ben.

The man said, "Yes, my name is Pete Wilson."

"I hear you have mules for sale," stated Ben.

The man said, "Yes, I do."

With that, Ben slid out of the saddle and shook his hand. "My name is Ben Sharp."

"Are you from Old Town?" asked Mr. Wilson.

"Yes sir," replied Ben.

"Do you know the Sharp brothers over there? I think they are in the gun business." inquired Mr. Wilson.

"Yes, I do, I'm the youngest brother", answered Ben.

"It is a pleasure to meet you, Mr. Sharp!" responded Mr. Wilson.

"Pete, I'm looking for 24 mules; two to three years old, somewhere around 15 hands high" stated Ben.

"Well, I don't know if I have that many in that age group and size. I might be able to come up with 15 or 20. I know a man over on the next farm that could take care of the rest. What in the world are you going to do with that many mules?" asked Mr. Wilson.

"I am planning a trip west. Well, how much do you want for them?" inquired Ben.

"Well, none of them have been shoed and at that age most of them have never been in harness - so you will have to do a little training," mentioned Mr. Wilson.

"That won't be a problem, I have a blacksmith that will see that gets done", stated Ben.

"Then I will take $10.00 a head for them. Could I pick them up in October?" asked Ben.

Pete said, "Yes! Not a problem."

"Could you have them ready around October 1st, and talk to your friend to see if he can fill the bill with the rest you don't have?"

Pete agreed saying, "I can do that, and I will see you in October. Thanks a lot for the business, and make sure you lock that gate good when you leave. Those mules will rub that wire lock off the post in a minute."

It was getting close to 12 pm when Ben headed out of town. He rode about ten minutes and spotted a big log alongside a creek bed. He reined in the mare and hopped down. He thought he would eat a little jerky and drink some water; he had plenty of time to get home. He sat there by the creek and let the mare rest and enjoy the long green grass growing by the creek bank before the long ride home. Ben had not had a lot of time to think much about the trip west. He was excited he had been able to do such a fine job on the guns. Most of all, he was happy his brothers had liked his work.

The wagons were coming along fine, thanks to Nate, and it looked like Elisabeth and Helen were doing a fine job on getting everything together; but this was going to be a hard trip. It would be cold, and the snow should be deep. The trail Ben had chosen would be called the Northwestern Trail by him and his people. It is known today as Highway 80. He thought he would have a wagon road all the way through the western Indiana Territory, but from there on, he had no idea what to expect. What about ditches and washout? Could they get wagons through that kind of landscape? It then came to mind that he could load the scooper, which could help them get across deep ditches. He would remind Nate to make some kind of a long drill to see how thick the ice would be on rivers and ponds. He surely did not want a team and wagon to break through in weather like that. Would Elisabeth and the boys be able to drive the wagons if he had to ride point? All of this and more ran through his mind. He would talk it over with Nate and see what he thought about it all. Besides, the warm summer air was making him sleepy. He had overstayed his welcome.

He got home a little before dark, and Elisabeth had a nice supper ready. He was hungry! After all, it had been a long time since morning. He told Elisabeth about some of his concerns, and wanted to know if she had any ideas. "No, I don't know much about something like that. That is a man thing," replied Elisabeth. Ben was left with the burden of his thoughts.

It was Sunday and church time. Ben and Nate were both very religious men. They did not wear their religion on their sleeves, but everything they did had God connected. Therefore, to not be in church on Sunday was a bad thing for them.

It was August, and they still had a lot of work before them. Nate had to see Mr. Adams and ask if he still wanted to buy the farm. Ben needed to find out if his brothers wanted him to sell his place, or if they would like to keep it and rent it out. Peter, the shop foreman, lived a long ways from Old Town and it would make it nice to have him a little closer. He would talk to them. The mules would be here next month, and he needed feed and harnesses and a first class muleskinner. He told Nate at church that after he had lunch, he would drop by for a chat.

Nate was sitting on the porch enjoying his pipe when Ben came down the hill. He sat down on the top step and said, "Nate, I had been thinking on my ride over to Low Berry yesterday that we could be short-handed on this trip. Since you have all girls, and Ben Jr. is too young to drive, what if I talk to Henry Wilson, who works for Mr. Hill on the north of town? Somebody should ride point a few hours each day, so we can see what we have to deal with before we get there. He is young, and from all reports is a hard worker," said Ben.

"Ben, you are right. It would not hurt to have another strong man in the group. Yes! See if you can reach him, and I will pick up his wages, since I'm the one short-handed," said Nate.

"Good, I will get word to him tomorrow. Now, I talked to a man over in Low Berry yesterday about the mules, and he thinks he has 15 or 20 of what we need. He said there was another breeder that lived a few miles from him, and he would try and get the balance from him. We should have them by the first of October," continued Ben.

"Good work, Ben," declared Nate. "Now all we need is harnesses. I will stop by Joe Smith's leather shop one day next week and place our order."

"What have we got left to do on the wagons?" inquired Ben.

"Not much, but we do need to order the canvas for the tops," answered Nate.

"Just give me the size, and where you want the ringlet, and I will get that on order, also," stated Ben.

"But Ben, I have a problem. We will have to sleep on the ground, because two wagons will be loaded with hay, and two wagons will be loaded with our tools and equipment. The other two will be loaded with household items and food. There are too many of us to sleep in the food wagon. I was thinking if we have canvas sheeting made with ringlets on the front end and sides we could lay that canvas on the ground under the wagon and put two bales of hay across the front, and two along the sides. Then we could have a warmer, dryer, place to put our sleeping bags", suggested Nate.

"That is a very good idea, Nate! It will provide us a warmer place to stand watch at night, and give us some cover if someone shoots at us. How many do we want?" asked Ben.

"I would say we need four, but better judgment tells me to order ten", answered Nate.

"Well, that will give us something to do this week! Now that we have that settled, do you want to work on the wagons the rest of the day?" inquired Ben.

"No! I just want to sit here and enjoy my pipe, and thank almighty God for all we have been able to do. Besides, I have not stopped since we started this project!" exclaimed Nate.

"It's okay with me, my friend. I can use a little break, too," agreed Ben. They just sat there and enjoyed the summer afternoon and talked.

Monday, Ben was able to get word to Henry Wilson that Nate Owens would like to see him. He stopped by the feed store and placed an order for 10,000 pounds of fall corn, and 100 bales of hay. He then went over to the gun shop to see if they had or could get four .45 caliber long barrel revolvers with holsters. Ben thought they would come in handy when they did not want to carry the long rifles. He also talked to Joe about taking three Sharp 44/40 rifles, just in case they wanted to shoot a buffalo. He then stopped by the saddle shop and placed an order for twenty-four harness sets for the mules in October.

This trip was costing them a lot of money. However, Nate had money in the bank from his Dad, and he made far more than he and Helen needed from the shop. Ben, on the other hand, had profits from the gun business, and that was a lot. Business was good and going to be a lot better. Money was not a problem.

Saturday came, and both men were busy working on the wagons when Henry Wilson rode up. Nate asked him if he would like to go west with them.

He said, "God, yes! When do you want me?"

"We want to leave the first of February," replied Nate.

"That is fine with me," agreed Henry.

"Can I ask how old you are, Henry?" requested Nate.

"Sir, I'm twenty years old," he replied.

"Do you know anything about mules?" asked Nate.

"Well, sir, I work them every day. Mules are different than a horse. A mule will try and bite you every chance he gets. He will kick the hell out of you, if you don't work him close," replied Henry.

"What do you do to keep this from happening?" asked Nate.

"Sir, if he tries to bite me more than once, I will hit him across the nose real hard," affirmed the young man.

"Henry, we have got twenty-four mules on order, and they are only two to three years old. Do you think you could break them to harness?"

"Yes sir, it will take a while, but I can do it," declared Henry.

"How long do you think it would take?" inquired Nate?

"Sir, I would say a good two months - or more," insisted Henry.

"Well, in that case, we would like to hire you as the O&S muleskinner. The mules should be here October first. We will pay you a dollar a day and your meals," insisted Nate.

"Sir, that would be fine. Mr. Hill only pays me two bits a day and my meals," declared Henry.

"When can you go to work?" asked Nate.

"Well, I'm cutting hay right now, and I would like to finish that up. So, how about next Monday?" asked Henry.

"That will be fine with us," agreed Nate and Ben.

September was coming to a close, and Ben said, "I will place the canvas order next week. I think we should have some 10' x 12' pieces cut just to cover things up, or lay on the ground. We don't have a barn anymore, and we need something to cover our feed and hay."

Henry showed up the last week of September as planned, and he and Ben thought they would ride over to Low Berry and check on the mules. If Mr. Wilson had any of them ready, they would try and bring back eight or nine. Pete was down at the corral when they rode up. Ben got off the mare and went over to shake his hand. "We are a week early, Pete, and I want you to meet Henry Wilson. He is going to be working for the O&S outfit as a muleskinner. Have you got any ready to go?" asked Ben.

"Oh, yes! I think I have 12 ready now, and I will have another 12 in a week," replied Pete.

"Can I pay you for the twelve and take eight with me today?" asked Ben.

"You sure can!" declared Pete.

"I will take all 12 if you think Henry and I can put six each on a tether," suggested Ben.

"If you tie three abreast, you should be able to do all right," agreed Pete.

"We will tie them close, and they should follow very nicely," added Henry.

"Well, you and Henry know mules - I know guns," acknowledged Ben.

"Speaking of guns, I sure would like to get my hands on that new Sharp long rifle," mentioned Pete.

"Well, I can take care of that. Next time I come down, I will bring you one", affirmed Ben.

Pete tied the mules off three abreast, and handed Ben a twelve foot tether to lead them with.

"Try not to spook them, and you should be fine," said Pete.

Ben let Henry take the lead, since he knew mules better than he did. He thought if he did well, the others would follow. As they came up on Old Town Henry stopped and said, "I think we should ride north a little bit and stay away from town, just in case someone in a buckboard would spook the mules. Six could be a pretty good handful, if they get wild."

Ben agreed. "A little more time - just might save us time."

It was dark when they rode up to Nate's barn. "Let's put the mules in Nate's corral for the night. We can deal with them in the morning," suggested Ben. Nate came out to see what was going on. All twelve had not been shoed yet. "You and Henry can cut out two or three and shoe them Monday," said Ben.

"It looks like they will take a number three or four shoe, and I don't think I have that many ready," stated Nate.

"Well, you fellows check that out Monday and I will take the wagon to work and see if I can pick up some harnesses. That way Henry can go to work Tuesday trying to break them," said Ben.

"Mr. Owens, I need a log hook. I would like to have the mules pull a dead load for at least two or three days, and I think a big old log would help take the fight out of them quicker," insisted Henry.

"I might have one; if not, I will make you one", answered Nate.

Ben said, "I will head up the hill and see what Elisabeth has got to eat, and see you both tomorrow night".

"Henry, Helen has got your supper on the stove, so let us call it a day," suggested Nate.

Monday morning Henry got a rope on three of the mules and tied them off at the hitching rail. "While I shoe these mules, why don't you take the wagon into town and pick up whatever canvas they have ready? That way you can start to cover the wagons and tie it down. While you are there, stop by the feed store and pick up as many 40 gallon barrels as you can get on the wagon. Tell Mr. Jones Ben or I will stop by and pay him when we order the corn."

Henry asked him if he had tops for the drums. "They will help us keep the corn dry."

Nate said, "Oh yes! We will need tops."

Helen fixed something for Henry to eat on his way back from town, while he got the wagon ready.

Henry got to town in good time and had the wagon loaded by 1 pm that would still give him time to get the canvas on one of the wagons before dark. Nate had finished the shoeing job and the mules did not quite know how to act with all that iron on their feet. Henry had to get some 2 x 4's and make a place to hang the new harnesses. He would have to do the same thing for Ben later. There was lots of work going on, and the day was over before you knew it.

After Nate finished shoeing the mules, he started pulling canvas and mounting barrels on the sides of the wagons. It was now the end of the first week of October. Ben and Henry still had to go pick up the other 12 mules. The girls were so busy they did not have time to cook meals, but they managed to keep their boys fed. This would be their last Thanksgiving and Christmas in Ohio, and some time had to be set aside for that.

Elisabeth sent Tom down the hill to get a few of the drums Henry had brought back the other day. She needed them to pack dishes and canned goods in. Elisabeth was thinking, "If I had known it was going to be all this much work, I might have told Ben I did not want to go!"

Ben was working hard at the gun shop. He felt he needed to do all he could to get the new gun to market before he left. The patent had been filed, and Joe and Jim were on cloud nine with the orders they were getting on the long rifle; but most of all, there were two contracts with the army that were being renegotiated to buy the new five-shot gun. That alone would keep them in business for the next five years. Things were good for the Sharp family and their friends.

With November coming into view, their plan was to be done with the wagons and the mule training. All they would have to do is load the wagons and make last minute plans. Mr. Adams had bought the shop and farm. He would take over the shop on January 1st. Jim and Joe had agreed to keep Ben and Elisabeth's house and rent it out for them. They would make sure it got good care, and the money would go into Ben's account.

November and December were spent getting things like the tools loaded. The hay was loaded onto two wagons. A layer of hay was spread on the wagon floor of the household wagons and canvas spread over that. Forty-eight barrels of corn were loaded, and oil cloth was spread over the tops and tied down. This was to keep water out. They still had to make room for water barrels on the front of two wagons. Since the trip was being made during the winter months, they did not have to fight dust, but all the wagons had to be snow and water tight. Any barrels left would be used for food supplies.

Thanksgiving came and a big dinner was planned. Ben had everyone at his house. After dinner he called everyone together and said, "I need to go over our plans for the trip. Nate and

I have been to the State Land Office and have filed claims to homestead one section each south of Omaha and West of Lincoln, Nebraska. We have chosen that part of the country because it has better land choice, and because there still should be plenty of timber from which we can build our homes. I figure it's 650 to 700 miles to where we want to go. Nate and I estimated that by taking the wagon trail South of Chicago we could have more wagon roads since its closer to Chicago. If that is the case, we could make better time and get there before it's too late into the growing season. I have estimated that it is 100 miles or so to the Indiana border. With good luck that will take us four days," stated Ben. "I hope to travel 25 miles per day. Our day should start at 5 a.m. and end at 5 p.m. It should take one and one half hours to break camp, and one and a half hours to make camp. It's about 140 miles across Indiana - that is six days with good luck. It's about 210 miles across Illinois - that is another nine to ten days. Across Iowa, it's another two hundred miles or 10 days. We should try and cross the Mississippi River at Sarasota, and go south 75 to 100 miles to our new home. Nate and I have decided to go south rather than North to South Dakota. We feel the winters will be a little warmer and save us 400 more miles to travel. Total time on the road, 33 to 40 days - if all goes well.

Then he continued, "I will take the lead wagon, followed by Ben Jr. in the hay wagon. Tom will bring up the tool and equipment wagon. Elisabeth will have the lead wagon with me. That way she can better care for the baby. Helen can drive the lead wagon in Nate's group. Henry will take the hay wagon and Nate will bring up the end of the wagon train. I have put Henry on the hay wagon because if he has to ride point, we can let Elisabeth drive the hay wagon until Henry gets back. If anyone has a complaint with the wagon assignments, please speak up now."

After a slight pause Ben said, "When we get ready for camp each night, I will start the ring, making it as tight as I can; Ben Jr. will pull his wagon up close to mine with the tongue turned a little bit to the right, Tom will be behind Ben Jr., and so on until the circle is closed. We must make the circle as tight as we can. This will give us better protection and cut down our walking between wagons. Nate and Henry will take care of the animals. The boys will gather firewood for the night. I will take care of the fire and water the animals and help Nate and Henry where I can. This will be our duty assignment every night and day unless you speak up."

He then continued, "For our sleeping arrangements, we have ordered canvas that will be locked just behind the front axle of the wagon. The canvas will also lock onto the sides of the wagon. We will then put two bales of hay across the front end of the wagon, and two bales across and along the side, placing them on the canvas to hold it down. This should provide a windbreaker and protection in case we get into trouble. The canvas on the ground should help keep our bedding and sleeping bags dry. If we need, we can put hay or grass under the canvas and on top to make it soft for our sleeping bags. Parking the wagons at night on high, dry ground will help. I will sleep under the hay wagon next to Elisabeth and the baby, Tom and Ben, Jr. under the equipment wagon, Nate and Henry under the other equipment wagon next to Helen and the girls. If we can, this should be our sleeping place every night."

"I think we should have two four-hour guard duties every night. Let's start with 9 p.m. to 1 p.m. and 1 a.m. to 5 a.m. Tom and I will take the 1 a.m. to 5 a.m. We can trade shifts, if we want more sleep. If we camp next to a wooded area, we will hobble the mules next to that; if not, they will have to be hobbled next to the wagons. We should not be on the trail more than 45 days," stated Ben.

"When we arrive we must pick the plot of land each of us wants; where we will build our homes, barns, corn cribs, and smoke houses. The land we pick should have a good supply of trees and good water. We will be there for the rest of our lives, so the girls should like the places we pick. Let's stay safe and take care of one another - God will be with us. With all that said, I will let Nate offer a prayer, and we will enjoy the rest of the day," concluded Ben.

December was spent getting ready for Christmas, doing more packing, and talking to family and friends. January was spent loading tools, corn, hay, and clearing out from Nate's shop what was thought to be needed. The weather had not been too bad, and everything was set to go on Monday, February 1, 1804.

January 31st found everything in place. Mr. Adams was very excited about the new shop. Since Nate and Helen had loaded everything from the house, they were to spend this last night together at Ben and Elisabeth's. That way, everyone would be ready to go at the same time. All the bedding had been loaded for the trip, so everyone would use their sleeping bags and sleep on the floor. It was fun! Jim and Joe had brought their wives over to say goodbye, and everyone was having a good time. The mules had been bedded down, half in Ben's barn and half in Nate's barn.

4:

Henry and Tom were up at 4:30 a.m. to get the mules hitched and ready to go. Helen and Elisabeth made sure everyone had good coats, gloves, and footwear. Ben and Nate got the pigs and cattle tied to the wagon and made a last minute inspection of everything. Some of the people living around came by to see them off, including the Adams from down below. At 6.30 a.m. February 1st, 1804, Ben popped the whip for the first time and the mules came to life. Regardless of what lay before them, it was too late to turn back!

The day was cold - about 28 degrees. The sun was just coming up. They hoped it would get a little warmer as the day went by. Everyone was dressed warmly, and 28 degrees didn't seem bad for that early in the morning. There was 6 inches of snow on the ground, but the wagon trail had been used the day and night before, so the trail was broken. Nate had shoed the mules with cleat shoes so they dug in very well, and with four of them on the tongue, it did not seem they were working that hard. Ten minutes turned to thirty minutes, thirty minutes turned to an hour. The trail was flat most of the time, but every now and then they would come up on a slight grade. You could see the mules throw their shoulders into the harness, and the muscles on their rear hindquarter stand up. All in all, it did not seem they were overloaded.

After the first hour, Ben raised his hand to stop the wagons. He thought it would be a good time to check with everyone and see how they were doing. All seemed to be doing quite well and were still happy. The sun was up, and it felt like it was getting a little warmer. Ben felt he had two weak spots in the train; one was Ben Jr., and the other Helen. He spent a little more time with each of them. They both seemed to be doing well. Ben Jr. thought he was all grown up and was having a good time. Ben was thinking as he walked back to speak with Nate, *I'll bet he will sleep well tonight!* "How far do you think we have come in the past hour?" asked Ben.

"I think it is a good three miles, maybe four", answered Nate.

"Well, it's 7:30 am now; why don't we go another hour and I will take over Henry's wagon and let him ride point for a few miles, and see if we can find a good place to pull off and have something to eat?" suggested Ben.

"That sounds good to me. I'm hungry already," responded Nate.

Another hour went by, and the landscape stayed about the same. Ben pulled up again and talked to Henry. "I think we have come about seven to eight miles in the last two hours. I would like for you to ride a half hour out and a half hour back and see what things are like out that far. We will keep on going. If we find a good place for our midday meal, we will pull up," said Ben.

Henry made it back in an hour or so, and Ben figured they had traveled 12 miles since morning. Henry said he had come upon a creek about 8 miles up front, and it looked like they could water the mules and eat a bite. So far, everything was going pretty much as they had planned. They had given the mules a little rest each time they stopped, and the day had warmed up to maybe 32 degrees or so. That was good for them, but bad for the road and mules, because it began to make the dirt soft.

At 11:30 am, they came to the creek Henry had said was out there. After watering the mules, they pulled up on the far bank and gave each of the mules a feed bucket. Everyone got to get down and walk around a little bit. Ben and Nate agreed they had traveled a good 20 miles, and if everything went that well for the afternoon it would be a good day. Henry would ride out again after dinner, and see how far they could go without problems.

In an hour, Henry rode up saying the snow was not near as deep as what they had already traveled through and that he had crossed two more creeks, and that the trail was still clear. He had seen two farms about five miles apart - one on the left side of the trail, and one on the right. Ben said, "Go ahead and drive for awhile and we will see what's up there."

The day had warmed up well, and as Henry had reported, the snow was only three inches deep and you could see the ground in many places. After traveling two more hours, they pulled up for a rest. It was almost 3 pm and Ben and Nate figured they had traveled a good 30 miles. Mary Sue was doing just fine in her snowsuit. Elisabeth had just gotten her up from a nap, and she was holding her doll and wanting to get down from the wagon. Nate and Henry were very happy with the way the mules had handled the loads. They felt as the hay and corn were consumed, the load would get lighter, and it would even be better. At 3:30 pm they moved out, hoping to find a nice campsite around 5:30 pm. After a few more miles, they came to the first creek Henry had reported. Ben got down and checked the water level in the creek bed. It looked like only a foot or so deep, and the bed was rocky. He did not think it would give them a problem. They would cross slowly, and let the mules drink if they wanted too.

Another hour went by, and the second creek came into view. This one had a higher bank on the west side. They would not let the mules drink and hit the water at a good, fast, pace. After an hour on the other side, there was a clump of trees and a large field. It would be a good place to make camp. The ground looked high, and the snow had cleared off in big spots. Ben started the circle and everyone followed. The boys got some wood together and started a fire. Helen and Elisabeth got food ready, and cups and plates. Nate and Henry took the mules over to the wooded area and made a corral out of rope and hobbled them down.

Corn, hay, and water were brought up. The cattle were left tied to the wagons after milking. The milk was stored in jugs and placed in a snow bank. Everyone was doing their work as if they had been doing this for years. After supper, everyone got their beds ready and returned to the fire for some talk. This was the first night to sleep outside, and the beds had to be made correctly. The canvas Ben had ordered was laid on the ground and tied up under the wagons. Then, the hay bales were placed in front and on the sides. This would keep the wind out. A little hay was then placed on top of the canvas; this could be used to feed the animals tomorrow. Next, a blanket was double folded and the sleeping bag placed on top. Two more blankets were provided in case anyone wanted to cover up. Ben slept in the wagon with Elisabeth and the baby; Nate and Henry slept under the hay wagon, and Tom and Ben Jr. under their hay wagon. Henry and Nate would take the first watch. Tom and Ben would take over at 1 a.m.

After returning to the fire they reviewed notes on the day. Nate reported that the wagons looked good, and not one double tree was out of place. Henry checked on the mules after supper and reported they had eaten, drunk, and were now lying down. Mary Sue was full of life and wanted to play in the fire after her nap. The long day of driving the mules had tired Ben Jr., and he went to bed. Helen took the girls and her son, Bill, off to bed. Henry, Nate, and Ben took out the map he had gotten from the Land Management Office at home, and thought they would try and figure out where they were and how far they had traveled. There were no roads marked on the map - only what was called the Northwest Trail. From the looks of the map, the trail ran well past Chicago and looked like they had traveled 28 or 30 miles, placing them about halfway out of Ohio. Not bad for the first day. The next day looked about the same, except for a good-sized river or creek.

Nate offered a short prayer thanking God for his blessing and asked that He watch over them through the night. Ben thought he would check on Ben Jr. before going to bed. He found him sleeping sound, warm, and safe. He said goodnight to Tom and said he would wake him up at 1 a.m. Tom took his boots and coat off. He had made his bed next to Ben Jr. with just enough space between them to prevent waking him when he went on guard duty. He took his sidearm off and laid it just under his pillow and placed his rifle alongside his sleeping bag, sort of tucking it under the side.

Tom had inherited his father's brains and was quite mature for his age. He felt a sense of peace of a job well done as he made himself comfortable in his sleeping bag. His mind raced back to the start of the day and the life he had just left. He wondered what tomorrow would bring. The next thing, his father was bending over him saying, "Tom, it is time to go." It seemed he had only been asleep ten minutes, but three hours or more had passed by.

Ben gave Tom some instructions. He told him to take the other side of the train. That way, he would not sit in the warm shelter of the wagon bed and go back to sleep. "Walk up and down the inside of the train from the tongue of our wagon to the end of Nate's equipment wagon", said Ben. Then, he should walk from back of his wagon to the front of Nate's equipment wagon. He was to stop every now and then and look into the night through the scope and see what he could see. In the event he spotted danger, he was to fire at the danger if it was great enough, or into the air if he wanted help. Tom felt tired, and knew he should go to bed each night right after supper if he was to make it. Those three to four hours of sleep were not going to be enough and then drive all day.

The night was a little cold, so that kept him awake. The sky was clear, and there were no sounds except the animals. Tom could look across the train and see his Dad doing the same thing as him. It didn't take long to figure that he needed to be at the equipment wagon, while his Dad was at their wagon. That way, someone would be on each end of the train at all times. The four hours went by quickly, and Tom thought he would go lie down for one more hour or so. Henry and Nate would take care of the mules, and Ben Jr. would get the fire going. His mother would get him up to eat just before they hit the trail. Everyone gathered around the fire for something to eat, coffee, and milk. The big question was - how did every one sleep? Quite well, was the report. Henry said it was better than his cot!

It was nearing 7 am when they were ready to go. Dousing the fire with water, it was time to roll out. Day number two on the trail was to be much the same as yesterday, they hoped. They were still in Ohio and would be all day. The only real change was there were more people on the trail. Every time another wagon came down the trail, they had to move off to the side to let them by. The trail was not wide enough for two wagons side by side. It was not bad, and everyone wanted to know where they were going and where they were from.

That night Nate, Ben, and Henry looked at the map and the best they could tell was that Indiana was about twenty miles out. That meant that by 3 pm tomorrow, the train should cross over into a new territory.

The past two days had been much the same, and day five saw the train 60 miles into Indiana. Nate said he wanted to check the mules' shoes to see how they were holding up. The last thing they needed was a lame mule. It took him a good hour to check all twelve mules. Henry took their harnesses off and hung them on the front and back of the wagons. That way, everything would be ready in the morning.

After supper they sat around the fire for some talk, when Henry noticed two riders approaching the train. He told Nate and Ben and then moved away from the fire to the equipment wagon. He stood just outside and watched the two men ride in.

It had just begun to turn dark. Both men were carrying side arms and rifles alongside their saddles. Henry did not like the looks of the two.

One of the men yelled out, "Can we approach the camp?" With that, Nate walked up to meet them, while Ben and Tom moved out of the firelight to the other side of the wagon train. Then the man asked, "We would like to know if we could share your fire, and maybe some coffee."

Nate said, "Sir, this is a Christian family train and we have rules".

"Oh yeah, and what are they, if I may ask?" inquired one of the men.

"You tie your horses off outside the train and leave your side arms and knives in your saddle bags," replied Nate.

"How do I know I can trust you?" inquired the stranger.

"You don't - but those are the rules, if you want coffee and heat," declared Nate.

"You are pretty damn sure of yourself!" admonished the stranger.

"Oh, I forgot to tell you, there is no swearing in camp. We have women and children here and there are three more men watching every move you make. So if you would like to step down and follow the rules, you are welcome," stated Nate strongly. The men looked at one another for a long time, and then stepped down.

Both men had big bed rolls and saddle bags that looked full, which told Nate they were used to sleeping outside and were carrying food and clothing with them. Their clothes looked like they had not been washed in months. He did not like the looks of this, but was glad he had stated the rules before allowing them to step down.

Tom had moved up to the lead wagon and had a much better view of the men. Ben was sitting under the equipment wagon, ready for anything. The men tied their horses to the wagons, took off their gun belts, and hung them over their saddles. Then they stepped across the wagon tongue into the train circle and headed for the fire. Nate walked a little to the side and about a half step back. As they approached the fire one of the men said, "It sure is nice to feel a little heat."

Nate agreed, "On these cold nights it's good to have. By the way, my name is Nate Owens and this is my family."

The taller man spoke up and said, "My name is Bill Jones, and this is Jess Tyler".

"Where are you fellows from?" inquired Nate.

"We are from down the Missouri River area", answered Bill.

"What brings you up this way?" inquired Nate.

"We have been looking for work. Thought we would go up to Dayton and look around. Where you folks from?" asked Jess.

"We used to live up in Ohio in Old Town. We are on our way out to the Nebraska area," responded Nate.

Then Nate asked, "Would you men like some coffee?"

Both said, "Yes".

"We have just finished our supper, and I don't know if there is much left," said Nate.

Helen spoke up and said, "We have some potatoes, beans, and gravy left. Would you like some?"

Jess said, "We have not had food like that in a month." Helen filled a couple of plates and handed them to each man. They sat their coffee cups on the ground, and sat down on a barrel. Joe said, "It sure is good, Ma'am, and we thank you very much".

"By the way, where are the rest of your men folks?" asked Bill.

"They are out there in the dark, walking the train", answered Nate.

"Do you walk all night?" Bill asked.

"Most of it", Nate replied.

"Well, that should make you pretty tired for the next day, doesn't it?" remarked Bill.

"We manage pretty well," stated Nate.

"By the way, would it be all right if we bed down next to your fire for the night?" asked Bill.

About that time, Ben walked up with his rifle tucked under his arm. He said, "If you keep the fire going - and we have a look at your bed roll".

"Damn, you people drive a hard bargain," declared Bill.

Nate spoke up quickly saying, "Remember the rule - no swearing!"

By now, the girls had drifted off to bed. Only the four men remained around the fire. Ben and Nate walked the two men over to their horses, and asked them to untie their bed rolls and throw them on the ground. Then they were to unsaddle their horses; throw the saddle blanket over the wagon wheel, and put the saddle on top of it. While they were doing that, Ben inspected the bed rolls. The rolls were thick because they had another blanket in each of them.

Joe said, "What do you want us to do with the side arms?"

"Put them in your saddle bags and lay them over the wheel," replied Ben. They did not like that, but did as they were told. Ben rolled up the bed rolls and handed them over as they stepped over the tongue into the circle.

"That is a fine looking rifle you have there, Mister. What kind of gun is that?" asked Bill.

"It's a Sharp semiautomatic long rifle", answered Ben.

"Where did you get a gun like that?" inquired Bill.

"I made it," replied Ben.

"You made it!" Jess remarked.

"That's right - I made it", Ben pointed out.

"Can I see it?" asked Jess.

"No, I'm afraid not. I don't let it out of my sight," Ben said.

"I'm not going to run off with it, I just wanted a look at it," declared Jess. "No, I can't do that. I don't give up my piece to anyone. Keep the fire up and sleep well", rebuked Ben boldly.

With that, Nate and Ben walked over to where Henry was watching the whole show from his sleeping area. The three of them sat down under the wagon to talk. Nate spoke up, "I don't know if they are telling the truth, or not. Their clothes are dirty, and their saddle bags are full of something, but we have no grounds to turn them away since they have asked for shelter."

"You are right, but we have to keep a close eye on them all night. If they let the fire die down go over and throw a log on, and don't be quiet about it. That way, they know you are out there doing your job," cautioned Ben.

The two strangers slept well, and the camp began to stir at 5 a.m. The men were served coffee and food, and Ben walked them to their horses. They thanked him again and rode off.

There was another big day in front of them, and with good luck they would be 110 to 115 miles into what is now known as Indiana. It was a nice day, with the sun shining. After two hours on the trail, they came upon a pretty good sized river. Ben pulled up and got down to see how deep the water was. Henry and Nate walked up and it was decided the water was not too deep, but they needed to know how deep the mud was in the bottom. It was determined that Henry would ride his horse across the river to check for mud and water depth. He reined up and started a slow walk across the river. It was 50 feet wide and had a medium bank about three feet above the river bed. The gelding did not like the water, but after a few spurs he did as he was asked.

The water came up just above the horse's knees, and it looked like from the bank that he was not struggling to pull his feet out of any mud. Henry crossed and waved from the other side that it looked good. After crossing back over, it was agreed they would wrap the corn barrels with canvas and tie canvas under the bottom of each wagon. However, there was not enough canvas to do all six wagons. Someone would have to ride a horse over and bring the canvas back. Nate said, "I will take my equipment wagon and Ben Jr. over. He can hold the team for us, while I cross back over on the horse."

"That sounds fine with us," agreed Ben and Henry.

The next wagon to cross was Tom with the other equipment wagon. The water came up just under the wagon bed, but was not strong enough to float the wagon. Nate followed with one of the hay wagons. Since three wagons had gone over without a problem, Ben decided that it was safe to take Elisabeth and Mary Sue across. Nate followed with his girls, and then Henry crossed with the last hay wagon. The whole crossing had taken up three hours of their travel time, but it had been a safe crossing.

They gave thanks to God for his blessing, and got ready to move out. Nate said, "Why don't we have something to eat before we have to stop again?"

Helen said, "We have ham, and lots of bread, and over three gallons of milk - and more tonight. If we don't drink it, I will have to give it to the hogs." Henry gave the teams a little corn and some water, as the river water was too muddy to drink.

After another hour on the trail, Nate was suddenly surprised when a rider passed him in a gallop and reined up in front of his mules. As he was trying to figure out what was going on, the second rider pulled up next to his wagon with a gun pointed at him saying, "Throw that rifle down here you have leaned up in your wagon!"

Nate was not a fool, and knew it was no time to put up a fight. He picked the gun up by the barrel and handed it down to the rider. By now, Nate recognized the two men as the riders they had given food and shelter to last night.

Henry was driving the next wagon and knew something was wrong. He turned his wagon just a little bit to the right and then turned back to the road. That way, he could get a better look at what the problem was. He pulled the team to a stop, set the brake, and grabbing his rifle, he hit the ground on the run. He ran to the back of the wagon, laying the rifle on a water barrel. He could see they were beginning to ride off in a gallop. He sighted the rider in the shoulder and fired. It was like slow motion as the rider fell from the horse in a full run and hit the ground hard on his butt.

Rider number two turned his horse a little to the right, and kept on the run. Henry wasn't worried. The rider was only two hundred yards away, and he knew he had time. He sighted the same area and fired. The rider lunged forward but did not come out of the saddle. Henry did not want to kill him, but he had made up his mind that if the rider did not rein in his horse and ride back to check on his partner, he would drop him. Just as he finished sighting him in the back of the head, he turned his horse.

Henry untied his gelding from the back of the wagon, slid the rifle into its holder, and jumped in the saddle. He covered the two hundred yards in seconds. He rode up to the man still in the saddle, pulled his .45, and took the rifle out of the riders' rifle holder. The man lying on the ground was beginning to move and was crying out in pain.

Nate walked up and said, "Good job, Henry! Get their guns and toss them out there in the grass."

The man that called himself Jess Tyler asked, "What are you going to do about us?"

Nate said, "Nothing! You do the devil's work; you get to collect the devil's pay. You had better thank God the man did not kill you. You are not far from the river. Camp there, and get well."

"But we need a doctor!" exclaimed Jess.

"Well, you had better hope you get lucky and one comes along. If you ever show your face around my train again, you won't need a doctor!" exclaimed Nate.

With that, Nate and Henry walked back to the train. By now the train had stopped, and Ben was on his way to see what the problem was all about.

"Are you just going to leave them out there?" inquired Ben.

"Yes sir!" Nate replied. "The Book says you reap what you sow"

By the time they got the train back on the trail it was five pm, but they wanted to put one more hour on the trail before dark.

There had been a lot going on to delay them, and they needed to get some distance between them and the two robbers.

As they bedded down Ben asked, "Do you think they could be coming up on us again?"

"No, I don't think so. Henry hit them pretty bad, and they need time to get well. No, I think they have had all they want of us."

It had been a bad day with the river, and the robbers. They estimated maybe 15 or 20 miles was all the day had to offer.

Next morning they were up early, and it looked like a good day to make some good time. Ben decided to let Elisabeth drive for a while, and he would go back and ride with Nate. He needed to talk to him about the supplies, wagons, and the mules' shoes. It was agreed supplies were holding up well; water had not been a problem, and letting the mules rest a few minutes every hour was a good thing. It looked like they were in good shape. Ben Jr. had put a lot more hay in the chicken pens, and there had been a few eggs from the deal. The hogs didn't like being dragged along by a tether but were getting used to it. If things got too bad, as the hay wagon load went down they would put the hogs in with the hay. Nate said, "Don't worry about the mules' shoes. It takes three to four months to wear out shoes and that is on rocky ground. The ground here on the trail is soft and should not be a problem."

Day eight saw them on the trail with a little more wind than they had been used to, but it was February. The weather was 28 to 30 degrees but the day was bright, so everyone buttoned up tight and westward they went. Since it was Saturday, Ben wanted a nice campsite with plenty of wood for the fire, and good water to fill the water barrels. They would sleep late tomorrow morning, have a late breakfast, and give thanks to God Almighty for his many blessings. Maybe if all went well, someone would take a long ride out front to see what the countryside looked like.

At straight up 6 pm they came upon a small creek, a good clump of trees, and some open ground. You couldn't ask for more, and Ben was not going to try. Bringing the wagons into a circle was routine now, and the boys soon had a nice fire going. Since the day had been cold the ground was hard, and the mules had made good time with some down hills in the mix. It looked like maybe 35 miles had been covered.

After supper they sat around the fire and talked about how far they had come, and how far they had to go. It was decided Henry would ride out tomorrow around noon, and get a read on what lay in front of them. Everyone went to bed early, and since it was cold it would be a good time to test the bedding. Nate and Henry would keep the fire going all night, until Ben and Tom took over.

Next morning, Ben made coffee since he was just coming off guard duty. Helen and Elisabeth got up and made a nice breakfast with bacon and eggs, and fresh milk for the girls. Helen said, "I want everyone to enjoy the eggs, because starting the middle of next month we will have no more eggs. I have to start saving them for nesting, which I hope will take place in April."

Ben spoke up and asked how Nate and Henry had slept. "Very well," Henry said, "I used one more blanket to cover up with, and I was fine".

Nate said, "My feet were a little cold for a while, but did warm up after an hour. I plan to take care of that tonight."

"Oh yeah, how do you plan to do that?" inquired Henry.

"I'm going to lay two pieces of iron by the fire, and after they get warm I will wrap them and put them in the bottom of my sleeping bag. I hope they will hold the heat for a few hours", answered Nate.

"You might know a blacksmith would come up with an idea like that!" laughed Henry.

"Since we are going to stay in camp this morning, I think I will catch a little shut-eye," said Ben. Everyone else had a good time exploring the woods and the creek, which was covered in ice except for the very middle. Henry saddled his gelding and hobbled the mules, so they could roll and eat a little grass. It was close to noon and he bid everyone farewell and said he would try and be back by suppertime.

Henry spurred the gelding to a nice trot and looked out over the landscape. It was a nice afternoon. The trail was clear and the ground hard. He slowed the gelding down to a walk and let him catch his breath. Everything looked good. He would ride two hours, and then turn around and head back. The land was flat, and the grass was high on both sides of the trail. He had not even come across a creek. Henry did not like the tall grass on both sides of the trail and wondered if there were any Indians in this part of the country. The tall grass would make a good ambush place. He rode on with no sounds except the geldings' hooves on the hard ground. After another half hour or so, he came to a good size ditch leading off to some trees and brush. He reined the gelding up and stepped down. It looked like a good place to take a break.

He was enjoying a drink from his canteen when he heard sounds down by the woods. He pulled his rifle from its holder and dropped down on one knee. A hundred yards down the ditch he saw a herd of deer sliding down the bank and heading for the woods to bed down. He thought for a minute he would take one, but it would be late when he got back to camp and he did not want to skin a deer this late in the day. All sounds were gone after the deer crossed the ditch, and it was quiet once again. A light breeze was blowing and it looked like snow was on the way. He slid the rifle back into its holder, pulled the gelding in close, and grabbed the saddle horn. It was time to go back.

It was getting dark when he returned to camp, and Nate had begun to worry. He was right. It had begun to snow, and the fire felt good after two hours of cold wind. Helen brought up something to eat as he asked about the mules.

Nate said, "I took care of them. They are fine." Then Nate asked, "What did you see out there?"

"Well, to tell the truth, not much. The trail is clear for a good day's travel. The trail is hard and was dry until it started to snow.

The grass is tall for about two miles, and around the end of the day, we will come to a deep ditch. It looks like we can scoop it out a little bit on each side, and we should be fine. It would not be a bad place to camp, except I did not see any water. I did see some deer, in case we want one for supper. Other than that, it is a good trail," replied Henry.

While Henry had been gone, it was decided that it was time for everyone to take a bath. The girls spoke up, saying, "Are you crazy? Take a bath out here in a field when it's this cold, and everybody can see us? NO WAY!" they exclaimed.

"Well, we will see if we can't fix some of that," said Helen.

"Oh yeah, how?" asked the girls.

"Well, you just wait and see," replied Helen. She then asked Nate and Henry to remove the big black kettle from the equipment wagon, and set it up next to the fire as close as they could. Tom and Ben were to drive three or four poles in the ground, and tie canvas around them. They were to leave one end open next to the fire. The kettle was filled with water, which Henry carried from the creek. Ben brought a big wash tub from the equipment wagon and sat it as close to the opening as he could.

All agreed that Elisabeth and the baby would be first, and no men folks would be near the bathing enclosure while the girls were getting their bath. Once the girls were done, the water was changed and it was the boys' turn. Ben Jr. went first; then Tom, Henry, Bill and the others followed. It was not that bad after you got into the warm water - it was drying off that you got cold. It sure did feel good to wash off after eight days, and get some clean clothes. Elisabeth made some tea, and she had some shortening bread she had made and wrapped in oil cloth before they left home.

It had been a nice Sunday, but the snow was coming down good when they started off to bed. Nate and Henry took the first watch. By the time Ben and Tom took over, there was a good inch of snow on the ground. After the watch was over they had three inches on the ground, but it did look like it was beginning to slow down. Ben did not think three inches was enough to give them much trouble, so he woke up Henry and Nate to get their viewpoint. It was agreed they would move out as always. Tom lay down while breakfast was being prepared, and at 7 a.m. the train was on the move.

The mules had to pull hard to break the wagons from the frozen ground, but once moving, it was not bad. The trail was hard to read with the snow covering the tracks. Ben had to keep his mind on the task at hand to keep from guiding the wagons in the wrong direction. Wind had blown the snow around and if you knew what you were looking for, you could read the wagon ruts up front. The day went on much the same as another. Ben stopped the train every hour or so to let the mules rest.

About 4 pm, the ditch Henry had warned them about came up. Ben looked around and pulled the train down by the trees and got ready to camp. They unhitched the teams, except for two mules that they were going to use to scoop out the ditch banks. Nate and Henry took the saw down to the trees and cut five logs, eight feet long. Ben dragged them up to the ditch and rolled them in. He thought doing this would make the bottom of the ditch a little higher, and keep him from scooping out so much dirt. He would put a little dirt on top of them before he was done.

The work took a good three hours or more, but the ditch now would be an easy crossing. Before Ben started the ditch, he had scooped some of the snow off the inner circle so everyone could get around a little better. By the time the ditch was finished, the boys had a good fire going and Helen and Elisabeth had gotten something to eat together. It was not a bad trip so far. They had planned well and brought almost everything they needed. Everyone was well, and the girls were as warm as they could be and still be outside.

After supper, the men sat around the fire and looked at the map. Nate figured they had traveled a good 30 miles in the snow and thought it was a good day. Ben looked at the map hard and tried to see what he thought about the trail, and how far it might go before it ran out. The map looked like it was five years old or older, and Nate said, "Since we are this far north near Chicago, the trail could go all the way to Saratoga, since that would be a major river crossing." He thought after five years, enough people had used the trail to make it passable. "The only thing we can do is push on - time will tell."

Next morning would see them on the trail for 8 days, and all was looking good. Food was holding up well, and everyone had a bath. The only thing that had not been done was the washing of their dirty clothes. Helen said, "We can take care of that the first time we get to stop a few days." The snow was still three to four inches in places, but it was not holding them up. They had no idea what the trail was like up front; after all, the ditch had been the end of Henry's ride on Sunday. It would have to be just one mile at a time.

All day had not brought them near good, clean water, so the train had to use the barrel water. There was enough water to last them for three days. If worst came to worst, they could melt snow. Ben brought the train to a stop a little early, because in his mind he was going to make a night ride up front to see what he could see. Elisabeth got him some food together and he saddled his mare. Tom wanted to go with him, so he asked Henry if he could ride his gelding.

Henry said, "Yes, and he is a little high strung in the hands of a stranger. Don't let him jump out from under you!"

"If you will shorten the stirrups for me a little, I'll be fine," said Tom.

Ben thought it would be fine to have a little company along on the ride. After an hour it was still light, so Ben pushed on. After all, he did not need the light to find his way back. The trail was clear, and the snow was not quite as deep as it had been for the past two days. There was not much to see. There were no houses and no one else on the trail, so it was quiet. There was a small stream after another fifteen minutes' ride. They would be able to fill the water barrels tomorrow, but they had not gone far enough along to camp; maybe for lunch - but not camp. Ben said, "So let's head back; it looks good enough for me".

On the trail back, Ben noticed a small fire surrounded by three men in a clump of trees about three hundred yards off the trail. He reined the mare in and stepped down. He walked around to the front of the mare and took out his bandana and wrapped it around the mare's nose.

"Why did you do that?" Tom asked.

"So she won't snort. You do the same to the gelding. Stay here and hold the horses. I'm going to walk out there in the grass a few yards, and see what they are talking about," replied Ben firmly.

After a hundred yards or so, he bent down low in the grass and snow. He could clearly see the three men sitting around a fire. The problem was they were not western men - they were Indians! Well, that told him there was some in the area. He made his way back to Tom and told him to walk the horse a few hundred yards before mounting again. Tom knew there was something wrong but did not say anything.

A mile down the trail he pulled up and said to Tom, "The reason I did not say anything back there was because there were three Indians around that fire. I didn't want to make any more noise than what we had to", stated Ben.

"What do you think that means?" asked Tom.

"Not much, I hope. It looked like the Indians were just passing through", answered Ben.

"What makes you say that?" inquired Tom. "If they had a camp nearby, they would not have stopped for the night. No, I don't think they mean any harm," declared Ben.

It was 8 p.m. when they pulled into camp. They unsaddled the horses and threw blankets over their backs and joined the fire. Nate walked up and asked, "What did you see out there?"

"Not much. We found a place to fill our water barrels tomorrow. Other than that, it looks like a good trail."

Tom could not hold himself any longer and blurted out that they had seen some Indians on the way back.

Nate spoke up. "Are you sure?"

"Yes, it sure did look like it to me. They were camped alongside the trail, and looked like they were passing through. I don't think they have a camp around here, or they would not have been camping out. We will be a little careful tomorrow", answered Ben. Then he said, "I'm going to lie down for a while. My shift will be here soon."

Nate said, "Go ahead and sleep another hour. Henry and I will stay a little longer."

"Ok! I will tell Tom," agreed Ben.

They had covered a good 35 miles per day. At the start of the day it was cloudy and cold. It felt like snow was in the air. They had good weather so far on the trip, but it was February, and anything could happen. Ben did not like it, but they were at the mercy of the times and there was nothing they could do.

Good time was made during the morning, and when they stopped for lunch light snow had begun to fall. As lunch was finished the ground was beginning to be covered, but they moved on. There was no wood for a fire at this campsite. By 4 pm the snow was two inches deep and was coming down hard and fast. Ben knew a campsite would have to be found soon, or they were in trouble.

Another hour went by, and the mules were getting tired. Snow was now a good four inches, and there was no sign of let-up. Ben stopped the train to let the mules rest. As he did, he saw some woods about half a mile off the trail on the left side. He got down and went back to ask Henry if he would ride down there and see what he could find.

Henry untied the gelding, and headed out through the field. Everyone had moved inside the wagon flaps and was watching Henry. He pulled short of the woods and turned the gelding hard to the right. Ben was wondering why he did that, when he could have ridden straight forward. After a few minutes in the woods he came back; but again, he went wide and rode out into the field a good two hundred yards. Ben could not figure out what he was up to. In the bat of an eye Henry and the horse were gone. My God, where did they go? No Henry and no horse. Elisabeth said, "Where did he go?

"I don't know be quiet!" He thought he heard the gelding snorting and making sounds. Once again the sounds of a horse in trouble were clear. Ben jumped from the wagon and headed to the back of his where his mare was tied. He pulled himself into the saddle and pushed the mare as fast as he could in the snow. It seemed like weeks before he got close enough to see what the trouble was. As he got closer to Henry he could see the gelding had fallen into a lake and was fighting with all his strength to climb a steep bank. He could not see Henry at all. As he searched for Henry his eyes caught a glimpse of Henry's hat twenty feet to his left, lying on the ice. Henry was nowhere to be seen. The gelding tried and tried again to get a foothold in the steep, muddy bank. You could see the horse losing his strength as he fought with all he had to get out. In another second he spotted Henry bobbing up and down in the water, holding on to a chunk of ice.

Ben slid from the saddle and grabbed his rope tied to the back of the saddle. As he threw the loop at Henry and the ice block he could now see blood running from Henry's head as he struggled to hold on to the rope. Ben was pulling with all his strength when he felt Nate in back pulling also. As Henry was dragged out of the water, Nate said, "We have to get his clothes off or he will freeze to death".

About that time Nate heard Tom and Ben Jr. making their way through the snow as fast as they could. As they dragged Henry to shore he yelled at Tom, "GO GET SOME BLANKETS! HURRY!! HURRY!"

They removed Henry's clothes, took off their coats, and wrapped him up. Nate pulled out his bandana and tied his head up.

The gelding was still trying to get a foothold in the bank but was losing his strength fast. Nate said, "We cannot save that horse unless we can get a rope on him."

Ben wound up the rope and threw it at the horse's head. As it went around his neck and they began to pull they could see the already-winded horse could not breathe. Nate said, "If we can get that rope around his front legs and the saddle horn we can use the mare to pull him out. With that Nate slid down the bank of the muddy lake into the icy water. He removed the rope from the horse's neck and threw it over the saddle horn. He reached under the gelding's belly and pulled the rope up under his front legs. Ben tied the rope on to his mare's saddle and pulled her forward. With a few tries the mare was able to pull Nate and the gelding up out of the lake.

By now the boys had made it back with some blankets and a half bale of hay. Tom kicked the snow out of the way and laid the blankets on the ground. By now Nate had his clothes off and they put both men in the blankets. Ben made three piles of hay while Nate lit it. Tom and Ben got some wood together. They built three fires around the men and sent Tom back to the wagons to get horse blankets and some dry clothes for Henry and Nate.

Ben wiped the gelding off with Henry's shirt and they covered him with horse blankets. The fires were beginning to get hot and Nate and Henry were talking about being too close together in those blankets. Ben said, "It looks like they are going to live, so let them get some clothes on".

Ben Jr. was walking the gelding up and down the path they had made to get him warm and it looked like everyone was going to be fine.

Ben said to Henry, "I thought you were old enough to know not to go swimming in the middle of winter. Let's have a look at that head."

With that Ben untied the bandana and took a look. It was skinned pretty badly but not deep. "I think you are going to be just fine if you don't get sick on us. You and Nate stay here by the fire while we get the wagon train a camp site."

Henry spoke up and said, "I think we can camp next to those woods over there, but you had better look around for more water holes."

Ben said, "I will walk the mare out there a few yard and see what I can see. We know we have water. Ben, you stay here and Tom and I will bring the wagons up."

With in another hour they had the wagons in place and Nate and Henry were helping Ben Jr. gather more wood. "Let's keep this fire going until we get the camp setup," Nate said to Henry. "Then we can move in close to the fire and get something warm to drink."

Ben pulled the wagons up 25 yards or so from the woods and hopped down. It was snowing hard. He wanted to get the scooper down and clean off the circle before the mules were put up. *I guess I had better clean off a place for them also*, thought Ben.

Helen and Elisabeth got things ready for dinner, while the boys got the fire going. "You kids stay in the wagon until we get things warmed up," insisted Elisabeth. Mary Sue did not like that, and Elisabeth took her over to Helen's wagon where the other girls could watch her.

Ben got a circle for the mules cleaned off, put away and fed, then joined Nate and Henry by the fire. They decided to deal with the lake in the morning, so they went back to see what the women were cooking up and got Nate and Henry some warm tea.

Tom had taken some wooden polls and made a tent where they could sit out of the snow and eat. The snow was coming down hard and was between three and four inches deep. After eating, they all agreed that if the snow was too deep, they would remain in camp until things got a little better. Everyone began to drift off to bed, which was the only place to be on a night like this. Nate had found a few pieces of iron and laid them around the fire to get hot. He thought they would help Henry and him-self stay warm overnight.

The snow was still coming down hard. Guard duty would be light tonight, since they had pulled off the main trail and the weather was as bad as it was. It was good sleeping weather. The only sounds were every now and then a cow would bawl, or a mule would snort.

Ben threw the wagon flap back and checked the weather. Much to his surprise, it was still snowing and it was a good foot and a half deep. Nate and Henry were the closest to the fire, so they kept it burning through the night. He noticed the wood had been placed under Tom's tent to keep it dry, or to keep from digging it out of the snow. There was no need to hurry in getting up--no one was going anywhere--but the animals had to be taken care of.

Ben Jr. milked the cows, while Nate's oldest girl took care of the chickens and pigs. The men had picked the hogs up yesterday when the snow got deep, and placed them in the hay wagon. Ben harnessed one of the mules and cleaned off the circle one more time. He also cleaned out the mule area and put out some hay. He would fill the feed sacks tied around their necks, and give them water after breakfast. It was still snowing when he sat down to eat.

Nate walked up and said, "How long do you think we will be here?

Ben said, "God, I don't know! If this snow would quit I would say it could be two days before we could move out." Right now, I don't know what to say."

Elisabeth and Helen had made pan cornbread, ham and eggs, and hot coffee. Not bad for a fellow away from home!

Henry stated, "I'm going to take a shovel down and clean off the lake, or what we think is a lake, and see how deep the ice is".

Nate said, "I will go with you just in case you fall in. Maybe I can get you out!" They laughed and headed off to the lake.

The snow was deep, and it was coming close to two feet. It was hard to walk as they made their way to the lake, and it was hard to tell exactly where the lake was. Henry found a spot and started shoveling. It was not long until he struck ice. He shoveled out a spot 6 feet by 6 feet, and Nate took the drill he had made and started a hole. The ice was deep since it was a lake, and the water was not moving. It was a good foot deep.

Nate said, "Let's drill a few more holes in a straight line. Then I will get a saw, and we will check to see if the water is any good down there." After that, they walked back to camp and got a saw and some buckets. The path was not so bad this time, and the snow was beginning to quit.

When they got back, Tom and Ben Jr. wanted to tag along. Nate sawed a hole in the ice two feet by three feet, and Tom moved some more snow out of the way. The ice block was too big to pull out of the water, so Nate had to cut it again. When they got the ice out, Henry dipped some water out, and it was clear and had no smell. As he did so, he saw fish - not just one or two, but many of them were swimming around the hole. Nate said, "They are hungry. It won't be hard to catch them."

Tom said, "Dad has got some things in a box in the wagon that he takes with him when he goes fishing, if I can find it." They filled the buckets and headed back to the camp. They would have water, anyway. Who knows, maybe they would have fish tonight for dinner - that would be a change!

Back at camp Ben was told of their finding, and he was happy everyone would have water if they had to camp a few days. Now fish - that was something else! He had not had fish in a long time. Tom came back with his dad's fishing box, and it had everything they needed. The path was now clear, and walking was not a problem. Since all the excitement had cleared away from the hole, there were all kinds of fish hanging around. Nate did not know for sure, but thought they were crappie.

Tom took a piece of bread he had gotten from his mother and dropped it into the water. It did not get more than a foot down and there was a big fight as to who got the food. A nice big one won out, and Tom pulled him up. Nate thought he was a good three pounds or more. More bread was dropped into the hole, and again a big catch! "How many do you think we need?" Tom asked.

"I would think 8 or 12 at least. There are eleven of us. We can always come back and get more," replied Nate. The water seemed deep where they had cut the hole - maybe six feet, or more. This had turned out to be a good campsite, even if it did almost drown Henry.

Ben looked at the buckets full of fish and said, "You fellows caught them. I will clean them."

Ben Jr. got two more buckets of water, while Elisabeth's washboard was brought up to clean the fish on. Ben thought twelve would be enough, since they were so big he could cut them in half. Helen and Elisabeth would roll them in cornmeal with a fresh egg or two. They were going to have a fish fry tonight!

The snow had stopped, and the sky was beginning to clear, but Ben and Nate did not like the two or three day delay. It would put a strain on their feed and hay. The girls did not care; they had washing to do, and this would be a good time to catch up. They had ham and coffee for lunch, and the day went by. There was not much else to do, so Ben took a nap and the kids played around the fire.

Henry went with the boys and cut a big stock of wood, and brought it to the campsite. He got the idea to use the scooper to haul the wood with, and Tom and Ben could ride down to the wood site. It was fun for everyone today.

The girls had decided that it was too late to start to wash clothes, so they would save that for tomorrow. Besides, the kettle needed to be put on the fire to heat water. Helen checked on the kids and they were playing games, and even Bill was playing with them. It had turned out to be a good day, even though it was such a mess when they woke up.

That night, everyone gathered around the fire while the fish were being fried. God, they smelled good! Helen asked, "How long do you think we will have to stay here?"

"I don't know at this time. Sunday night I will have a better idea. The snow has to come down where we can read the trail and not kill our mules. If the weather warms up, it could be Tuesday. Other than that, I have no idea," replied Ben.

"How far do you think we have come?" asked Elisabeth.

Ben answered, "I figure between 400 and 450 miles".

Then Elisabeth inquired, "How much more do we have to go?"

"I would say about the same distance," declared Ben.

"What if we get to where we are going and someone else has taken our land?" Helen wanted to know.

"They would have to have papers on the land given to them by the Government Land Office," replied Ben.

"What if they have given the land to two people? Will the government make it good? How much land has the Land Office granted us?" probed Elisabeth.

"One square mile, this is 640 acres. That will be 1,280 acres for the two of us. The law says we have to mark it off and farm the plot for the next five years before we have title. That is why we want to get a crop in the ground this year. That way, we will only have four more years to go," stated Ben.

"That is more land than I ever thought we could own!" exclaimed Elisabeth.

"We must watch what we are doing. We should have water, a small stream, creek, or river. We should have a spring, or be able to make a spring. I think it is best if we camp for a few days, before we stake our claim," said Ben. Everyone sat around the fire and ate fish, biscuits, and gravy. Not bad for people on a wagon train!

Next day the snow had dropped 1 1/2 to 2 inches, but it was still far too deep to travel. Henry and Ben Jr. got down the black kettle and set it up for the girls. Nate and Ben inspected the wagons and mules. Tom uncovered the potatoes and turnips in the hay wagons so the girls could fix what they wanted for dinner. Everyone was busy doing what needed to be done.

When they woke up the third day the sun was shining, and it looked like if all turned out well they could move on after the fourth day, but the snow was still close to a foot deep. Ben said, "We will see what the day brings. What do you say we have one more fish fry before we lose that?"

It was agreed by everyone, so Henry and Tom took buckets and went fishing.

Sitting around the camp fire at night was the most fun, and everyone got along very well. Every night they had started their meal off with a prayer, but tonight Nate thought it would be a good time to sing and have a longer prayer meeting. He would read from the Bible and give thanks to God for their many blessings. Everyone rejoiced and gave thanks to God. It had been a good day because the sun had been bright most of the day, and the snow was down to 6 inches or so. Henry had ridden the trail for three hours, and reported he had marked the trail well. If they would rest the mules every hour or so they would not get a lot of miles in, but time was of importance.

On day four, everyone was up early and the mules were well rested. Most of the items taken down for the four days were put back in place the night before. Helen and Elisabeth had breakfast ready with coffee, bacon, and eggs. They moved out at 7 am. The wagons were frozen to the ground, but with a little more effort than normal they were on the move.

Things were not that bad. The mules were able to move along the trail quite well and were rested. Ben felt the day would go all right. Sometime after the second hour out, a wagon came down the trail loaded with corn. The man said he was on his way to Chicago to a mill. He also said that he had come from a farm in Iowa 50 miles from where they were, and that the snow was not that deep farther down the trail.

Ben said, "Yes, but it will deepen the closer you get to the turn off to Chicago. This is the first day in four days we have been able to travel." After wishing each other luck, it was back to business.

With that report Ben figured he was in Iowa, or very close to it. That meant 300 more miles and they would be at the river crossing in Saratoga. He guessed 10 more days would put them close to the river. They were making good time after being snow bound for four days. He pulled up after a few more miles and went back to share the information he had just gotten with Nate and Henry.

Chicago had incorporated as a city in 1782 and people were on the move, but they had not expected this kind of movement of people and wagons this far west. The more he thought about their move, the better he felt about the whole thing. It was going to be a great time to expand and grow. Henry and Nate were glad to get the news and after some small talk, they moved on. Ben said, "The next time we stop, we will see if the women have anything to eat."

The day came to a close at 6 p.m. It had been a good day for travel. As they sat around the fire, talk came up on what they might find at the river crossing, and what kind of crossing could be expected.

Nate said, "The closer we get to the river, maybe we can ask someone if they crossed, what kind of boat or ferry was available; how much did it cost for a wagon, how many wagons could they take per crossing, and how long would it take for a crossing." All this information and more were needed.

Ben estimated the day trip had covered 25 miles or more, and that they were in the Iowa Territory by 15 or so miles. Nate was worried that the four days in the snow had eaten into the corn and hay supply, and they might not have enough to see them through the summer.

"Maybe we will come across a farmer with some corn for sale," suggested Ben.

"Let's hope and pray, for that; it sure would make me feel better," stated Nate. Everyone drifted off to bed. Nate and the men sat around the fire for a little while, and then went on guard duty.

Next day all were up early. The snow was not bad any longer and other wagons that traveled the trail had left it clear, and well marked. Let's hope it will be a good day and we can make up some of those four days lost, thought Nate.

The trail was wider now and every hour or so a wagon or men on horseback rode by. Most of them waved and said where they were going. When the noon hour came, rather than pull off the trail and build a fire, Helen and Elisabeth got some cold biscuits and ham together.

It was not long until a family came down the trail on their way to Chicago. Ben flagged them down to ask about the river crossing. Yes, they had crossed and there was a ferry. The charge was five dollars per wagon, one dollar per animal, and two bits per person. The ferry could take two wagons, but you had to unhitch the teams. The mules might get spooked and cause an accident. The man said it took almost two hours per trip by the time you got the wagons on board and the team unhitched. The crossing took a good thirty minutes. By the time the ferry was loaded on the other side and made its way back, you had spent a good two hours, sometimes three.

That night, Ben and Nate talked about planning the crossing. They figured with six wagons, it would take three hours for the wagons and two trips for mules and cows. That meant it was going to take five to six hours to get everyone across the Mississippi River. So whatever time they reached the river, they would camp and talk to the ferry operator and get his views, decided the men. They would try and start the crossing early in the morning. Maybe it will take longer than five hours. What would the ferry operator do with the other people that needed to cross? What about the next day? Since the day would be spent crossing, maybe it would be best to camp and leave early for the last leg of their trip.

Ben spoke up. "That sounds good to me. I would say we have eight more days just to get to the river."

Next day, it was back on the trail early. The weather had been getting just a little warmer, but the wind was picking up. It was the 20th of February and spring was just around the corner. Ben wanted to get to the homestead before the ground started to get soft, so he was going to push the mules hard today and see how far they could get. All went well, except for the people coming and going. It was going to be hard to find a good campsite tonight with this many people on the trail. He would start about 5 pm looking for a spot that had some trees for firewood.

It was almost 6 pm when he spotted a nice place about one mile off the trail to the north. He headed the wagons out over open ground, so he had to watch where he was going to avoid ditches and creeks. It was a good campsite, but there was no water. Everybody would have to drink from the barrel tonight. Tomorrow they would refill the barrels at the first clean stream along the way.

Nate figured a good 35 miles had been covered for the day and they were maybe a good 50 miles into the Iowa territory. It was not going to be long now until the big Mo was in front of them. The kids were dancing and singing around the fire, happy the trip was coming to an end. Ben had pulled far enough off the trail that no other travelers would bother them, but the guards still went on duty as always.

The next day was Saturday and the weather was still holding, so it would be another long, hard day. They got off at 7 am, and after the first two hours Ben spotted a house and barn off the trail about two or three miles to the north. He stopped the train and went back to ask Henry if he would ride over there and ask the man if he had any hay or corn for sale. "If he has got it, we will take 30 bales of hay and fifty bushels of corn."

Henry was glad to get out of that wagon seat for a while, and untied his gelding and rode off.

The train was pulled out into the field a short distance, and everyone waited for Henry to return. They waited on him a good hour, and Nate was about to ride out to see if he had gotten into trouble when he saw a wagon and rider coming toward them. A few more minutes, and they pulled up with a wagon loaded with hay and corn. The man was a big Swede and did not speak very plain English. Ben was able to understand him and soon found out he wanted 15 cents for a bale of hay, and 25 cents for a bushel of corn. Nate was so happy he was ready to jump up and down! God had answered his prayers. They now were almost at the end of their journey, and the wagons had been restocked with feed. What a blessing!

Henry spoke up, saying, "When he said we could have it, I stayed around to help him load his wagon. Sorry it took me so long, boss."

"Henry, you did great!" declared Nate. The man's name was Josh Smithwater, and he wanted to know if they would come up to the farm and have dinner with him.

Ben said, "No, we have to try and make up some time." Therefore, he paid Mr. Smithwater, and they went on their way. Four hours had gone by, and he needed to get some miles behind them. As the day came to a close, Ben spotted a good campsite with wood and water. Tomorrow was Sunday, and he thought they would take the day off and worships God. Nate and Ben both needed this day to pay thanks to the Almighty, and spend time with their wives.

Sunday came and went, and Monday everyone was up early and excited about having only two more days left after today before reaching the river crossing. The day was long, and people were moving up and down the trail. Wagons were turning north and south, all going to new homesteads or hauling something somewhere. They did not stop for lunch. The girls had made something to take with them, so they ate on the go. At one stop to rest the mules, a family came up from behind and wanted to know if they could join the train. Nate said he did not see anything wrong with it, but if they wanted to camp with them they would have to supply their own food for their animals. The man said he had no problem with that, and would tag along.

Ben found a nice campsite off the trail a mile or so. As they pulled into the site, Ben noticed his wagon train had grown by three new wagons, so the circle had to be larger. Everyone hopped down and went to the center of the train to meet the new people. The man introduced himself as Homer Martin, his wife as Sarah, and his two boys as Joe and Sam Martin. He said they had left a town west of Chicago where he had gone to medical school, and that he wanted to move and set up practice some place in the west and get a homestead to let the boys farm. The boys were 17 and 19 and needed to start their life.

The boys got the wood together for a big fire. Ben told the boys that since there was a lot of wood at this site, they should cut plenty and store it in the hay wagons. That way, if there was no wood at the river crossing, everything would be fine with a supply on hand.

The night went by fast with their new friends, and there was a lot to talk about. Homer asked where they were going, and Ben said, "We are trying to settle somewhere around little Blue River. We have talked about trying to go south after crossing the Mississippi along the Dredge River, and then cross the Platte River and head north to see what the land is like."

Homer said that was pretty much the same route he was going to take, and would like to tag along until they got west of the Platte. Ben said it was fine with him, and Nate said it would be nice to have a doc on the trail.

It had been a long day, and everyone thought that they had covered 35 miles. Ben thought the most they could be away from the river was one or two days. Nate said, "Let's stop someone coming down the trail, and ask if they have crossed, and how far it was". They all agreed that sounded good.

Doc Martin was surprised to see the way the train had arranged the sleeping places and the guard duty. He said he and the boys would be glad to take their turn at the watch. That way, duty time would be cut to three hours instead of four. Next morning breakfast was prepared, and Mrs. Martin contributed her share of the food for her people. At 6.30 am, it was time to hit the trail. Everyone was excited that it was almost time to see the big river.

After two hours, there was a rider that came along that wanted to stop for a few minutes and rest his horse. Ben pulled the team to a halt and asked if he had crossed the river. The man said yes he had, and that it was fifty miles straight down the trail. "But", he said, "don't expect to cross right away!" He said that with only one horse and himself he had waited three hours to get over, and that people were everywhere waiting their turn. "There are lots of wagons on this side, with lots of horses and riders on the other side. There are a lot of wagons going west and riders going east to find work and other business - so don't expect to cross right away."

The man wanted to know if he could buy a bucket of corn and some water for his horse. Ben said, "You cannot buy, but we will give it to you for the information".

They talked for awhile, and the man said the reason there was so many people waiting to cross was the ice floating down the river. He said the two teams on the banks had to be stopped while they waited for large cakes to float by. They did not like that, but there was nothing they could do about it. After a cup of coffee Helen still had in a pot, it was back on the trail. Ben said, "We will go for a couple more hours and stop for something to eat".

The temperature for the past three days had been close to freezing, and today the wind was back on the howl; after all, it was wintertime. It was bad for traveling and being outside, but it was good for the mules. The ground was frozen and it made pulling the load much easier. While they ate Henry gave the mule's water and corn, and a handful of hay in each bucket. It was kind of funny to Henry. It seemed everything he did for the animals, Doc, and the boys would soon pick up on. After all, they had been raised in town and did not know frontier life the way they did. He did not say anything and offered to help, if they wanted it.

The day came to a close at dark. Ben wanted to get as much trail behind him as he could; campsites were harder to find that had water and wood. After an hour of watching the landscape, he found what he needed for the last day on this side of the river. He pulled the wagons in next to a nice creek. It was not that deep, and most of it was frozen, except for two feet in the middle. There was some brush, and a few small trees about one half mile to the north. With the extra wood the boys had cut the night before, he thought they would be all right.

After they got the fire going, Henry and the boys took a lantern and walked over to the wooded area. It was pretty thick with good size brush, and a few downed trees. Henry made an A-frame out of some brush, and they cut and piled it on. They thought two A-frames of wood would be enough for the night, and put the rest on the wagon for later.

The two Martin boys could not get over the rifle Henry carried everywhere he went. One of the boys asked, "Where did you get that gun? I have never seen a gun that pretty."

Henry answered, "Mr. Sharp made it"

"Are you crazy? How could a man make a gun like that?" asked the boy.

Henry replied, "He is a gunsmith, and a very good one, if I might add. He made six of them. He gave one to each of us and one to his brothers, who are in the gun business."

"What is that thing on top of the barrel?" questioned the boy.

"It's called a scope. It allows me to see farther than I can with the naked eye. The gun shoots 800 yards, and it's hard to see a clear target at that distance - that is why it has a scope", answered Henry.

"Do you think he would make me one?" inquired the boy.

"I don't know. You will have to ask him," replied Henry.

Back at camp, the men talked about the 40 miles they had put behind them for the day and tried to guess what was left to go. It was just hard to tell. The only thing they could do was push on. Sarah felt much better with other women around, and soon was getting along with Helen and Elisabeth. It was much nicer planning the meals and making sure everyone was fed. She thanked them over and over for allowing them to join the train. The nights were much better also; with more people to pull guard duty, everybody got more sleep. The wind had died down as the sun went down, and it did not seem as cold as it was early in the day. Nevertheless, it had been a long day and everyone started off to bed. Tomorrow would be a big day.

Five am comes pretty quickly, and there was lots of work to be done each morning. Cows had to be milked, animals had to be fed, mules had to be harnessed, and all their belongings picked up from the night before. Breakfast had to be cooked and even with everyone doing their part, it still took two to three hours to move out. At 7 a.m. Ben popped the whip, and the mules leaned into their load to break the wagons from the frozen ground - and it was river, here we come!

They had been on the trail for 23 days, and Ben estimated he still had a week or more before the trip would come to a close. He was not disappointed. Good time had been made, even with the loss of four days in the snow. However, he worried about the river crossing. He was also concerned about crossing the Platte, and what kind of land formation could be expected along the Mississippi River. Was it going to be high ground, or full of lakes and soft river lands? He pushed those thoughts out of his mind, thinking God had brought him this far, and He would see him the rest of the way.

After an hour, Ben pulled the wagon to a halt and let the mules catch their wind. Some people came by and he asked how the river was. The man said, "You will be looking at big muddy by the noon hour".

"How many people are waiting to cross over?" Ben asked.

The man said there were maybe ten to fifteen wagons waiting to cross over. That sounded bad and sounded good. He thought maybe by the time he got there some of the wagons would have crossed. If he got there by noon, they would camp and start the crossing at first light, but he would have to talk to the ferry operator.

Four more hours, and he could see in the distance the wagons and people. Yes, it was a busy place - people and wagons everywhere! He pulled the train to a stop and went back to talk to the other fellows. Ben said, "This is what I think we had better do. Because there are so many people trying to get across, I think we had better wait in line; otherwise, someone is going to try and get in front of us and that would only cause bad words. Let's leave the teams hitched to the wagons, and stay in line until the ferry quits running for the night. Then we can unhitch the teams and tie them to the wagons, build a fire, and eat. In the morning, we will be the first to cross - or close to it."

Everyone agreed it was a good plan.

5:

Ben, Nate, and Homer turned the driving over to their wives and went up front to talk with the ferry operator. As they walked up the line, Nate counted 8 wagons and quite a bit of livestock waiting their turn. The ferry was on the other side and was just getting ready to offload when they walked up. It was some sight to see for the first time. Lots of the men were lined up against the rail chewing tobacco and talking about the river. They stood there talking about the trip and what might lie in front of them.

It was close to an hour before the ferry got up near enough for them to see what was going on. It was a strong looking boat or ferry, made out of logs with large planks fastened to the logs. As a matter of fact, it looked like two layers of planks going in different directions. There was a two-log rail running all the way around the ferry except the two ends, which had a chain gate across the opening. In the middle of the ferry were another two logs going across the middle only. It had a pole gate. Animals were led up and tied to the pole in the center. Mules and horses would pull the wagons up close to the rail, and then were unhitched and tied to rail. The wagon brake was locked and the wheel choked. The ferry could take four wagons and the teams.

A large post was on the outside of the ferry, with large angle braces down to the floor - one on each side. There was a large rope that ran all the way to shore where it passed through two large pulleys attached to the top and bottom of another large post. A team of four mules was hitched to each side. As one team pulled the ferry across, the other team kept the ferry from going too far off course. What an operation - but it worked, and they were busy!

In a few more minutes, the ferry tied up at the dock and they went down to talk to the operator. He told them the charges and said they could cross first thing in the morning. The charges were agreed to, and Ben would pay when they got off. Women and children could ride across in the wagons. It was safer in the wagon than running around on deck. With that business behind them, they headed back to see what the girls had cooked up for supper.

Back at the train, it was discussed that the wagons would load as they were in the train at this time. That meant that Doctor Martin would have one wagon that would have to cross with three other wagons that he did not know. It also told them that if the first wagon was loaded on the ferry at 6 am, they would all be across by 1 or 2 pm this would give them enough time to find a campsite and prepare for the trip south. Since Henry was the best muleskinner in the train, he would drive the wagons onto the ferry, and Nate would unhitch the teams and tie the mules off at the rail. Cattle and hogs would be taken care of by Ben and Tom.

At 5 am, everyone was up and fed. The day looked like another cold windy one, and as soon as the ferry was offloaded, Henry started the first wagon to the dock. The mules' hoofs made a hollow sound and they jumped around a little; but with his skills and the sound of his voice, and a snap of the whip, they took to the dock in stride.

Next step would be the moving ferry. The ferry was tied off sound and did not move much, but it was still strange for the team.

The first wagon had to be driven between the center rails and backed into a parking spot on the right. The brake was then set and the wheels blocked. Nate unhitched the team and tied them off at the rail in a close tie. They did not have a lot of room to jump around. Henry brought up wagon number two, while Nate secured the team and wagon number one. The pole gate was closed, and the next two wagons were loaded in the same manner. The hogs were left in the wagon, and the cattle and bull on the back rail. The ferry was loaded! It looked like it took three fourths of an hour.

Tom and Ben would stay on the other side and take care of the teams. Everything went well, and they were all over by 2 p.m. This was a great time in history for all of them! Nate said, "Let's all bow our heads and give thanks to Almighty God for a safe crossing of the great Mississippi, and ask that He guide us to our new home in safety".

They had talked to the ferry operator while they were loading. He had told them to go southwest toward the mouth of the Dredge River where it dumped into the Platte. "It's 20 to 25 miles over to the river, and you might find a crossing at that point."

Nate thought that would be a good idea, and he figured they could be close to the spot by dark. It was agreed, and they were off to find a new home in the Nebraska Territory, with God as their guide.

6:

It was 5 pm when Ben spotted a nice, clean creek just a little off
the trail, if that was what you could call it. The landscape had
changed a great deal from the flat open land. There were hills and
trees--lots of trees--and grass as high as a mule belly. He did not
know what to think of this as he formed a circle for the nightly
camp. I guess when we get up in the morning, we had better send
out a scout to see if there is a crossing, and what the land has to
offer, thought Ben. He told Elisabeth to have the wives cook up
a good meal, and they would have a party of sorts.

That night around the fire, there was talk of when Homer
and his family would turn north. It was agreed that would have
to take place after tomorrow, if everything went well. Ben said
from here on in, he would ride point, as he had a better idea
what kind of land they were looking for. He asked Henry if he
would trade wagons and bring his wagon up front, because he
did not feel Elisabeth was that qualified to drive the lead wagon
on an unbroken trail. So tomorrow, they would make the switch
on pull-out. He then warned everyone that they were in Indian
country, and that the guard duty would have to be wide awake.
He also said when Doc and his boys did guard duty, they would
loan them their night rifles. Joe couldn't wait to hold that pretty

rifle! Ben said, "Do not fire the gun unless you have to!" With that, they went to bed.

Nate and the Doctor took the first watch. Henry and Joe would follow, and then Ben and Tom. The night was cold, and it was damp being that close to water. The high grass held the wind back, but Ben did not like it because an Indian could slip right up onto the train and never be seen until it was too late. Nate said, "Let's untie the canvas covering the hay and move some hay around, and we will be high enough to see danger and still have some protection".

For now most of the guard duty would be spent on the wagons, instead of the ground.

Next morning after breakfast, Ben saddled his mare and got ready for his point duty. The mare was a little jumpy since she had not had a saddle on for over two weeks. Henry had done most of the riding, so all she had to do was eat and sleep. He had not been on the ride more than one hour when he came upon the mouth of the Dredge River. It was not a good place to cross. It was wide and deep as it dumped into the Platte. He thought he would ride north, and maybe it would not be so wide and deep.

The wagon train did not know he was swinging north. If he rode back to tell them of his plan, he would lose two hours or more. He decided to let them come to the river and see what he had seen. How would they know which way he went? He came up with the idea to pull two or three grasses together and tie them off with some rawhide. Two or three of these would point the way he had gone.

He was right! Ten more miles upriver and it was much narrower and not near as deep. He found a good spot where wagons could cross and rode over to the other side. Again, he tied the grass on both sides and set out straight ahead. Five more miles and he came upon the Platte River. Much to his surprise the river was not that deep, and what was there was full of ice. It looked like in the spring when the snow would melt up north; the river ran full--but not now. He rode over and found a lot of dead trees and wood about 100 yards away. It would make a good camp.

As he rode back, he noticed the grass was all beaten down and there were hoof prints in the dirt, everywhere. Hundreds of them! Why would there be that many cattle here by the river? He got down from the mare for a closer look and soon found that the droppings on the ground around him were buffalo, and lots of them. Well, he hadn't seen any Indians, but there sure were lots of buffalo and where there are buffalo, there are going to be Indians.

With all this information, he thought he would head back to the train. He reached them around noon, and they had not quite made it to the Dredge. Ben stopped the train, rode down to the middle, and told the boys to meet him up front. They all gathered around Henry's wagon, and he reported what he had found. It was not bad news, but he wanted everyone to know they were now in frontier land, and things were not going to be the same.

After the meeting, he tied the mare off to the back of his wagon and took the lead once more. Ben knew he was one half mile from the Dredge, and he also knew they could not cross at that point. He turned the train to the north so it could arrive at the crossing he had marked earlier.

It took an hour for the trip and since he had already crossed the river once, he pulled his wagon into the water and ice and crossed over. On the other side, he pulled up and gave the mules a rest. They had been on the trail for over four hours, so it was time for a little break before crossing the Platte. After all, when they were across the Platte they would be in the part of the territory where they were to make a new home, and very few white men had ever seen. Everyone was happy they had come this far and done that much. Ben warned them he wanted them to be happy, but to not lose sight that they were in dangerous country, and anything could happen at any time. They were not to leave the camp unless someone was with them, and the men were to keep their guns by their sides at all times.

After something to eat, the train pulled out for the last leg of the trip for the day. The Platte was 10 or 15 miles straight ahead, and with good luck they would be on the other side by dark. It was 5 pm when the train reached the grass heads Ben had tied off when he had crossed earlier in the day. Everything looked the same, so without much delay he started the crossing. At six o'clock, Ben brought the wagons into a circle for the night. The ground was dry and hard, except for some snow here and there. The grass was not that tall, as the buffalo had eaten it down, but droppings were everywhere. It was strange the buffalo did not seem to cross the Platte. Ben and Nate did not know why. It seemed they would eat and drink and move back into open country. They were not buffalo men, and this was their first encounter with their habits.

The boys built a big fire, and their nightly meal was prepared. It was too dark to fill the water barrels, so that would have to wait until morning. As they sat around the fire, Doctor Martin seemed to have something troubling him. After a long silence he spoke up, "I do not know what to do. I have talked to the family about it, and they have asked me to talk to you. They have told me to talk with you fellows, and whatever we decided would be all right with them."

"What is on your mind?" Nate asked.

"Well, to tell the truth, I don't know what to do. Since we are in Indian country, I'm somewhat concerned about the welfare of my family. If we go north, we will be in open country for a week. First, we are not as skilled as you fellows in the ways of the frontier. If we had to fight, I don't know if our guns and equipment would withstand the battle. I do not know if my boys can load and stand off a charging Indian tribe. My feeling at this time is to ask your permission to go with you. I'm sure the boys can stake a claim somewhere close to your claim without interfering. Besides, I have fifteen people here to care for. I may be able to do more for the 15 of us than to try and find fifteen people that need me in the new town. After a few years and after the boys are settled, my wife and I can make the move to the new city if we wish," stated Doc Martin.

Ben was the first to speak. "Doc, I do not have anything bad I could say against that. You are welcome as far as I'm concerned. There is enough land here in the west for all of us."

Nate said, "You have my vote one hundred percent."

"Then it is settled. We will travel with you and support you any way we can. I would like to say thank you on behalf of my two boys and wife. You have been kind to us in every way, and we will help in any way you see fit. God bless us all!" stated Doc.

Nate felt much better to hear him use that word. He had not heard him express his love of God before. With that business done, they went about their guard duty and to retire for the night.

At morning breakfast, the rest of the group was informed of the decision made during the night and that cooperation and understanding of each other's feelings would be the order of each day from here forward. According to Ben's calendar, it was the 1st of March, and things were changing fast in this part of the world.

Chicago had become a city in 1782, and the territory they now were in had been bought as the Louisiana Purchase. There was a rumor that the President would soon dispatch an expedition to map and explore the territory. They would be one of the first settlers to be asked to go west and stake claims to the western territories. No one knew what was on the other side of the hill. It was an exciting time, and no family had ever traveled this far west to build and settle the land.

It was a bright day. As the sun began to come up the March wind was a little raw, but there was a spring feeling in the air as Ben popped his whip for the first time. They had looked out over the land last night, so Ben did not need to ride point just yet. As he moved forward he could not believe what his eyes revealed. It was beautiful! They had never seen country like this before. There were rolling hills, tall grass, and every now and then a small lake, and pine trees that seemed to reach to the heavens.

Prairie chickens were frightened from their feeding and flew off to a safe distance. It was so quiet you could hear the person next to you breathing. There were no people, only the sound of the wind and the mules. Ben was proud he had led his people to such a wonderful place. After an hour and a half, he pulled the mules to a stop and asked Henry to take the lead wagon once more.

Ben saddled the mare and got ready to ride point once more. As he stepped up into the saddle, he pulled her head to the west and heeled her to a trot. It was a nice day, and he wanted to cover as much ground as he could. His plan was to head west and a little to the south toward the Big Blue River. It should make a good place for their home, and he thought it would be two to three days travel. The river would provide a mill for corn grinding and water for the animals in the summer.

He had ridden for an hour and a half when he pulled the mare to a lake up ahead. He stepped down to allow her to lower her head to drink. As he was looking out at the landscape, he spotted five or six Indians on a hill about a mile away. He almost jumped at first sight, but instinct told him being afraid was not going to save his life. They did not seem to be making any moves to come after him. His mind was racing a mile a minute. If he went forward, he would only increase the odds in their favor. If he turned and ran, they might look at him as a coward and come after him.

He let the mare finish her drink and pulled her head around so he could look over her back. As he stepped up into the saddle, he allowed her to keep her head down to smell the grass. He did not want them to think he was in a hurry. Reaching around to his right side he removed the leather string holding his rifle in place. They were too far away for him to shoot at, and he would rather let them make the first move.

He brought the mare's head up and started a slow walk back up the trail he had just covered, keeping an eye on them over his left shoulder. He did not want to get killed today and he did not want to kill anybody, so he let the mare walk. After a hundred or so yards they were still there, and he felt a little at ease. If they had not made a move on him up to now, he thought he might be in the clear. He let the mare walk. It was best to let them know he was a lone rider just watering his horse. He took his eyes off them for a minute, and the next time he looked they were gone. With that, he heeled the mare into a trot. He did not want to take too much wind out of her just in case he had to run, but he needed to get back to the train as soon as possible.

After twenty minutes or so, he pulled up on some high ground and halted for a better look. There did not seem to be anyone on his tail, so he rode on. He spotted the train a mile up front of him after another half hour more. His heart came out of his mouth and went back in place. He was safe, and he did not have to kill anyone!

He rode up to Henry's wagon and asked him to stop. He then rode down the train to ask Nate and the Doc to come up front for a powwow. He told the men what he had just seen and what he thought they needed to do. Ben stated, "Tonight when we close the wagons I would like for you, Henry, to hobble the stock inside the circle. That way, they cannot be cut free during the night. I would like to increase the guards to four per shift. What I think has happened is they seen our smoke last night and sent out a scouting party to see who is in their land. I talked to the ferry operator the other day, and asked him what band of Indians lived in this part of the territory. He said they were mostly Arapaho and that they mainly were buffalo hunters and traders, but every now and then some of the young warriors would rise a little hell and more so if they could get something to drink. So let's be safe and hope for the best. I think after tonight, we have only one more day on the trail, so let's keep a tight hand on things!"

Ben took the lead once again and with four hours of daylight, he would like to make it to the lake where he and the mare had stopped for a drink. He did not see a lot of wood, but a big fire could wait one more day. They had plenty of wood on the hay wagon that would see them through the night. The land was beautiful, and he was happy to call it home. Most of all, he could see the happiness in Elisabeth's face with what she saw and that they had a doctor with them. What more could you ask for?

After stopping the mules three more times, he spotted the sun shining on the lake only a mile up front. He brought the train in close to the lake; that way if there was trouble, they only had three sides to defend. Everyone brought their wagon in tight and turned the tongues in toward the circle. That way there was little room for the stock to get loose, or for anyone to break through. Ben Jr. and the other boys soon figured out what was going on, and pitched in to help.

A small fire was started. Ben did not want to light up the inside of the circle too much, and everyone was asked to stay away from the fire except as needed. The guards were asked to look into their night scopes more often to see if anyone was trying to slip up on the train. The night wore on and there was no trouble.

Next morning at daylight, about ten or so Indians showed up to the north on a knoll. The women were getting something to eat together and did not pay much attention to Henry when he came to tell Nate and Ben about the war party. They walked over to have a closer look and decide what action to take.

Ben had a good glass, and could make out ten to fifteen Indians all standing in a row. The one in the middle had a large headdress on with lots of feathers. They guessed he was the one in charge. No one did or said anything. After a few minutes, the man with the large headdress and a man on each side of him rode forward. The man on the right side held a long pole with a white flag blowing in the wind. Ben said, "It looks like they want to talk."

It took only a few minutes until they were in front of them. Ben and Nate asked the other men to cover them as they walked out to see what they wanted. Ben or Nate had never seen an Indian this close up, and were ready for whatever came. The man in the middle looked to be 50 years old or so, while the other two were in their mid twenties, or maybe thirties. It was hard to tell. Each carried knives, spears, and tomahawks.

The one in the middle carried lots of beads and silver around his neck. He kept touching the things, and making gestures that he wanted to give them to Nate. After talking with Ben, Nate stepped forward to take one of the gifts. It was clear he wanted something back for the gift. Nate did not have anything to give him so he said to Ben, "What if we gave them a ham or some corn? Do you think that would help?"

"I don't know, let's try", replied Ben. He told the Indian to get down, while he sent one of the boys to get a ham. Elisabeth was not happy with that, but thought now was not the time to discuss it with her husband. She then told Ben Jr. where they were, and to take the smallest one he could find. Ben Jr. got the ham, and ran back to his father.

Ben showed the Indian the ham, and he quickly nodded it was a good trade and gave him two of the beads strung around his neck, but he wanted to trade more. Nate said, "Why not some corn for the horses?"

He made a move toward the horse's mouth, and the Indian nodded, "Yes". Ben Jr. then ran off to get two small bags of corn. The Indian liked that very much, and gave him two of the silver pieces in exchange. They wanted more, but Nate said, "No, that is all we have for now". With that, they turned and rode off.

Nate and Ben got behind the wagons quickly, and watched to see what they did. When they got back to the other Indians on the hill, it was powwow time for awhile and then they rode off. The men were happy they did not have to fight, and went back to the campfire to tell everyone what had just happened. Ben still did not trust them. He knew because they could not understand one another very well, the slightest thing could make them mad. He still wanted to watch his back.

After a while the wagons moved out. It was now 8 am they had lost three hours with this powwow, but it could have been the whole day--or worse! So who was crying? Ben took the lead and moved out around the lake and headed south. If his instincts were correct, they would come to a river soon. Around noon they came across a small creek, and he noticed the water was running to the southeast. This told him he was headed right toward the headwaters of Big Blue.

They stopped and got something to eat, and talked about Indians and how pretty the countryside was. The land was a little more flat in this area but still had a hill every now and then. After dinner, they were back on the trail. In an hour Ben stopped the train to let the mules rest, and about a mile up in front of him was a sight he could not believe. There, in a valley of two or three miles, were more buffalo than any man had ever seen. There were hundreds of them, maybe a thousand - who knew? They were grazing and moving to the north like a giant cloud. He did not want to get them excited and thought he would wait and allow them time to move farther north. Everyone had to come to have a look. Never before had they seen such a sight! After half an hour, it looked like they could go on south without bothering them.

The sun was going down and Ben did not want to camp but one time, so he pushed on. The country to the southeast of him was full of trees and woods, while the land to the west was open, flat, and full of grass. Another half hour went by, and he was beginning to get nervous when he spotted the river. He had come out just a little west of the tree line, and in a nice, low valley. He pulled the wagons up next to the trees, and put them in a nice, tight circle. It looked good, but it was getting too dark to tell what was all around them. He would camp, and they would explore the area tomorrow. For the night they would bring the animals inside one more time, until they made up their minds.

A big fire was made, and this time it was made at one end of the train next to the woods. He felt a riding attack could not be done from there, leaving only one side Indians could come in on. They were tired, hungry, and happy they were where they should be. Since they were going to be here all day tomorrow, Helen and the girls had promised cornbread, ham and beans, and if the boys would shoot a couple of prairie chickens, they would have a good meal.

The weather was good but still cold. Ben was very happy with the weather on the trip. He had lost three days with snow, but all had gone well for such a long trip. They wanted to get to bed and get up early to explore the area. It was decided that Ben, Nate, and Doc would saddle up in the morning and see what the area looked like. The rest of the boys would stay close to the camp and keep a good lookout.

They were only about two hundred yards from the river, and from the looks of it in the dark, it was about 25 yards wide. They could not tell how deep because of the ice and darkness. Tomorrow would come soon enough. Everyone made a bed and a place to sleep. The trees helped hold the winds back to the north and east, and the tall grass did a fair job to the west. Nate and Henry took the first guard, followed by Ben and Tom. The rest would take the night off.

The camp started to stir at daybreak, except the children. They could eat later. Ben divided up the work for the day, and no one seemed unhappy. The three men would check out their claims. Tom and Henry would build a pole corral for the mules and horses. The cows would be hobbled for a few more days. Joe and his brother would milk the cows, feed the hogs, and care for the chickens. Ben Jr. would stay with the girls and keep an eye on things.

As the men rode out it was decided they would check out the river first, come back through the woods, have some lunch, and then head northwest. They would not stake any claims today, only explore the area. As they rode, it was hard to believe what was before them. The river, as thought, was 25 yards wide and it was about three to five feet deep in this area. It had a rocky bed, and looked as if it would go to 40 or 50 yards wide in the spring when the snow melted upstream. It could be full of trout, but the ice covered it pretty thick and it was hard to see. As they crossed the river, there were more trees - thick as hair on a dog. It was hard to ride through.

As they rode south another stream came into view. This water was running toward the Big Blue, so they followed it. This took them almost due east for a few miles, and it was still very woody when it ran into the Big Blue. Big Blue was about 50 yards wide here. Before the other steam dumped into Big Blue on the south west side, it was still about 25 yards wide.

Crossing over, they rode into the woods a few hundred yards, trying to keep the river in sight since they knew their camp was next to it, but did not know how far. It was six hours since they crossed the river, when they heard the children playing. Everyone was glad to see them and wanted to know what had been seen.

Nate stepped down from his horse and said, "Well, there is not going to be a shortage of wood and water. We have got more than we will ever need."

Ben said, "It looks like there could be some good hunting, also. God only knows what is in those woods. They are too thick for man or horse to get through without planning. Water - there is a good flow, and plenty of it." In the back of his mind, there was a plan to build a corn and wheat grinding mill using the water for power, but that will have to come after we get our lives together, thought Ben.

"We will ride west after lunch and see what lies in the open land. Since you boys have got the corral pretty well under control, I would like for you to check the area for weeping water coming out of the ground headed for the river. We need three locations, if you can find them. It does not have to be a lot of water; we can always dig them out and line them with stone. I will check with you tonight on what you found. If you find some good ones, we will build springhouses and have a place to keep our milk and butter."

After lunch they rode out as planned.

The day had turned out well. It was a little windy, and the temperature was around 32 degrees. From here on, it would get warmer with each day, and everyone would have a full day of work. Doc turned his gray mare to the north to get deeper into the prairie. The grass was tall and the land flat and it seemed to be going uphill just a little bit. Doc inquired, "If we were to consider our camp the start of our land, how far would a mile take us from the camp?"

"It would be 265 of our wagons end to end, or 1,760 steps or paces, but don't forget, Doc, that is only one way. When you get to that point you have to turn right or left, and go another 1,760 steps, and then back to the starting point. Don't forget that is just one claim, we have to make three claims that size. The rules say we do not have to go in a straight line just as long as it comes to 640 acres", answered Ben.

"My God, Ben that is 1,920 acres! What in the world would we do with all that land?" asked Doc.

"We will farm and graze it. There may come a time when we wish we had more," replied Ben.

"Well, all I can say is, this is new to me. You fellows know farming far better than I do. After all, I'm a doctor from the town of Chicago. I was born there and grew up there. I do not know much about this great land we live in. I'm not afraid of work, so you guide me, and I will care for all of you," declared Doc.

As they rode over a little knoll, there came into view a good size lake. It lay between some hills and had a small creek running off toward the river. My God, what a pretty place! There were no trees anywhere, except along the river a good half mile to the left and behind the camp. It was a perfect place to build a home and raise kids. Nate did not think Lincoln was more than a hard day's ride to the southeast. They would not be totally by themselves. He said to Ben, "Let's take it. I just don't think we could do any better. We will go back to camp and see what the boys have found, and talk about how we should plot the land off." Back at camp the boys had found two nice springs in front of the camp about three hundred yards, but had not had much luck in finding the third one. Maybe time and the weather would reveal the third one.

It was 5 pm and the wives had supper on the fire. They had lots to do: clothes needed to be washed, and their food supplies had to be checked and stored correctly. As soon as the ground got soft enough, a cellar or hole had to be dug for the potatoes and turnips, and a garden had to be planted. Everyone was so happy that this was going to be their new home!

The men sat around the fire and talked about business, and plotting the land. After all, Ben and Nate were good at business, having been in the gun and blacksmith business all of their lives. They knew about agreements and contracts. Henry knew there was to be a lot of trees cut for building, so he got Tom, Joe, and Sam to get all the tools off the wagons while he sharpened the saws and axes that were to be used. Ben Jr. got the kettles down and set them up. He then got lots of wood together for the fire to heat wash water and cook.

Around 10 pm the men were done with their meeting and Nate called everyone together to inform them what had been decided. He wanted to give thanks to God Almighty for his blessings. They sang songs and prayed. The doctor and his family did not know quite what to think of all this, but went along with the group. He and his wife Sarah had noticed the love of God these men had, and thought how blessed they had been to come upon such a group.

After the meeting, Ben took over and told everyone their plans. It had been agreed that Ben and his family would take over the tract of land next to the river and crossing over the river a half mile. Nate and his group would take the tract next to Ben and parallel to him. Doc and the boys would take a tract southeast of Nate and Ben taking in some woods and lots of open ground.

They would all work together and build the first house for Ben. It would be a large house with four bedrooms, two porches, and a center fireplace. The house would be built next to the right hand side of his plot, and if there was good weather it should be done some time in April. The next house would be built for Doc and his family, and would be in the back of Nate and Ben's homes, in the back middle of his plot. They planned to have that done by the last of June or middle of July.

Next, they would build Nate and Helen a home on their plot next to the left side and about two hundred yards from Ben's and Doc's places. This would get everyone close to one another in case of fire, sickness, and Indians.

"Does anyone want to change any of this?" asked Ben.

Ben continued, "Tomorrow four of us will take one of the wagons and the scooper and go to the river to collect rocks. We will take twelve or fourteen posts and mark the boundary of our land, piling the rock around each post. Joe and Sam can start to cut and clear grass from fifteen acres, so we can burn it off and get ready to plow as soon as the ground is soft enough. Do not burn any grass or set fire to the field we wish to plow unless you have plowed a dirt barrier around the field fifty feet wide. We do not want to set the prairie on fire. We need to get corn in the ground by April 30th, if we can."

"We will choose Joe and Sam for the farm work, since this is the area they wanted to be trained in. Henry and Tom will start cutting logs for the building projects. I have estimated at least 100 logs, each 20 feet long and 8 inches thick, will be needed for each house. Fellows, don't worry about cutting too many; we will use all you cut. Just as soon as we get the boundaries marked, we men will start the building," stated Ben.

"The first job will be to lay out the size of the house and dig a foundation trench for the first logs and flooring. By the way, Henry, we will need eight to ten 12 or 14 inch thick logs for that lower base. One of us men will bring logs into the building site. I will ask Ben Jr. and Barbara Ann to debark the logs as we bring them in. Folks, all I can say if we work hard as a team, we can get all of this done in a few years," declared Ben.

"You are right; this is not a ten minute job, but at least three years before we are done. Then other work will take up our time. The garden will have to be taken care of by the girls and kids. That still leaves the animals to feed and water and cows to milk. I'm going to leave all that up to you girls. Good luck, God bless you, and let's go to bed. The morning will come soon enough", finished Ben.

Next day everyone took up their duty as outlined the night before. Nate tied a piece of iron to a rope and hung it from a post. That way the girls could ring when they were ready to eat, or if there was any trouble. The men were back by noon and started to lay out the house foundation. Some rope was found, and a straight line 16 inches wide was made around the area where the house was to be built. Picks, mallets, and shovels were used to dig the trench. By nightfall, they had pretty well finished the digging. Tomorrow the trench would be filled with rock from the river, and the first logs laid for the flooring.

Joe and Sam reported that they had stepped off what looked like 15 acres to them and had started cutting the tall grass. Joe came up with the idea that one could cut one way, and the other in the opposite direction. After the grass dried, maybe it could be raked and rolled into a ball to be taken up to the corral for the animals.

Henry and Tom reported they had downed ten trees and cut them into logs. Henry said if Ben Jr. could drive the mule, he would wrap the chain around the logs and they could be brought to the site for debarking. The men could take the chain off here at the house, and all Ben Jr. had to do was drive the mule. With that, maybe the foundation logs would be in place tomorrow. Everyone complained about sore muscles but thought they would sleep well. Tomorrow was Sunday, so they would take most of the day off.

The same thing took place day after day, and soon it was March 15, 1805. The house was almost half done, but the weather was turning for the worse. Snow was in the air, and this time of the year it could get deep for the last snow before spring. Everyone was dug in pretty well, and the animals had lots of grass. Hay and corn could be cut back since the mules were not working that hard. Tom and Ben, Nate and Henry had made their beds in the tool wagons with hay on the sides and canvas over the tops so they would have nice warm places to sleep. As the weather got warmer they would not have to worry about snakes trying to get in bed with them. Things were not bad. So let it snow! Maybe when it melted, the ground would start to get soft and the boys could start to plow. They had cleaned off 15 acres and burned the ground. They had so much hay it, too, had to be burned.

It snowed most of the day Sunday, and late into the night. Next morning it was hard working, because the snow had to be cleared off. Trees could still be cut and the logs dragged into the work site. Another fire was built next to the building site, so most of the bark and small ends could be burned. Much to everyone's surprise Doc was a good stone worker, so he was given the job of building two fireplaces in the house. One was in the kitchen and living room. It was a large one built as a see through. That way Elisabeth would have a fire and oven to cook with, plus the backside would heat the living room. Another one was built at the end of the hall, so between that one and the living room most of the house could be kept warm during the winter.

People were beginning to be seen in the prairies. It seemed every week or so, a wagon or two would pass by. This one family stopped to see if they had a doctor with them. It seemed one of their sons had fallen off a wagon and broke his leg. Somebody told them that a doctor lived next to the Big Blue River about five miles to the Southwest. They wanted to know if he could set the leg.

Henry greeted them when they drove up. He asked to see the boy. He was lying on some hay in the back of a wagon. He looked like he had thrown up a time or two and looked pretty bad. Henry asked, "When did he break the leg?"

"Last night when we were getting ready to make camp," the woman said. The team suddenly moved forward and he fell off the back.

"Well, let's get him over to the doctor and see what he can do", Henry said as he picked him up in his arms and headed over to where Doc Martin was working. Doc brushed his hands off and walked over as Henry laid the boy on the floor.

"What seems to be the problem?" asked Doc.

"He fell off the back of the wagon last night and broke his leg," Henry said.

He then turned to Sarah and asked if she would get his bag and some bandages. Elisabeth brought up a pan of warm water and some soap so Doc could wash the leg and clean his hands. Doc asked Henry as he washed his hands if he would cut him 4 or 5 sticks about 18 inches long. He gave the boy a little morphine and waited a few minutes before he asked Henry to hold his arms down and Ben to take charge of the other leg. He then set the leg and wrapped it with bandages, then placed the sticks alongside the leg in four places. Ben placed him on some blankets so he could rest. He then told the father he could camp here for a few days and let the boy get his strength back.

Doc said, "I should watch him a few days, anyway. You need to keep him as still as possible for the next two weeks."

The man said, "Thank you very much. How much do I owe you?"

Doc said, "Not a dime. I was getting tired of laying stone for that fireplace so it was nice to get a chance to do the work I'm trained for."

The man looked down at the ground and in a shy way said "We sure do thank you. I don't know what we could have done if you had not been here. By the way, would you like to have some puppies? My old dog had six puppies last week and we just don't need that many dogs."

Doc said, "I don't know; the kids might like to have a puppy. What do you say, Ben?"

"God, yes! They need something to play with and help keep the snakes away from them. Yes sir, we will take them."

In a few minutes the man came back with three little puppies in his arms. He said, "They are crossed between a German Sheppard and a Missouri Hound. They should make good watch dogs."

Doc said, "The kids are going to be happy with them".

"Well, since you won't take any money, I feel better giving you something. By the way my name is Jeff Boyer. We are miners from Missouri on our way to California and now we had to have this luck.

"My name is Homer Martin and this is Ben Sharp. We have staked out a land grant here on Big Blue and are trying to build some farm land."

"Well, I'm sure glad I found you. Would it be all right if we camped down by the river for a few days while the boy gets a little better?"

"Yes sir, that will be just fine, and if you need anything just let us know.

Henry had talked to some trappers last week, but they could not speak English. He thought they were Frenchmen. For some reason, it seemed like they had gotten here just in time. Ben said, "In another year, most of the land would have been taken!"

Ben and Elisabeth had moved into their new house, and Doc was hard at work building his own fireplaces. The gardens had been plowed, and five acres of corn was planted. Every now and then, someone would spot a few Indians. They would not come too close but would stop and watch from a distance, and most of the time they were hunting along the river. Since the snow melted it was running wide, and the catfish were hungry. They had been trapped in the ice all winter.

Henry and Tom came in from the log cutting job and reported their first encounter with the red men. It seemed three of them had snuck out of the woods and were eyeing Tom's rifle leaned up next to a tree. Henry was the closest to the gun, so he stepped between the Indian and the gun and made a sign not to touch it. They did not like that. The one that had been left in the woods drew an arrow from the holder on his back, and stuck it into his bowstring. Henry placed his hand on his .45, and they turned and went back into the woods. Tom did not trust them and made sure his gun was not far out of reach. They were very sneaky and watched every move that was made.

After they reported what happened, Ben said he did not want anyone far from a gun at any time. He asked Doc if it would be all right if Joe or Sam wore a sidearm while attending the fields. Doc said he did not see anything wrong with that, but thought some practice was needed. Ben said, "I can take care of that!"

The whole 15 acres of corn was planted, and the first 5 acres were beginning to break through the ground. With this done, they decided to plow 7 acres for potatoes and beans for the girls. They would need a lot of potatoes to feed 15 people for the winter. All four sows that Nate and Ben had brought with them had pigs, with each sow having 6 to 8. Some kind of a pen had to be made for them or they would eat all the potatoes planted last week! Spring rains were now here, and the river was running high. Just as soon as the water went down, a trout line would be run across the river to catch a few of those big catfish that had been seen.

Doc's house was finished, and work was in full swing to build Nate and Helen a home. All the bark Ben Jr. had been taking off the logs was burned. The ash was then cooled, mixed with clay, salt, and chopped grass. This mixture was used for daubing and filling cracks between the logs on the building. Everything was taking place as planned. Once Nate's home was done, work would take place on the barns and one smokehouse.

With summer coming on the girls were busy planting the garden, and Sam and Joe were hoeing weeds from the cornfields. It did not take long for days to pass, but they were all happy and well. Everything was needed! Chairs were made by cutting short logs and standing then on ends. Nate had taken some sideboards from one of the wagons, and loaded them on logs to make a table. This fall, Ben and Nate would build a shop for Nate, and get the lathe in service to make real chairs and tables!

October was just around the corner and the corn and potatoes had to be picked. The pigs that were born in the spring were ready to be slaughtered and smoked for ham and bacon. Two barns were finished, and work had started on the third one. The men had also started to build a corncrib and smokehouse. It had been a good summer now that the corn was almost finished!

Joe and Sam were complaining that someone was picking the corn on the far side of the field. Ben said it was possible to lose a few ears to hungry travelers, but he was sure it was the Indians.

"What can we do about it?" Doc asked.

"We will set up a guard system until we get most of it picked. We will start by picking the rows next to the prairie and cutting the fodder for cattle feed. That way, they will have to cross more open ground to get to it," replied Ben.

The Indians were getting braver by the day, and they did not like it. They had nothing to live on except buffalo meat and fish. Most of them were not farmers and stock people; therefore, they must live off the land or steal from the white man.

"I don't like it, and would rather give it to them than let them steal," stated Ben.

7:

Monday was a full day with most of the women in the garden or washing clothes. The men were building a corncrib. Joe and Sam were picking corn, and Tom and Henry were still cutting logs and wood. Sue Marie and Bill were playing just outside the wagons, which were still mostly in place from where they had been parked in the spring. No one was paying any attention to their games and fun until Helen rang the dinner bell. Sue Marie and Bill were nowhere in sight! Nate got up from the table and started calling their names. No sound or sight of them anywhere! He came back to the table and reported they were nowhere in sight. Within an hour, every place in and around the grounds was searched. Nothing was found!

Henry went toward the river just in case they had gone that far from the camp. He waded into the river and checked the other side. As he came back to the river bank, he noticed Sue Marie's whistle she carried around her neck laying there in the mud. Along with the whistle were two sets of tracks leading off toward the woods and the high grass. The steps were long, meaning someone had been running. He followed the tracks to the woods where he found pony droppings, and signs someone had tied two or more horses at that location. He was sick and he wanted to throw up! He knew what Indians could do to white girls, but he had to fight his way back over the river at a half run. Nate and the others had to be told what he had found.

Back at the camp, Henry broke the news to everyone. Helen let out a scream that could be heard for miles. She started crying and screaming at the top of her lungs. Nate tried to hold her, but she would not have any part of it. Elisabeth went to Ben and threw her arms around his neck, crying, "Oh God, why have you done this?"

Doc and Sarah took Helen and led her over to their house. There Doc gave her something and waited until she fell asleep.

Ben asked, "What do you want to do?"

Nate said, "I'm going after them! Its high noon and the sooner we get to their camp, the better chance we have of getting them back! Tom, Sam, and Doc will stay here, and the rest of us will ride out now!"

The four of them saddled their horses and headed to the open prairies.

The Indian camp was a good 30 minute ride to the northwest. They covered that distance in a short time. The camp lay in a valley with a high bluff to the east. The Indians liked this kind of campsite because it protected them from buffalo stampedes. Buffalo knew the land well, and would not run into trees or canyons, so it made a good campsite for the Indians. They dismounted and tied the horses to some mesquite brush 25 yards from the bluff.

Crawling in the tall grass and looking down on the campsite three hundred feet below them through their rifle scopes, they could see every move the Indians made. Everything looked normal. Kids were playing along a creek bank a hundred yards to the east. Everyone was doing something. There seemed to be two teepees where more people were going and coming from than all the rest. Ben said it looked like the big one with all the drawing on it could be the Chief's teepee.

After five more minutes Nate said, "I'm going down there"

Ben asked, "Are you crazy?"

"No! Just mad! Here is the plan - you fellows wait here and keep an eye on me. If anything goes wrong, I want you to kill every damn one of them. Do you hear me?" replied Nate.

"I hear you," Ben said, "but I don't like it!

"Well my friend, I don't care what you like! We have two kids down there, and I'm not going to give them up without a fight! If it means my life - then so be it!" stated Nate. With that, he rode off to the east so he could get off the bluff and get down to the creek.

Nate Owens was a strong man. Swinging a three pound hammer all day and building three houses within a year had him in good shape, and he was no match for man or beast when he was mad! He rode quietly as he made his way off the bluff. He approached the creek with a grove of cotton woods in front of him. He stayed in the woods until he was only a few yards from the kids. He knew as soon as his horse hit the water, the kids would run and warn the camp.

As the horse came out of the woods, Nate reached down and grabbed a five or six year old boy by the arm. The boy was screaming and kicking, but he was not a match for Nate's strong hands. He sat him down hard in the saddle and put his left hand over the boy's mouth. The kid bit his finger, and Nate slapped him hard across the legs with the rings. The kid shut up and the others were soon left behind. He rode into camp and headed straight for the teepee with all the pictures.

It was not long until a crowd had formed. The kid started screaming again, and Nate put his hand over his mouth once more as he drew his Bowie knife and placed it in the kid's ribs. Two braves walked up as if they were going to pull him from his horse, and he made a sign that if they came any closer he would cut the boy's throat. He did not know if anyone spoke any English, so he made signs that they had two of his kids, and unless they gave them up he would kill the boy. Over next to the Chief's teepee, a brave drew his bow and pulled an arrow from his back.

Nate turned his horse toward the shooter, and did not take his eyes off the brave.

"I have three men on the hill with rifles," said Nate as he pointed to his rifle on his side. "Give me my kids, or you die and the boy goes first!" declared Nate. Still watching the brave, he saw him let the arrow fly. He ducked and the arrow missed its mark. Before he could reach for another one, he fell kicking and quavering on the ground like a squirrel shot from a tree. A squaw ran over to him and started screaming. With that, the Chief came out of his teepee to see what was going on. He told the braves to put down their weapons.

Nate once more repeated what was wrong. The chief then made a sign to a woman nearby. She ran to the teepee that seemed to have all the traffic he had observed from the bluff. Within a few minutes, a woman came to the teepee opening with Sue Marie and Bill in hand. Sue Marie let out a yell and ran to Nate. Nate dropped the Indian boy to the ground and slid out of the saddle. He then put Bill on behind the saddle, and got back on the horse, lifting Sue Marie up in front of him.

He could see how confused the Indians were with the dead brave lying on the ground, when they did not hear a rifle shot. This made them wonder how he had died so quickly after shooting the arrow. The white man had great power, but they did not understand how this could be done. The closest shooting point was three hundred yards away, and there was no one in sight. Nate rode out of the camp, slowly crossed the creek, and headed for the bluff. When he arrived he asked, "Who fired the shot?"

Ben spoke up and said, "I did! I did not want to kill him, but I knew if one brave fired, all the others would join in. I thought it was better to take one out rather than many with you in the middle. I did not have a lot of choices." They quickly mounted and rode back into the prairie.

It was getting close to dark when they rode back into camp. Helen was still under Doc's care. Elisabeth fell down on her knees and took both of them in her arms. She kissed and kissed them, and held each one to make sure what she saw was real. By now Helen had come around. "Thank you! Thank you! Only God knows how much I love you!"

Nate said, "I thank all of you for your help. A special thanks to Henry and Ben. They are the ones that made all this possible."

Ben spoke up. "I want each of you to watch each other's backs. Do not let anyone be alone for long. These people get braver with each passing day. Now that we have had to kill one of them, I'm sure they will want to even the score. So tonight, and every night, day and night - we must watch over one another!"

8:

The corncrib was almost done. It had been built on the downside of a small hill. That way a wagon could pull up alongside, and the corn could be shoveled into an opening on the side. It would hold more than this year's crop, so it looked like they had enough feed for everyone, plus the stock, for the coming winter. They had planted 15 acres, and it looked like 30 to 35 bushels to the acre, giving them more than needed.

The smokehouse was different and was started next. For this year they would only build one, but next year they would build two more - one for each family. The smokehouse had a stone-lined bottom on three sides, with stone running up the side two to three feet so the fire built to smoke the meat would not burn down the smokehouse.

Nate had brought some steel with him that was used for a grate 36 inches above the fire or coal bed. The house had no windows, and the roof was steep and pointed. Nate had installed a damper in the roof to trap smoke during smoking time. All these things had to be done in order to take care of the things that were needed to survive a long, hard winter. Temperatures would drop to 0 and below, and snow would be so deep a mule could not walk or feed itself. Ben and Nate were businessmen as such, at a time in history when not much was known about business. They knew what they wanted and how to get it. It took hard work and planning to get where they needed to be.

With the smokehouse finished, a large, strong skinning rail had to be built. In October they would slaughter 15 or 16 of the pigs that were born in the spring to provide ham, bacon, and grease - known as lard in that time of history. The fat, or lard, was used for cooking and to make soap. It was rendered from the skin and fat taken from the pigs. The cracklings were used in cornbread mixes, and to eat as a snack.

Nate had brought blocks with him of different sizes. Blocks were two wheels that allowed you to hang things from a barn or skinning rail. A rope could then be threaded through the blocks with a hook, so that a 300 pound hog or 800 pound calf could be raised up to be skinned. The meat was then salted or treated with sugar and spices to be smoked. When the smoking process was finished, the hams were hung in the cooler side of the smokehouse and kept all winter long to weight the table.

They had a good summer and still had the fall to go. They had built three houses, three barns for the stock, two springhouses, one smokehouse, two chicken houses, a large hog pen, planted 15 acres of corn and seven acres of potatoes and a garden. They had dug a cellar and lined it with logs to store the potatoes and canned goods.

Yes, they had worked hard for the past seven months, but there was still a lot of work to be done. Land had to be cleared and plowed for winter wheat and barley, a shop had to be built for Nate and Ben, and a corn mill needed to be built to grind corn and wheat for bread. One more springhouse had to be found and built. The wood that Tom and Henry had cut had to be moved closer to the houses for heat and cooking, and heating bath and wash water. It was not easy being a frontier family, and it was all about just staying alive.

Sometime before it got cold and snowy, they would have to travel thirty-five miles to the east to a trading post and see if they could buy salt, sugar, and lamp oil, just to name a few items they needed. Since there would be some ham and corn that might not be needed, they would try and trade these items for the things they needed. They had no idea what the trading post might have, but the trip had to be made. They had no idea what kind of money the post would take, if any, and the danger in going or just how to get there. After hog killing time, they would plan the trip in November.

It was decided that Nate, Henry, and Joe would make the first trip, leaving behind the rest to care for the settlement. The trip would take three days. November 15th was the date set for the trip. They put 50 bags of corn on the wagon, and six hams. Ben said they should set the price of two cents per pound for the corn, and two dollars each for the hams. That meant there would be $62.00 to buy things with. Nate took another $100 with him, but did not know if they would need it.

Sleeping bags and food were prepared, and one barrel of water and corn for the mules. At 5 am they were on their way. At 3 miles per hour, they should see themselves at the trading post by 3 pm. Much to their surprise, they arrived at noon. The trading post was a good three hundred yards from the river and not only had a trading post, but houses, a saloon, a blacksmith shop, and a good gun and saddle shop. They did not expect all this.

Nate got down from the wagon and went inside. A group of men were standing outside, and a few Indians were hanging around a corral on the right side of the trading post. There were three men in the post; two were talking with each other, and the third was talking to the trader. The trader looked to be in his forties and spoke with a German or Swedish accent.

Nate heard the man he had been talking to call him Mr. Hammersmith. "Would you like to buy some yellow shelled corn and some hams?" asked Nate.

The men's faces lit up and Mr. Hammersmith said, "Yes! By all means, yes! We have a lot of requests for both. If they are good hams, I will pay three dollars each."

"We just smoked this fall," Nate replied.

"That is good. I have a little smokehouse out back, and I will hang them in there for a few more weeks. They will bring good money this winter. Corn, sir, I will pay 3 cents if it is in bags, and 2 cents per pound if it is in a barrel," stated Mr. Hammersmith. "I have 50 bags outside," stated Nate. "That is good. You can unload out back on the porch. What can I sell you?" asked Mr. Hammersmith.

"Well, let me unload, and I will look around," replied Nate.

Nate went outside and kicked his heels together! He was very pleased. Henry pulled the wagon around back, and they unloaded in a few minutes. Back inside Nate asked Mr. Hammersmith if he could take federal dollars. He said yes, that federal dollars, silver and gold were all he would trade in. "Well, I have federal money, but no gold or silver", Nate said. "Mr. Hammersmith, if it is all right with you because it is so late in the day, I would like to look at what you have to trade and do my business tomorrow. Would that be all right with you? We will find a campsite tonight, and be here early in the morning."

"That will be fine with me, I will be here at 6 am", replied Mr. Hammersmith. With that, Nate left the post and joined Henry and Joe in the wagon. They headed to the outside of the area to find a place to camp. There were no hotels or places to rest, so they would camp where they could build a fire, unhitch the mules, and sleep in the wagon.

As they sat around the campfire Nate said, "I found barbed wire at the post, and burlap sacks. I also saw sugar, and salt, and dried beans. I could not help but wonder how and where these things came from. Then it came to me - the river! Tomorrow, I would like both of you to come in with me, and if you see something we need let me know."

They were out of their sleeping bags and ready to go at 5:30 am. Nate wanted to get the trading done and head back home as soon as they could. At a little after 6 am the three of them walked into the trading post. Nate said, "Mr. Hammersmith, I did not bring a list with me, so if you will write this down and if you have it, we will take it. Sir, we need 2 rolls of rope: one roll one inch in diameter, and one roll one half inch in diameter, four bags of white flour, four bags of salt, two hundred pounds of lye, four bags of sugar, four blocks of licking salt, two bags of coffee, 500 hundred burlap bags, and Sir - how much do you want for the barbed wire, and how many feet are there in a roll?"

"What did you say your name was?" asked Mr. Hammersmith.

"My name is Nathan Owens, and we have a little spread 35 miles southwest of here on the Big Blue River," replied Nate.

"How long have you fellows been out there?" inquired Mr. Hammersmith?

"It will be a year this April," responded Nate.

"Well, let me say this is a nice order, and I sure hope you folks come back!" stated Mr. Hammersmith.

"Mr. Owens, the wire is $5.00 a roll, and it says there is 1,000 feet in a roll," proclaimed Mr. Hammersmith.

"In that case I will take ten rolls, and 10 pounds of staples, and I will take 10 gallons of lamp oil," Nate said, then added, "Sir, I think that will do it, unless my boys see something they want."

Henry said, "I could use a few of those files over there, and a new ax. I think I wore out ours this summer."

"In that case, put them on the list," said Nate.

Mr. Hammersmith said pull the wagon around back, as a lot of the stuff was on the back porch. Henry and Joe loaded the wagon while Mr. Hammersmith marked off the items. He said, "Mr. Owens it looks like I owe you $93.00 for the ham and corn, so if you have $60.00, our business is done".

Nate said, "No sir, I would like to have two pounds of that hard candy you have over there."

"I will just throw that in for such a nice order," declared Mr. Hammersmith.

Nate said, "I thank you very much, sir, and yes, we will be back next spring. I think we may bring some of our wives when we come back. I'm sure they would like some of that cloth you have over there, and maybe some cotton."

"It has been nice meeting you and I look forward to seeing you in the spring," stated Mr. Hammersmith.

It was about 10 o'clock and with good luck they would be home by sundown. Nate was as happy as he could be. The trading post had far more items than he expected, and it looked like Mr. Hammersmith was a fair man. The place did not look like much, but it was close to the river and there was building going on. Mr. Hammersmith said it looked as if they would get a post office if the U.S. Government bought the territory. He said with a post office, the trading post area would grow.

When they arrived home, everyone ran out to see what they had new. Nate told the girls what a good trading post it was and about all the cloth and cotton that he saw. Doc wanted to know if he seen anything a doctor might want or need. Nate said, "No, but I didn't think about looking for things like that. I did hear that they are going to build a post office there next year. We might be able to send and get mail now and then. We will go back in the spring and take two of you wives along."

Nate said, "Unload the wagon at my place, and we will divide up the supplies. Leave the wire in the wagon until we find a good, dry place for it."

Doc asked, "What are you going to do with all that wire?"

Ben answered, "Fence off grazing fields for the cattle and mules. That way, we do not have to hobble them anymore. We also so can put a couple of runs around the hog pen."

They still had a little time before Christmas, so Nate's workshop was started. The lathe was needed to make furniture, and the sooner the windmill could be put into service, the happier all the wives would be. The plan was to build a much bigger shop than he had in Ohio. He wanted to pull a wagon inside if he needed to work in the winter.

Between the shop and other work, Tom and the boys needed a place to shell corn, so a building was built next to the corncrib where not only could they shell corn, but they could sack and store it. Joe and Sam had come in out of the fields now that winter wheat and barley had been planted, so they could give Tom a hand with shelling.

It had been three months since the kids had been taken, and no word from the Indians. Ben said they might have moved southwest to keep up with the buffalo. Now that it was getting colder, the buffalo would move south for the winter.

Christmas was just around the corner, so it was planned that only one tree would be put up in Ben's house, and everyone would eat and do church services there. Since Nate did not have Christmas on his mind when he was at the trading post, Henry and Joe would ride up there and see what they had to offer.

Doc said, "In that case, I would like to go also. I need to check that place out. They might have something a doctor could use." It was thought they could ride up and back in the same day, so it was planned for Friday morning.

Since Nate and Ben were good at making things, Tom had talked to his dad about a corn Sheller that was on his mind. His thoughts were that if he could put a whole corncob with the corn on it into the worm turning device, that when the device reached the end, the corn would be off the cob, and all that was left would be the cob. It would drop to the floor, while the corn was caught in a bucket. That way, he could turn the thing by hand, and feed it much faster than taking it off by hand. Nate said, "Tom, you are a chip off the old block. Yes, I think I can make something like that. Let me get the shop up and going, and I will see what I have for steel.

The boys made it back from the trading post all happy. They had gotten some candy and things the women wanted; plus Doc had found morphine, liniment, quinine, and some new tools used in opening a wound. He, too, thought the place was a godsend. Everyone would have a good Christmas, thanks to Henry and Joe!

When they built the barns, they had been made with eight stalls down one side, with hay and fodder in the middle. This left the eight stalls on the other side for pigs and chickens when the weather got bad. Snow had already fallen in a light coating, but they were not concerned and thought they were ready. Barrels would be filled with water and brought into the house, so the water would not freeze. They were hoping the two springhouses would keep running under the ice and they would still be able to keep milk and butter.

Helen and Sarah would hold school for the kids and make quilts to keep warm. The men would make furniture, buckets, and drums for all three houses. The four month winter should go fast. It would soon be a year in their new home. Next spring would not be as hard on them, since most of the building was done.

Ben and Nate wanted to get a lot more corn in the ground next spring, and if Nate and Tom could get their Sheller to work, maybe the corn could be sold to the trader and the Army Post not too far from them. If that happened, Ben had his mind set on a big stone grinder run off a water wheel in the river. That way they could grind bone meal, corn, barley, and wheat for white bread, and make feed for the stock that no one else had.

9:

Winter came Thanksgiving Day. The snow began to fall and did not quit for three days. It was so deep that if they had not built a porch onto the house, the doors to the outside could not have been opened. It was cold! The temperature had dropped down to 18 degrees. Ben said, "Thank God we do not have to sleep on the ground this winter. We may not have a bed, but we have a fire and warm sleeping bags. So let it snow!"

Everyone stayed close to the houses, but still the men had to take care of the animals, feed the chickens and hogs, and milk the cows. All the animals plus the chickens had been brought into the stalls of the barns, so everyone was doing well compared to last winter. Everyone stayed in the house for the first day. Then the men got the scooper out and made a nice path to each house, the springhouses, and Nate's workshop. Elisabeth gave school assignments and the other girls made and repaired clothing.

Christmas was only two weeks away. Since it had been decided to be at Ben's house, the girls were busy planning the meal, and how and where they would seat everyone. It was agreed upon that Christmas morning would start off with a big breakfast and prayer. They would then open presents and give thanks to God for all His gifts for the year. Each one was asked to give his thoughts on the trip to their new home and the best and worst part of the trip for them.

Henry was asked to go first. "I would like to thank Mr. Owens and Mr. Sharp for picking me to come on the trip. No young man could ask to be around better people than you folks. I thank you again for giving me the chance I have had to be a part of this family. You have taught me the love of God, and what He can do for you. God only knows where I would be if it had not have been for you people."

Ben then spoke and said, "Well, thank you Henry! You are a good man, a hard worker, and we are proud to count you as one of us; however we knew that after only 300 miles of the trip. That is why I could not let you freeze to death when you fell into the ice."

Everyone got a big laugh out of that.

The doctor then took the floor and said, "I do not know why my wagons came upon you on the trail. It was as if the power of God was saying, 'Doctor you cannot make this trip without help, and just up in front of you is the help you need.' I am a Doctor - a man of healing - and know nothing about the frontier. In the past nine months, I have learned more about life and people than I did in all my schooling years. I am a better man than I was, and I now know and trust God with a different light than before. I would not have come west if it had not been for the boys. They wanted to farm and get out of town. I was just starting my practice, and I said why not? We can all start together. We planned a trip with the help of some friends, which I now know was poorly planned. I thank all of you for taking us in and teaching us the things we have to know. I now pledge my life to you people and my family and will serve as long as God will allow me. I like our new home, and there is not one of you that I dislike. May we live in peace and good health forever?"

"Well, Doc we have not had to use you to much as a doctor just yet, but I'm sure the need for your skills will come in due time. You are not only a good doctor, but a hard worker and we welcome you and your family. We thank God for sending you," said Ben.

Winter would last three to four months, and it would be back to the garden, canning, and planting potatoes. This New Year would bring in 1806, and Henry and Doc had heard at the trading post that the U.S. Government had made the Louisiana Purchase. This made the men happy, because they would now get their land in four years or less, free and clear.

Spring would come, and Nate had been busy building two new plows so the fields could be plowed much faster. Ben said, "You keep saying how good I am, but my friend you are worth your weight in gold as far as the O&S Feed Company is concerned. You have made two plows, three large harrows to break up the clods, a weed plow, and a mule-pulled row plow. My God, man - one more winter and we will be able to sell farm equipment! We could not have a better man with us than you. We all thank you from the bottom of our hearts."

Nate had been able to do all this with steel Henry and the boys brought back from the trading post. It seemed the Army needed the steel for the forts, and some work they were doing, so Mr. Hammersmith had been able to get his hands on some of it." Well, Mr. Sharp, I could not have done it without your lathe and your skills. God has made us a two-mule team to lead our people to a better life. So as long as He allows us to keep our health, we will work for the good of all."

The same thing went by year after year, and the next thing 10 years had gone by before you could bat an eye. It was now 1816. Changes had taken place that could not be stopped. It was noted that Mr. Henry Williams was making more trips to the trading post. It seems every time something was needed, he and Joe would be the first to say, "I will do that next weekend!"

As the summer wore on, it seemed that not only did they go on Friday, but lots of the time they did not make it back until Sunday afternoon. Nate thought he had better pry into the long stays just a little bit. He asked Henry, "What is taking so long and keeping you at the trading post?"

He said, "Mr. Owens, Mr. Hammersmith has a daughter one year younger than me, and I guess she has taken a liking to me. I get to the post on Friday night and spend most of the day with her on Saturday working around the trading post. Joe and I sleep out in Mr. Hammersmith's barn Saturday night, and I go to church with her on Sunday and then ride home."

"Well, what does Joe do?" asked Nate. "Well, sir, I think he has been talking to a girl at church. I think she is the preacher's daughter. You would have to ask him," replied Henry.

"So you have got a girlfriend?" inquired Nate.

"I guess so, sir. It kind of looks that way", answered Henry.

"Well, it's all right with me, but just remember it's a frontier town and anything can happen! So watch your P's and Q's!" warned Nate.

"Yes sir! I will do that!" agreed Henry.

10:

All the boys except Joe and Sam were doing something, so Ben thought he would start to plow corn ground on Monday. It was a pretty day with the sun shining, and he wanted to get the crop in early this year. Nate had made a new plow and he wanted to test it out. He threw the plow, his water jug, and whatever else he needed into the back of a wagon and headed out.

They had taken the canvas and rails off some of the wagons last fall to haul corn, so the wagon was open. He dragged the plow off the wagon and hitched the mules to it. It was a big deep bottom plow, and Nate said if it worked well, he would try and make it into a double one next year. He had made three or four passes around an acre square, and things were working well.

When he was coming down the backside of the square, he spotted four or five Indians riding along the river. He watched them as they came up the river. He noticed they did not seem like a hunting party. They were riding bareback, which most Indians did, but they all were wearing feathers and paint. He hurried the mules a little so he would be close to the wagon, just in case they came across the river. His rifle was leaning up next to the back wagon wheel, so he wanted to get as close to it as he could. He was wearing his sidearm, but he did not want to use that unless he had to. They were a good three to four hundred yards away from him. As long as they stayed on the other side of the river, everything would be fine.

Another hundred yards, and the Indians suddenly turned their horses into the river. He had now reached the wagon and tied the mules off on the plow handles, so if they tried to run they would pull the plow in deeper. He did not want to act as if he was afraid of them, so he reached into the wagon bed and came out with his water jug. He uncorked the jug and started to drink, watching them from around the end of the jug.

The Indians pulled the horses to a stop, and watched for a few seconds. Then all of a sudden they let out a yell that could be heard for miles, and put the horses into a full run. Ben knew they were after him. He picked up his rifle which they had not seen, and began to fire. There was about two hundred and fifty yards between them. The first one went down with a bang! He did not take his eyes off the group, and kept firing; two, three and number four hit the dirt. By now, the fifth one was on top of him, and he dived underneath the wagon as a tomahawk struck the wagon bed.

The mules were jumping around trying to get the plow out of the ground. The last Indian did not want to stick around, since four of his friends were out of the fight. He put the horse in a full run, and headed back to the river. Ben wasn't in a hurry; he knew he had one more round and lots of yards left. He leaned the rifle on a wagon spoke, and took a nice, long aim. When the Indian's head came into view, he pulled the trigger!

By now, the field was beginning to fill up with men. Tom rode up on a bareback mule. Nate and Henry were on the run, and Joe and Sam came running across the field. Ben crawled out from under the wagon and said, "Fellows, where were you when I needed you?"

The fight was over, and the land was once again quiet. Nate spoke up and asked, "What happened?"

Ben said, "I don't know! Five of them just decided to attack me!"

Nate said, "I don't think they just decided to attack you. I think they have been planning it all winter. You see, they went west for the winter, staying with the buffalo. When they got back into camp they put together a little war party and decided to get even for the death of their brother last fall."

"So now what?" inquired Ben?

"Well, I will tell you. Here is what we are going to do. I want you, Henry and Tom to get a wagon. Line the bottom with hay and bring some canvas. Tell Elisabeth I want five roses from her garden just ready to bloom. I want the five bodies loaded onto the wagon bed and covered with canvas. We are going to take them home, horses and all. I want all of you to saddle up and ride with me. I will drive the wagon, and we will leave Doc and his boys here," declared Nate.

Within an hour, they had caught the horses and were on their way. An hour and a half later they were at the camp, and sure enough, it looked like it did last fall. They pulled the wagon up under some trees and laid the canvas on the ground. They placed all five bodies on the canvas, folded their arms over their chests, and laid a red rose on each one of them. They then tied their horses to a tree. With that done, they got back into the wagon and headed home.

Ben asked, "What do you think is going to happen now?"

"I don't know, but if they have any sense they will see that six of their men are now dead, and that they were brought back to their family with honor. I don't know what they will do. I do not know Indians, but I will guarantee you, we will find out sooner or later. Right now we are going home to make sure all stays well!" stated Nate. Doc had put the mules away, and Ben would start his work again in the morning.

It was hard to believe what was going on out there in the prairies. You could almost always see and hear the sounds of wagons everywhere. Last year they had killed five big rattlers, and they did not know if it was the wagons or what was making them come toward the houses and barns. Sam came up and said, "Mr. Sharp, I don't know if this is the reason or not, but last year while Joe and I were cutting grass, it seemed like every time we came upon a prairie chicken nest there would be a snake not too far away. We think they are after the eggs or baby chickens, or both."

"You know, I will bet you are right! That is their food supply, and that is why they are so big and fat!" declared Ben.

"Well, I don't like it. It also seems that where we have cut the grass, we don't see as many," added Sam.

"I'm going to have Nate make us eight to ten three prong forks that we can stick in the ground around the barn and houses. That way, we can place the fork over the snake's head and kill it on the spot. Please do not put your hands in places you can't see. If you walk outside, please walk with your head down and wear high top boots loose at the top if you can. I will talk to Doc and see what he knows about snake bites - so watch your steps!" stated Ben.

Doc and Tom were going to cut fence posts and start to build miles of fence. Deer, buffalo, and raccoons had to be keep out of the corn; they needed pastureland for the stock. Every time Henry went to the trading post, he would bring back five rolls of wire and five pounds of staples.

Everything was now on the farm. It was planned that a three row barbed wire fence would be used five feet off the ground. The first row would be twelve inches off the ground. The top row would be 6 inches down from the top of the post, with the middle row in between. Large posts would be used on the end of the run, with angle braces running down each side. The posts would be on ten foot centers with a large pull post every 100 feet, with angle braces on each side. They would start with the cornfields, then the gardens, and last, all pastures and programmed planting fields. It would be an all-summer job.

That night as Ben and family took their nightly meal, Elisabeth noted Ben looked a little beat and wanted to know if there was anything wrong. He said, "I feel a little down because I took the life of five men today and I'm sad about that, but I do not believe I had a choice. It was them or me. I think I did the right thing in taking the bodies back to camp, but I do expect to hear something one way or the other."

Ben then added, "I have been talking to Nate. He tells me he has spoken to Henry about his weekend trips to the trading post. It seems he has met a young woman. She is the daughter of Mr. Hammersmith, the trading post operator. He told me he and Joe arrive on Friday night, and sleep in Mr. Hammersmith's barn. Henry then gets up in the morning, and helps out at the trading post on Saturday, and then goes to church with her on Sunday. Then he and Joe ride home Sunday afternoon."

Elisabeth said, "I don't see anything wrong with that! Henry is 30 years old, and it is time he took a wife."

"I don't know, but I think she is in her mid to late twenties," Ben said, adding, "He also told me that Joe was seeing a young woman. He would not tell me much about the girl, saying I needed to talk to Joe."

"Well," began Elisabeth", it looks like we might have a little romance going on here at the farm!"

"What do you mean?" asked Ben.

"It just seems to me that Tom and Barbara Ann have been staying pretty close together. I notice every time she goes to the springhouse, Tom is not far behind."

"My God Elisabeth - they have been together all of their lives! Maybe he just wants to make sure she is safe," stated Ben.

"I don't know; they just look at one another differently than they used to. I'm sure it's all right," added Elisabeth.

"We will just keep an eye on things!" declared Ben.

It had been a month since the big shootout in the cornfield. Ben was coming out of the smokehouse when he noticed two Indians coming across the prairie. They were riding slowly, and it looked from where he was standing to be a child with whoever it was with him. He thought he had better ring the bell anyway, just in case. A few minutes later, he could tell one of them was carrying a white flag on a staff. He started to feel a little better, and by then the other fellows were gathering around him, or not far away. Now he could tell that one was a boy, maybe 8 or 9 years old, and the other was a woman. She looked to be in her twenties. She made a gesture of peace with the flag and her hand.

Ben spoke to her in English, but she kept shaking her head "no". Then words came out of her mouth, and Doc started talking in a language that no one else had ever heard. Ben asked Doc, "What is she is saying?"

Doc replied, "She speaks French - and not bad French at that!"

"Well good! It looks like the two of you can talk," said Ben.

"She said the Chief sent her here to see if you would have a peace powwow with him," said Doc.

"Tell her that if she can wait a few minutes, we will let her know," stated Ben.

With that, Ben turned to the others and asked, "What do you think?"

Doc spoke up saying, "She has come here in peace by bringing the boy".

"Ask her when," prompted Ben.

She said, "In two or three moons"

"Well, what is that - three days or three months?" asked Ben.

Doc asked her again. This time she said, "Three days at high noon.

"Tell her we will be there," declared Ben.

She said, "Thank you", and started to ride off.

Ben said, "Tell her to wait a few minutes". He then told Henry to get a ham from the smokehouse and wrap it in oil cloth. Ben handed her the ham and said, "Tell her this is for the Chief, and that we will meet him in three days at high noon".

She thanked Doc three or four times, and slowly rode away. She was very, very, pretty with long black hair that hung almost to her ponies back. Within minutes, she was out of view in the tall grass.

With her gone, they decided to have a little powwow of their own. Ben asked, "What do you think fellows? Doc, what did you think?"

"I think it is on the up and up and that they have had enough time to think about the five braves, and want peace instead of war," said Doc.

"In that case, here is a plan to build on", began Ben, "There are seven of us men here on the farm not counting Ben Jr. We will take Doc, Henry as our guard, and me into the camp. We will leave Tom and Joe on the hill with the long rifles. The rest will stay here at the farm and look after the women."

"Ok with me," agreed everyone.

Then Ben added, "Let's see what the next three days will bring".

Since the farm was so big and so much work had to be done in order to make sure everyone was doing the right thing, they would meet at Nate's shop to go over the day's progress and plan the next day's work. It was a fun time for everyone and took about an hour each day. It was early spring, and there was a lot of plowing and planting that needed to be done. The cattle herd had grown to close to 100 head. There were mules, horses, and hogs that had to have maintenance, to say nothing of chickens, gardens, milking, and butter making, which the women took care of. It did not take long for three days to pass.

The peace meeting was to take place on Wednesday, so Tuesday night it was planned that only light work would be done in the morning. They started saddling up at 10.30 am in order to be there by high noon. Ben had decided to take two sacks of corn, two hams, and some hard candy for the children, so Tom was asked to drive the wagon, and they would hold it back until more was known about the peace talks. If they were to bring the wagon into camp after talking with the Chief, Henry would go to his saddlebag and remove a bandana, which he would tie around his neck. At that point, Tom would bring the wagon down to the camp with the gifts.

Doc, Henry, and Nate rode into the camp carrying a white flag at a few minutes before high noon. Braves were everywhere, but none made any gestures toward the white men. Ben rode to the teepee he had seen before and asked Henry to get down and stand next to the teepee door. A brave was on the other side, as when Nate rode into the camp to get his kids. The brave opened the teepee flap and said something to someone inside.

Within minutes, the same Indian girl was outside. Doc had a nice greeting for her, and asked if the Chief was ready for the meeting. She said, "Yes", and invited them to enter the teepee. The teepee seemed much larger, once inside, than it appeared outside. The Chief was sitting on a blanket with a brave sitting on each side of him. Another blanket was spread on the other side, and a smaller blanket was in the middle to Doc's right side. The Chief made a motion for his guests to sit down.

After everyone was seated, the girl sat on the small blanket on Doc's right side. The Chief took three puffs from his pipe, and blew the smoke up into the air. Then he said, "My name is Chief White Head." He wanted to know their names, and he wanted to know if Doc was the Chief.

Doc said, "No!" and that he was a doctor.

The Chief then asked Ben if he was a Chief. Ben replied, "No, I'm just someone that speaks for my people."

Then the Chief asked which one sent the ham to him. Ben said, "I did."

"It was very good. Indians do not raise hogs; they are too much trouble to move from camp to camp. We must follow the buffalo," stated the Chief.

"Are you the one that brought the five braves back to our camp?" inquired the Chief.

"Yes, my men and I did it" answered Ben.

Then the Chief said, "We have never seen this before. Most white men leave the Indian where he has fallen. The women and the Arapaho Indian tribe thank you. I would like to say that the Arapaho would like to have peace with all the people that live in your camp, but you cannot kill our buffalo."

Ben declared, "We would like to kill one or two buffalo for meat every year."

"That is all right, as long as you do not kill and leave the meat in the prairie," stated the Chief.

Ben agreed for his people, "We will not do that."

"Then it is OK with the Arapaho", said Chief White Head.

"Thank you, sir! We will only kill what we need for food", assured Ben.

"If you will trade us corn, we will let you kill two buffalo every year," declared the Chief.

"Yes, we will have 20 bags of corn for your people," agreed Ben.

"Doc, can you ask the girl what her name is?" asked Ben.

"Yes. Her name is Little Flower," responded Doc.

"Where did she learn to speak French?" inquired Ben.

"She said from her mother, who was a French woman. Her mother belonged to the Chief, but died when she was twelve years old of the fever," answered Doc. "So, Little Flower is the Chief's daughter," said Ben.

"Yes, that is right," confirmed Doc.

"Tell the Chief we people at the O & S Farm are very glad to live in peace with the Arapaho and will not break this treaty," avowed Ben.

"Then we will smoke the pipe, and live in peace," agreed the Chief. The pipe was then passed around to all the men three times, and the peace powwow was over. Ben then informed Henry to bring the wagon in. Jim drove the wagon up next to the teepee and asked the Chief to step outside; that he had gifts to show his appreciation. The chief was very happy and gave Ben an Indian bow and a quill of arrows.

Ben, Doc, and Henry rode back to the top of the ridge very happy that the killing was over between the O & S Farm people and the Arapaho. This gave everyone at the farm a great comfort. Life once again could return to normal!

Nate and Tom had made their corn Sheller. The Sheller worked so well that Tom could clean out the corncrib and would be ready for next year's crop, but they had another problem. It looked like with the new double bottom plow Nate had made, they could plant twice as many acres as before. That meant two or three more corncribs had to be built during the summer.

In addition, Nate had also built two new harrows. The harrows were five feet wide and 6 feet deep. He had taken three feet long pieces of steel and rolled them into a spring-like tong. He then placed the tongs on a long piece of steel running across the six foot span. He had made four rows of the tongs and placed them behind one another but offset them by 6 inches. He then made a box on each side of the harrow to be filled with rocks to hold it down, plus a seat in the center for a driver. With the harrows done, Joe and Sam could use them to till all the wheat and barley ground without plowing. This meant they could rotate the corn crop and plant three times the acres as before. They wanted to give Mr. Tom plenty of corn to shell with his new Sheller.

A trip into town needed to be made by Nate and Ben to talk to the banker and mail some letters. They had not talked to anyone back in Old Town for over 10 years. They had plenty of money from trading with the trading post and all the travelers going west, but they just felt they needed better control over their money. Besides, Ben wanted to talk to Mr. Hammersmith about ordering a corn grinding stone. He had wanted to get a grinder for some time and needed to talk to the Army and Mr. Hammersmith as to who cut the stone, and the best way to get it to the territory. Nate had not been to the trading post in 8 years and Ben had never been. Since Ben's last trip, he had left most of the buying up to Henry and Joe. He just felt he was needed more at home, and Henry and Joe were doing a good job.

Friday morning around 9 am, the two of them left things in Doc and the boys' hands and rode out. Over the past few months, Henry and Joe had blazed a good road, so there was no trouble finding the way. Around noon they pulled up in front of the trading post. My God, this was not the same place he had come to 8 years ago! He could not believe what he saw!

There were people and houses everywhere. It was no longer a trading post, but a growing town. It had a bank, taverns, and even a hotel. Ben remarked, "When I came here 8 years ago, there were only three buildings - look at it now!"

Ben walked into the trading post, where he found a very pretty woman behind the counter working on some clothing. He walked up to the counter and asked if there was a Mr. Hammersmith around.

"Yes sir, he is out back working on some things," replied the woman.

Ben said, "My name is Ben Sharp. I have a farm 35 miles west of here."

"Oh my God, he will be delighted to see you!" exclaimed the woman, "He talks about you all the time. I will go get him."

"No, no! That is all right. I will just wander out there and see if I can find him," said Ben.

"As you wish sir, I would be happy to go get him for you," offered the woman.

"No, that is all right. I need to stretch my legs anyway," stated Ben.

"If I may ask, ma'am, what is your name?" asked Ben.

The woman responded, "My name is Mary Ann. I'm Mr. Hammersmith's daughter."

"Well then, do you know Henry Williams?" inquired Ben.

"Yes Sir, he comes in here about every two weeks or so. Henry works for us, and is a very nice man", answered Mary Ann.

"Yes ma'am, he has told me. Well, it was nice meeting you, and I will just slip out back and see if I can spot him," said Ben.

"Mr. Sharp, his name is Bill. If you don't see him just call out his name, and he will be coming up soon."

"Thank you very much," said Ben.

Nate and Ben walked out the door onto the back porch. It was full of everything you could think of. Looking around, they did not see Bill, but about two hundred yards down the hill was the river and a large dock. It looked like a boat tied up at the dock with another waiting up river. This was nothing like what he had seen 8 years ago. This was a booming town with a shipping dock. There were eight to ten men working the dock and there was lumber stacked up everywhere. Ben and Nate walked down to the dock and asked one of the men if Bill Hammersmith was around. "That is him over there checking that load of lumber," replied one of the men.

Ben did not recognize him. After 8 years he had put on some weight, and his hair was getting gray. As he walked up he stuck out his hand and said, "Ben Sharp".

Bill almost dropped the papers he was working on and said, "My God, Ben Sharp! I thought the Indians had you wrapped up in buffalo skins lying up on some poles somewhere in the hills!"

"No, not yet" was Ben's reply.

"What brings you to town?" asked Bill.

"Well, Nate and I have some business we would like to get your ideas on" began Ben. Then he said, "By the way, this is Nate Owens, my friend and partner."

"Well in that case, let me finish checking this lumber, and we will go up to the post and sit a spell," said Bill.

Ben and Nate wandered around the dock taking in all the scenes, and in about ten minutes Bill was done. They walked back up the hill where Bill said, "We have a little place in the back where we can sit down and have something to drink."

They walked into a room that looked to Ben to serve as a kitchen. There was a stove, table, and chairs, with two big cupboards along one wall. Bill asked if whiskey would be all right.

Nate said, "No sir, we are not drinking men. Coffee will be fine."

"Well, I think the coffee is old and cold. How about some tea?" offered Mr. Hammersmith?

"That would be fine," agreed the men.

Bill stirred up the fire and put some water on and some tea in a strainer ball. As he sat down at the table he asked, "What is on your minds?"

Ben said, "We would like to know a little bit about the bank. What kind of bank is it, and who owns it?"

"Well, I can tell you this much, it has been here four years. The bank is run by a man named Thomas St. Clair. I have been told that since the Army came to town, the Government opened the bank to deal with the army payroll. I think it is owned by the U.S. Government, but it does business with local merchants. Business has gotten so big in the past few years; I have had to use it. I don't want to leave money around here with all these drunken, crazy men."

"Well, I can't say I blame you, sir. We have a little money back in Old Town, Ohio, and would like to move some of it out here, just in case we need it," stated Ben.

"Well, Tom knows me well, so if it's all right with you, we will stop by there in the morning and I will introduce the two of you," offered Bill.

"That would be fine. I would like that very much," agreed Ben.

With that, the tea had begun to howl. Bill poured three big cups, and rounded up the sugar bowl. Ben told Bill about his desire to build a grinding mill for flour and corn. "My God, man that would be a Godsend. All the white flour we get now has to come from St. Louis and by the time it gets here it's beginning to get old. You get a mill setup, and I will buy all the flour and cornmeal you can grind!" said Bill

"Where do you think a man could buy a 42 inch wheel or bigger?" asked Ben.

"Well, I have heard that St. Louis has a stone cutter. I can make some inquiries and see what we come up with," said Bill.

"How long do you think it would take to get one?" asked Ben?

"I don't know, but just off the top of my hat, I would say a year," replied Bill.

"How much do you think it would weigh?" inquired Ben.

"I would think a 42 inch unit would weigh a ton for the top, and a ton for the bottom. Can you build the water wheel?" asked Bill.

Nate replied, "Yes sir, now that I see you have all this fine lumber here at the post!"

"Well, in that case, let's go to work. I will put out the word to the next boat captain from St Louis, and we will see who is making stones. Sending a telegraph would be much faster, if we only knew where to send it. Now that we have gotten that settled, would you and Mr. Owens have supper with us? It won't be anything fancy, but it will beat camping out!" offered Bill.

"What do you say, Nate?" asked Ben.

"It's fine with me; I'm always ready to eat", replied Nate.

"Also, while it is on my mind, I have a bunkhouse down the river a bit. This time of year I have some open cots that are not being used. Would you like to spend the night there? It will not cost you a dime. I make enough money from your account, I don't need to charge for supper and a bunk", said Bill.

"Sir, we thank you very much and we will take you up on both."

"Well, I will let the wife know there will be two nice men from up river for dinner. We will see you here at the post at 6 pm. In the meantime, you can see how much our town has grown," stated Bill.

"Thank you sir, we will be back at 6 sharp," agreed Ben and Nate.

With that, Ben and Nate left the trading post and went outside where the horses were tied. It was early in the afternoon when they rode east along the river. Ben could not believe what had happened to the town. There were people everywhere. There was a post office, bank, leather and gun shop, a blacksmith, taverns, and houses everywhere. There was even a lumber store.

They kept to the main road and a sign read "Army Post 2 miles upriver." They thought they would stop by and introduce themselves. Ben wanted to talk to the Commander about the Sharp rifle. They rode up to the front where a sign read, "Welcome to Fort Henry", there was a sentry at the opening as they started through. Nate asked, "Where is the Commander's Office?"

The solder said, "Straight ahead, sir, where the flag is flying".

"Thank you!" said Ben as they headed toward the building.

The fort was not large, maybe 75 to a hundred men. There were lots of buildings, barns, corrals, and barracks. Ben stepped down and tied his mare off. Nate followed. As they walked up on the porch, a soldier stepped forward holding his rifle up front saying, "What is your business, gentleman?"

Nate said, "We are here to speak with the Commander."

"Very well Sir. I will tell him you are here. Can I tell him where you are from?" inquired the soldier.

"Yes, we are from west of town at Big Blue and the York. We have a farm up there," replied Nate.

In a minute, the soldier was back saying, "He said come on in, he will see you now."

Ben and Nate walked into the room. To the right of them sat a medium build man in his mid-forties, or at least the best Ben could tell. As they entered the room, the man got up from his desk and introduced himself as Captain Kelly.

Nate took his hand as he reached out and said, "Captain Kelly, my name is Nate Owens, and this is Ben Sharp"

"Sharp? Where have I heard that name before?" inquired the Captain.

"I don't know, sir, I'm from Ohio, and my family is in the gun business," replied Ben.

"That is where I heard the name - it's Sharp rifles!" exclaimed the Captain.

"Yes Sir, I'm the second generation of rifle makers," proclaimed Ben.

"Well, what are you doing way out here?" asked the Captain.

"Well sir, I left the business to my brothers, and I became a homesteader. We got here in 1804, and we run O&S Farms 35 miles west of here. We came to town today on some other business, and thought since we are here we would stop by and introduce ourselves," explained Ben.

"Good, have a chair," offered Captain Kelly.

"Captain, Mr. Owens here has been able to give us a double bottom plow that allows us to plow a lot more land for planting than most. We are planning to sow a lot more corn this year. If we have a good crop, could we count on the Army buying some of that corn?" asked Ben.

"Yes sir, if it is good, clean corn, we will take all you have got," declared Captain Kelly.

"Well, that is good to hear. Between you and Mr. Hammersmith, that would put us in good shape," stated Ben.

"Mr. Owens, do you have any horses for sale?" asked the Captain.

"No sir. O&S has not put a lot of time into horses. We have a lot of mules but not that many horses. All we raise is cattle, hogs, and corn," replied Nate.

"How many cattle do you have?" inquired Captain Kelly.

"I guess well over a 100 head right now." answered Nate.

"We here at the Fort could take a few of them off your hands this fall," offered the Captain.

"You said something about being in the gun business. Is that a Sharp rifle you fellows are carrying?" asked the Captain.

"Yes Sir," replied Ben.

"What kind of rifle is that?" inquired the Captain.

"Sir, it is a Sharp long rifle, five-shot, semiautomatic .223. It has a kill range of 800 yards for small game and men. You can also see at night with this rifle," explained Ben.

"Mr. Sharp, I'm a soldier, and I know guns pretty well. There is no gun that can do that," declared Captain Kelly.

"Maybe so, sir, but this one does," stated Ben.

"Can you prove it?" asked the Captain.

"Yes sir!" said Ben.

"Well, we will go outside the Fort and see if what you are telling me is true," declared Captain Kelly.

With that, he got up from his desk and walked to the porch. He said, "Sentry, get Sergeant Jones over here now. Saddle my horse, and get a horse for you and the Sergeant."

"Yes sir!" replied the Sentry.

In a half hour, he was back with Sergeant Jones and the horse. "Sentry, go over to the armament and get me three targets!" ordered the Captain.

"Yes sir!" replied the Sentry.

"Sergeant Jones, this is Mr. Sharp. He is going to teach you how to shoot!" exclaimed Captain Kelly. In a few minutes the Sentry was back, and they rode out the gate to the back of the Fort.

"Mr. Sharp, how far is that tree from us?" asked the Captain.

"I would say 600 yards or so," replied Ben.

"Then we will back up 200 yards", ordered the Captain.

"That is fine, Sir," agreed Ben.

"Mr. Sharp, I cannot see that far, let alone shoot that distance," declared Captain Kelly.

"That is what this thing on top is for. We at the Sharp Company call it a scope. It makes things larger," explained Ben.

"Well, Mr. Sharp, you, sir, can be the first," directed the Captain. "Very good," agreed Ben. With that, Ben went down on one knee, placed his elbow on the other knee, took a nice long look, and fired. He thought to himself, *While I'm down here I will put the other four rounds in the target.* So as fast as he could keep his same position, he fired the other four rounds. He got up and turned to look at the Captain, and saw a look of surprise on the Captain's face that would surprise you - even if you were expecting it. "Mr. Sharp, I do not believe what I just heard. You fired five rounds in 30 seconds!" exclaimed Captain Kelly.

"Yes sir, and sir - there are five dead men down there!" stated Ben.

"Sergeant, go get that target now!" ordered the Captain.

"Yes sir!" replied Sergeant Jones. He galloped back, slid off his horse, and said to the Captain, "It looks like he only hit it three times, Sir."

The Captain took the target from the Sergeant and started to look at it. "Well, Sergeant, you are wrong - he has hit it five times!" declared the Captain. Then he reached down and got a small stick and pointed to the five clean holes. "Do you see what I see, Sergeant? Sentry, do you see it also?" asked the Captain.

"Yes Sir. I do not want to be the only fool here," replied the Sergeant.

The Sentry spoke up, saying, "Sir, you are no fool. What you are seeing just happened. I saw it with my own eyes."

"Well, Captain, it's your turn," said Nate. With that, Nate handed over his rifle and the Captain took the same position Ben had. The Captain looked through the scope and raised his head saying, "I cannot believe what I see with this crazy thing on top!"

"That is the point, Sir. If you are going to shoot into the next state, you need to see what you are shooting at," explained Ben.

"Well, I'm so nervous, I don't know if I can hit the target," stated Captain Kelly.

"Put your front sight on the bottom of the black circle, and squeeze the trigger," suggested Ben.

The Captain was not near as fast as Ben, but he fired three rounds and got up. This time the Sentry brought the target back for inspection. After the Captain looked at it he asked, "Mr. Sharp, how many of these guns can I get, and how fast can I get them?"

"I do not know, sir. We would have to ask my brothers. It has been 13 years since I talked to them", answered Ben.

"Thirteen years?" wondered the Captain.

"Yes Sir! I have been busy out there in the prairies, and we don't have a lot of mail out here," explained Ben.

"I understand," acknowledged the Captain.

By then Ben had loaded his rifle, and asked if the Sergeant wanted to have a shot. He said, "Yes", and the Sentry put the last target on the tree. It was clear the gun would do what Ben said. It was just good to have one more man shoot the thing. They collected the targets and rode back to the Fort. Ben did not have a lot of time left. He had promised Mr. Hammersmith that he would be back at the post by 6 pm.

"How can we reach your Company?" asked Captain Kelly.

"Well sir, I have to go over to your new post office and bank tomorrow. I will send my brothers a telegram. If you will give me your name and address, I will have them get back to you," suggested Ben.

"That would be just fine, Mr. Sharp," agreed the Captain.

"I will try and get a message out early in the morning, and maybe we can hear back tomorrow," stated Ben.

"That would be nice," said Captain Kelly.

"I'm sorry to leave so quickly, Captain, but a fellow has asked Nate and me to have supper with him, and we do not want to be late.

"Well, I sure am glad you fellows stopped by, and I hope to see you tomorrow," said Captain Kelly.

It was 5.30 pm when Nate and Ben tied their horses at the trading post, and Mr. Hammersmith was afraid he might have to eat all that food alone. He said he had just returned from the bank, and the banker said he would see them tomorrow. Ben told him that he would like to go to the post office first and see if he could get a telegram off to his brothers. Bill said that would be fine.

They locked the trading post and headed across town to Bill's home. "You don't have to worry about your bunks tonight. I have told my foreman to save two cots for you fellows, and he said he would. So you don't have to worry - it's all ready for you," said Mr. Hammersmith.

"Thank you very much," said Ben.

In ten minutes they arrived at Bill's home, tied the horses off. Mrs. Hammersmith was a nice, round lady who spoke with a German accent. The place smelled like some kind of bakery shop. She said she was just about ready and asked if they wanted to wash up. All of them said, "Yes", and Bill led them to the back porch. Mrs. Hammersmith seated them and asked Bill to bless the food. This made Nate feel good, knowing these people were Christians. It would make the food taste a lot better.

Mrs. Hammersmith had spared nothing. She had a big roast, potatoes, green beans, biscuits, and gravy. Now this was food fit for a king! They enjoyed their meal with small talk about prairie life. Mary Ann got up one time to get more biscuits, and Nate couldn't help thinking how lucky Henry was to find a nice girl like her out here in the prairie. They sat around and talked for a while when Ben said, "People, I have to go to bed. So if you fine people would let me say goodnight, I will find my bunk." They said their goodnights and rode off to the corral and bunkhouse.

Ben and Nate took their bedroll and saddles off the horses and took them into the bunkhouse where they met Harvey. He said he had gotten the message early in the day that two men were coming by for the night. He then said to take the two bunks up front next to the door. Ben thanked him and asked if it was all right to leave the saddles on the floor next to their bunks. Harvey replied, "Go right ahead" Then they walked the horses over to the corral, where there was plenty of feed and water.

On the way back Ben said to Nate, "You know, I have got to cut me a new yearling out of our horse inventory when I get home. My old mare is close to 15 years old and it's time I retired her."

"Ben, I think all three of us are in the same shape. Henry has been riding that same gray for as long as I have known him. So I think all three of us need new mounts," stated Nate.

"Who is going to be the bronco rider?" asked Ben.

"I don't know, we will take a vote when we get home." They unrolled their bedrolls, got undressed, and hit the hay. It had been a good day, but a long day.

Next morning, they met Bill at the trading post at 8 am after getting something to eat. Ben told Bill that he would like to go over to the post office and send a telegram to the bank back in Ohio, and to his brothers.

Bill said, "I will see you back here when you get done."

The post office was small, just a one room building with one man and a telegraph key. Ben asked him if he could send a telegram to the Old Town Post Office in Ohio.

"Yes, you can if they have a key", answered the man.

"How long will it take?" asked Ben.

"Let me look on my sheet here and see if they have a call station," replied the man. In a few minutes he came back and said, "Yes, they do. So if you will write out what you want to say, I will send it."

Ben sat down at the table and said to Nate, "I don't know what to say. It has been 13 years since we were there, and I don't know if the postmaster has changed or not."

"Why don't you write a short letter telling him how you are, and what you want and need done?" suggested Nate.

"Well, I can try it. We can start over if it does not sound right," stated Ben.

In a few minutes, he had written the following message: DEAR SIR, MY NAME IS BEN SHARP. I AM THE BROTHER OF JIM AND JOE SHARP AT THE SHARP GUN COMPANY THERE IN OLD TOWN. I NEED TO TALK TO ONE OF THEM. I NEED TO CONTACT THE OLD TOWN BANK AND TELL

THEM TO CONTACT ME THROUGH YOU UNTIL I GET A BANK ADDRESS. WE ARE ALL FINE. PLEASE GET THIS MESSAGE TO MY BROTHERS AND THE BANK TODAY IF POSSIBLE. I WILL WAIT FOR YOUR REPLY. BEN SHARP O&S FARMS BIG BLUE RIVER.

Ben handed the Postmaster the message and asked, "How much will that be?"

"That is 5 cents per word Sir, or $4.30," replied the Postmaster.

"How long will it be before they get it?" inquired Ben.

"I would say an hour or so, if there is anyone around to take the message", answered the Postmaster.

"We are going to go over to the bank and the trading post, so when you get an answer, please let us know," requested Ben.

"I will do that, sir," agreed the Postmaster.

With that, Ben and Nate left and headed over to the trading post where they found Bill waiting for them. They did not wait around and went over to the bank right away. It was a very small bank with just one window. The place was well built, and a soldier stood guard just inside the door. Bill nodded his head and asked where the bank manager was.

"He is behind the counter somewhere", answered the soldier.

Bill knocked on the bars, and a man came to the front. He said, "Thomas, I have two men out here I would like for you to meet." With that, Thomas opened the door and stepped out into the room.

"My name is Ben Sharp, and this is Nate Owens. We would like to talk to you about opening an account with your bank," stated Ben.

"Sure, let me get some papers together and I will be right with you." In a few minutes he showed up at a side door with papers in hand. "We can sit over here if you like," offered Thomas, pointing toward a table on the other side of the room.

Ben walked over and pulled out chairs for Nate and himself. The man held out his hand and said, "My name is St. Clair and I'm in charge of the bank. How can I help you?"

With that Bill excused himself and said, "I will see you fellows back at the trading post when you get done."

"Sir, my name is Ben Sharp and this is Nate Owens. We run the O&S Farms up on Blue River, and we would like to open accounts," stated Ben.

Mr. St. Clair then gathered information from them, and asked how much they would like to open the account with.

Ben said, "I would like to open my account with 100 U.S. dollars. Can I do that?" inquired Ben.

"Yes, you can, sir!"

"Can you telegraph my bank in Ohio and move money from there to your bank?" inquired Ben.

"If they have a telegraph station, yes sir, I can do that. What is the bank name and in what town?" inquired Tom.

"The name of the bank is the Citizen Bank in Old Town, Ohio," responded Ben.

"Let me see if they have a telegraph key."

Mr. St. Clair left the room and went back behind the door. In a few minutes, he came back with a book and said, "Yes sir! Your bank is listed. Would you like for me to send them a telegram and tell them what we would like to do?"

"Yes Sir!" replied Ben.

"What is your account number?" inquired Mr. St. Clair.

"Sir, it is number 17770421BS0468," responded Ben.

"Well, let's see what they say. How much money do you want to move?" inquired Mr. St. Clair.

"I would like to move $10,000.00, if my account has that much," specified Ben.

"Very well!" said Mr. St. Clair. He then turned to Nate and asked, "And how about you?"

Nate replied, "My account is in the same town, and my name is Nathan Owens. I would like to move the same amount."

"Gentlemen, those are pretty large amounts for a bank our size, but we will see what we can do," indicated Mr. St. Clair. Then he asked Nate, "Your account number, Sir?"

Nate replied, "17781012NO0675".

"Give me a few minutes, and we will have you an answer," declared Mr. St. Clair.

In a half hour he came back and said, "Gentleman, I'm sorry, but there does not seem to be anyone answering the call sign today. It is Saturday and later in the afternoon up there, and they may have gone for the weekend. I can try for you Monday."

"We are planning on leaving in a few hours, so we will have to come back. We have a man that works for us and he will be here on Friday. Can you give him the information?" asked Ben.

"Yes Sir I can, but I will have to put such information in an envelope and mark it to you. I cannot move the money until you fellows sign papers for me to do so," explained Mr. St. Clair.

"Can we do that now?" asked Ben.

"Yes sir, you can," replied Mr. St. Clair.

With that, he left the room once more and returned with papers to be filled out. They did so and said Henry Williams would see him on Friday.

"It has been nice doing business with you fellows, and I wish you all the luck in the world up there on Big Blue," said Mr. St. Clair.

"Thank you sir," replied Ben.

It was late afternoon when they rode up to the trading post and found everyone hard at work. Nate picked up some white flour and some candy for the kids; Ben got a few things and tied them on behind his bedroll. At 4 pm they headed for home.

It had been a good week for business. As they rode west, both men were pleased with what they had been able to get done. It was good to be alone and just talk. Ben said, "It will be nice to sleep in my own bed for a change!"

The men put their horses in the barn and said good night. Elisabeth, as any good wife, had been walking the floor and you could just see the strain and worry drain from her body when she saw Ben's face. "Ben! Thank God you are back in my presence! You have no idea how I worry about you sometimes. Do you know this is the first time in my life that I have not seen you or heard your voice in two days? You could be dead along the road, shot, or whatever! Only God knows what could happen to you!" With that she leaped from her chair and landed around his neck.

"Honey, God watches out for me when I'm away from you, the very same way you watch over me when I'm with you. I'm very grateful for both of your loves; but what I really would like to know is could a hungry man get something to eat around here?"

"Well sir that man can get anything he wants around here. I will cook for him, sew for him, and wash his clothes - anything he wishes is his!"

"Oh Elisabeth, be quiet, or I will have to marry you!" declared Ben.

"Ben Sharp! There is one thing in this life that I'm very grateful for, and that is you! God could not have done me better! Go wash up, and I will feed you!" exclaimed Elisabeth.

In a few minutes, Ben was back and sat down at the table. "Well, you tell me your story and I will tell you mine," said Ben.

"Well, to start with our son, Ben Jr., is spending the night over at Doc Martin's house," said Elisabeth.

"What is that all about?" inquired Ben.

"Well, he got snake bit yesterday afternoon. He went to help Mary Sue collect the eggs, and a snake bit him on his right hand. The two of them went straight over to Doc's place. Doc put a tourniquet on him, cut the wound, and sucked out the poison. He said he is pretty sure it was a dry bite," explained Elisabeth.

"What does that mean?" asked Ben.

"He said that for some reason, perhaps the snake had an egg in its mouth, and did not seem to break the skin too deeply. He said he would watch over him for a while, and see what is going on", clarified Elisabeth.

"Hold my food and I will go over and check on him," said Ben.

"No," advised Elisabeth, "he is all right; and besides, he is in bed resting and he doesn't need you over there stirring him up. You can go over first thing in the morning."

"Very well!" agreed Ben, and then asked, "What else have you got?"

"That is about it. The boys have gotten a lot of plowing done, and a lot of manure has been put on the fields that are awaiting the plow," responded Elisabeth.

"My! Maybe I should go away more often!" exclaimed Ben.

"Not if I can help it you won't," declared Elisabeth.

"Elisabeth, please don't spread this around, but I love you," said Ben.

With that he pushed his plate back and asked, "Could a fellow stay all night around here?"

"Anytime sir! Anytime!" responded Elisabeth.

With that, they cleaned off the table and got ready for bed.

"When do I get to hear about your trip?" asked Elisabeth.

"In the morning dear, right now with a full belly I'm butt tired. I need some sleep," declared Ben.

Next morning at breakfast Ben told Elisabeth all about their trip, and how happy he was with all they had been able to do. "Ben that is a windfall! Do you think we are going too fast?" asked Elisabeth.

"No! I only wish I could get more corn in the ground. We now have a market for all we can grow," said Ben then continued, "I will see you around noon." With that he headed out the door to check on Ben Jr.

Doc and his wife Sarah were having breakfast and enjoying small talk when Ben knocked on the door. "Doc how is my young man this morning?" asked Ben.

"He is fine. He slept well all night. We will get him up soon and feed him", answered Doc.

"How does it look?" asked Ben.

The Doc explained, "Ben, the best I can tell, he has a dry bite. That means the snake did not break the skin too deeply. There is very little swelling and from what I can tell, it looks like my bleeding of the wound was worse than the bite. I will keep him today, and you can have him back tomorrow if things stay the same."

"Doc, you are a Godsend. Thank you!" exclaimed Ben.

"How did your trip go?" asked Doc.

Ben sat down at the table with a big cup of coffee, and told Doc about the trip. "It was a better trip than I had planned. You see, we stopped off at Fort Henry and not only sold them some corn and cattle, but maybe got a big gun order. I have telegraphed my brothers and asked that they try and reach us through the post office telegraph key. I will ask Henry to go by there this Friday to see if they got the message."

"Doc, don't you think you should have some kind of a bank account? It would not hurt if you stop by the bank and set one up. We have talked to them, and it seems to be a good place to keep your money. You are a one third owner in all we sell here at O&S Farms, and we don't need all that money lying around," advised Ben.

"Ben, I will do that!" agreed Doc.

"Where are you working today?" asked Ben.

"Well, I had planned to take Ben Jr.'s place and help out Tom," replied Doc.

"Well, let me do that and you can run the Sheller. That way you will be here close to the house and your patient," offered Ben.

"That sounds good to me," said Doc.

With that, Ben set about to find Tom and see what was needed for the long day in the fields. Ben found Tom in the barn getting the mules and wagon ready. The plow was still in the field where he had left it Saturday. As they left for their work, they stopped by the springhouse to fill their kegs with fresh water for the day. Ben Jr. and Tom had done well last week. There was a good 15 acres turned, and if all went well between the two of them, there would be over 100 acres this year. The nice thing about it all was by using the barn manure, the land was much richer; and instead of the 30 bushels per acre, they could get 40 bushels this fall if the weather did not get too hot. Ben thought to himself that by using less for the stock to eat, he would have close to 3,000 bushels of corn for sale. At 50 cents per bushel, they could bring home over a $1,500.00 for O&S Farms. That would be over $300.00 per family, and giving Henry his share. This did not count any cattle that might be sold.

It had been talked about on the way back from town that a count would be necessary. They needed to see how many of the cattle were steers, and how many were old cows. They could be sold for $20.00 per head. Nate said his guess would be around 1,400 steers and 100 head of cattle - that would be another $30,000.00. This was not bad for 12 years. Each family could then bank over $7,500.00 each and still have all they needed to live on. That did not count money Nate got paid for shoeing horses, fixing wagons, and all the things he did. There were the passersby that stopped to buy things. Yes sir, they were doing just fine for frontier people.

The problem was there just was too much work for the nine of them. There was planting, weeding, haying, shelling, plowing, and cattle that had to be cared for.

Ben said, "Why don't we pay the Chief a visit and see if he has any braves that would like to learn farming?"

"Good idea," agreed Nate. "Let's go talk to him this week. If we can get three or four good men, we could get a lot more corn in the ground, and you need someone to help out at the shop," stated Ben.

"You are right. I shod over 10 horses and mules last week, and I was gone for one day."

Ben thought that if Ben Jr. was well enough to work tomorrow, he would take him and ride over to see the Chief. Nate was making good time building a hay cutter, and haying was coming up fast. If he could get a few good men, he would put one of the boys on the cutter and let the brave help with plowing. He had lots to things to talk about as he and Tom worked. It had been good for him out here on the prairies. He had been able to do more and make a better life for all. It sure was better than sitting at his work table, filing triggers. Yes, he and Nate had made the right decision to come here.

That night during the nightly meeting, Ben told the rest about what he felt would be a good year, and asked what they thought about hiring the braves. Some of them had a comment about protecting the women folks but would give it a try.

Nate spoke up, saying, "We will keep them so busy they will not have time to get in trouble. We have 40 acres of wheat, and 60 acres of barley, and 60 acres of oats to cut and shell. If we lose control of things, we lose everything. So let's try it."

Next morning Ben Jr. said he was tired of all this bed rest and sitting around, and told Doc he was going to work.

"Ok, you keep that arm clean and check with me tonight."

The week passed quickly, and Henry and Joe took off early and got cleaned up for the ride to town. When they got there, Mr. Hammersmith had moved them from the barn to the bunkhouse. He also said the bank and the post office had telegrams for Ben and Nate. Henry knew how much Ben and Nate needed those telegrams and told Mary Ann he would leave right after church Sunday - which he needed to get back to the farm.

During their talk, Henry asked Mary Ann to be his wife.

She broke down in tears, but said, "Yes! I will get the good news to Mom and Dad and we will make plans. Where would you like to be married; here in town at the church, or out at the farm?" Then she said, "You know, I think I would like to be married on the prairie. After all, it will be my home where we will raise our kids, and I will care for you. Yes! Yes, I will talk to Mom."

Henry had told Joe on the ride to town that he planned to ask Mary Ann to marry him and Joe said, "Do you know, I would like to do the same thing if I can get up the nerve."

"Just do it, Joe, and worry about your nerve later," urged Henry.

"Well, we will see," said Joe.

After church and a quick meal, they saddled up for the long ride home

Both families had been told about the weddings, and it was agreed to have them at the farm. Preacher Morris said that he would get one of the deacons to conduct services on that Sunday, and that they would make a weekend of the event. All they needed now was a date, and the women would provide that next week. Both men were riding high in the saddle and spurred their mounts to a nice trot as they left town. After all, they had lots of news for the folks back home.

They got home at 8 pm after leaving the dinner table at 1 pm. They stopped by Doc's house and asked him if he and his wife would meet them at Ben's house. They said, "Yes", but couldn't figure out what all the fuss was about. Henry and Joe rubbed the horses down and put them away. They pushed the door open in a few minutes and everyone wanted to know what was on these young men's minds.

Ben Jr. spoke up saying, "If it is all this great, I had better go get Nate and Helen."

In a few minutes, Nate and his group showed up. Henry was dancing around like a kid. He said, "First, I have mail for Nate and Ben." With that he handed them their wires. Ben opened his first, and jumped back as if a mule had kicked him.

"Well, what have you got there? Are you going to tell the rest of us, or do we just stand here and watch you?" asked Elisabeth.

Ben said, "No, its good news! It is just that I cannot believe it!" exclaimed Ben.

"Well, speak up, man. We are all family here. What is going on?" inquired Doc.

"It is the first news any one of us has had in over 10 years from the people back in Ohio. It seems my bank account has risen to over $150,000, and that they would be glad to transfer $10,000.00 to the Lincoln bank. The other telegram is from the post office, and it says all is well with business and families, and they would like to have a long letter or a telegram as soon as they could," explained Ben.

By then, Nate had read his mail and said his was just as good; and yes, they would transfer the funds he had asked for. He said Mr. Woods had a fire in the shop, and that it had slowed down his payments on the house and shop for one year while he rebuilt, but all was well and back to normal.

"Well, what else do you have that has got you in such a dither?" asked Helen.

Not being able to hold it any longer Henry blurted out, "Joe and I are going to be married! The ladies have agreed to have the wedding out here at the farm. The preacher will come and marry us, but we do not have a date just yet."

"My God people, we are going to have to build some new houses! We are going to have so many people living here it will be our own town!" exclaimed Nate.

Elisabeth had fixed some warm milk, and everyone was out of their minds with happiness. Their world was coming to a full circle. This was great news! Two more families will be raised here at O&S Farms.

"It looks like we will need our own church. What is next?" asked Nate.

"Right now it is bedtime; tomorrow will be a full day," said Ben.

"Oh, by the way Ben, Mr. Hammersmith said he had not heard anything from St. Louis, but was told a boat will be in on Monday or Tuesday and that he hoped to have news then."

"Well, let us pray that it will be good news," said Ben.

Ben had talked to Ben Jr. the night before about him going over to see the Chief, and Ben Jr. said, "Yes sir! I will be glad to go with you!"

After breakfast, they saddled up Nate's black horse and Ben's mare and off they went. As they rode into the camp, Ben saw Little Flower coming out of a teepee. He waved at her and rode over to ask if he could speak with the Chief. She nodded yes, and went to his teepee. In a few minutes, they were invited into the teepee and again, Little Flower sat on Ben's right.

He said, "I would like to ask the Chief if there are any young braves that would like to work on the farm for the summer."

The Chief's face lit up with a big smile, and said he had many that needed something to do.

Ben said, "I will take four of the number one braves."

"All right, when would you like them?" asked the Chief.

"Tomorrow would be fine Chief, if they can be ready" answered Ben.

"I will see that they are at your camp at 6 Am." stated the Chief.

"Thank you sir" said Ben, then continued, "I have brought your people some hams this morning, and some corn for your animals."

The Chief said, "You do not have to bring me gifts every time you call."

"Yes sir, I know, but we have done so well thanks to the big Chief in the sky, and you, sir. So I feel I should return something," stated Ben.

"Very well, be it as you wish," said the Chief.

Ben sat a while with the Chief and talked about the buffalo, and how the hunting had been the past winter as the buffalo moved south. The Chief said it had been fine, but that the white man was taking too many buffalo for the skins and leaving the meat to rot, and that soon there would be no more buffalo.

Ben said, "I guess that is why the Indian needs to learn to farm." Ben sat a little longer, and then said he needed to return to his work.

As they rode back to the farm Ben Jr. asked, "Where are the Indians going to stay? They are not going to ride back to the camp every night after a hard day of work, are they?"

"Ben Jr.! That is a very good question. As a matter of fact, to tell the truth, I have not thought much about it, but you are right. We will have to make room for them somewhere. I will talk to Nate when I get home, and we will make a plan." It was mid-afternoon when they rode into camp. Not having anything to eat yet, the first stop was Elisabeth's kitchen.

Next morning things really got busy. Not only did the Chief send four good men, but he also sent Little Flower to talk for them. Doc and Sarah would take Little Flower, since Doc spoke French. The four men would bunk down in the shelling house and corncrib until a bunkhouse could be built.

Next would come their work assignments. Little Bear and Tom, Henry and Wolf Man, Jim and Big Bear, would run the double bottom plows. Running Paw and Joe would run the harrows. Meals would be taken on Ben's back porch. If the weather was too bad, then meals would be moved to Ben's kitchen and front porch.

Little Flower was to ask if anyone did not like their job, or did not understand it. All four Indians spoke up, saying they did not know anything about farming.

Ben said, "That is why you will work with one of us for as long as it takes to teach you."

That left Ben, Doc, and Ben Jr. without a job.

Ben said, "Since we have some weddings coming up soon, I think the three of us will build a big bunkhouse so some of the people will have a place to sleep." It was agreed that Doc and Ben would cut logs, and Ben Jr. would drag them to the building site. The week's work was planned, and everyone went to their assignments.

With this many plows in the ground the planting field would be ready soon and a lot of hoeing would be needed. Nate was asked to hold up on the hay cutter and give them one or two more harrows. That was agreed. Doc and Tom had been asked to build fence only as filler, or when they were rained out. A well-organized farm work load was under way.

Within the next two weeks, the corn was in the ground and the bunkhouse was well under way. Two big loads of lumber were going to be picked up in town so the roof and flooring could be done much faster. They may have been new to the frontier, but these men knew what they were doing.

Henry and Joe took two wagons and Little Bear to town on Friday, so they could pick up the lumber and things needed to finish the bunkhouse and other buildings. Little Bear did not know what to do with himself. He had money O&S had paid him for his work, and to have a chance to go to town was more than he knew how to deal with. Indians liked to drink firewater, and Henry had to hold him tight to keep him away from it.

While there, Mr. Hammersmith reported that a boat captain had given him the name of a company who made corn stones, and more good news. "Not only do they make them, but they have a 42 inch set on hand, plus a telegraph key station where they can talk to the maker about the stone. He has provided me with station call sign and company name, address - everything needed to order the stone."

With all that, Henry was on top of the world!

When they got home, the first reports were in about the new Indian hired hands and what they thought about the white man's way of life - what he eats, how he sleeps, how he lived compared to the Indian way of life. It was different for them. When asked by Little Flower what they had to say, they all reported it was very good and they wanted to stay forever. They liked the work. The boys reported that they learned the work quickly. Ben and Nate found some old hats and gave each Indian one of them. The

Indians liked the hats, and would wear them to bed if someone did not ask them to take them off.

That night Ben sat down and wrote the stone cutter a letter. He wanted to know how the stones would be shipped so they would not crack or break, and what was the weight of each stone? Since this was his first experience with grinding stones, how long would a set of stones work before they had to be reworked? How could he adjust the coarseness of the corn or wheat that was being ground? Could he buy insurance on the stones in case of breakage in shipping? How much did they cost? If he placed the order, when would they shipped, and how long before they arrive? Can payments be made - one third when I place the order, and one third when the stone arrived, and the balance in 30 days? He would like the answers to as many of these questions as soon as possible by way of a telegram.

He then gave the post office call letters, and said he would await their answers. Since he was in the letter writing mood, he then wrote a nice long letter to his brothers. He needed to know if Captain Kelly had gotten in touch with them and what the outcome would be. With all of this out of the way, he would ask Henry to mail the letters when he went to town, and with that he went off to bed.

Work was going well with everything. Ben would wait to hear from the stone cutter before making any plans to build the mill house. The house would have to be large and reach well beyond the river so it could be used during high water.

Ben Sharp was a man of thoughts and plans. His mind never seemed to stop working. The families had been there long enough to have title to the land, but he knew they would outgrow it soon and wanted to get more. The title papers had the U.S. Government address on them, so he thought he would write to see if he could buy 1,280 acres to the north of Doc's place and northwest of the farms. He would write one more letter to go out with Henry this Friday.

Three months had gone by since the boys had said anything about the weddings, and the girls were wondering if something had happened. Helen said she would bring it up to Henry, and maybe some word would come back this Sunday. From the best the girls could tell, it looked like there would be three marriages on the same day. What a day that would be! If all took place as planned, three new homes would have to be built. It looked like most of next year would be taken up building; Nate wanted a church and schoolhouse for all the new kids that would be coming up.

Doc also wanted a small cabin with a cot for infectious diseases, in case the kids came down with something and he needed to isolate them from the others. He did not like treating strangers in his home. What started out to be two old friends and their families had turned into 21 or more people. Almost a small town! No one was complaining; it just seemed like a lot of people. Since the Indians had started to work for O&S Farms, there were a lot more teepees down by the river in the summertime.

Two weeks had gone by, and Ben had gotten word from St. Louis on the stones. It seemed most of his questions had been answered. Shipment could be made at once, and the price was $1,000.00. They would be created in heavy oak with two lifting eyes on each stone. Yes, he could get insurance, and it was $25.00 per year; if you had to ship the stone back to the mill, you would not be required to pay shipping. Ben then wired them back, saying he would pay for half of the stones now, and that shipment could be made in the spring. In the meantime, he would like to get a drawing of the support system so he could start building the mill. Reworking would most likely not be required for 10 to 15 years.

With all this information, Ben started his plans for the mill. He wanted to get it on paper and go over it with Nate. He wanted to select a narrow part of the river where the water ran deep and fast. He did not want to scoop out any more of the river than what was needed. Next, he would select large timbers on each side of the river and plant them deep into the riverbed, then surround them with large rocks. He would then tie the timbers to one another by drilling a large hole through both of the timbers, driving a steel pin through them, and wrapping one inch hemp rope around the two timbers. This was done for all four legs. The mill house would span the river by 50 feet and be 40 feet wide. This meant the timbers across the ends and across the river span had to be spliced, drilled, and tied in the same manner. He also wanted two support posts under each splice, surrounded by large rocks. With this now done, he could start the flooring uprights and roof.

The mill house had to be kept dry in all types of weather. A large ramp would be made to allow a wagon to come to the floor for loading and unloading. He would then build the water wheel. It would be made 8 feet in diameter, and three feet wide, with 12 buckets holding 10 gallons of water each. This was thought to give the wheel enough power to grind heavy loads. The wheel was really two wagon wheels with buckets in the middle.

With all this done, he couldn't wait to show Nate and start to build the wheel. It would take all winter to build the house, along with their other work. Ben was happy the St. Louis people said the wheel would grind 30 bushels of cornmeal and 20 bushels of flour per hour. This meant the mill could make over $4,000 per month, 12 months a year. Everyone should be very happy about that!

Nate looked the plans over and asked questions like, "How will you feed the corn to the mill?"

Ben's reply was, "As the corn arrives at the mill house, it is transferred to a large funnel shaped container with a door on the bottom of it. The container is lifted by block and tackle over the wheel receiving spout. The door is then opened just large enough to keep the wheel supplied. As a matter of fact, two of these containers will be used so there is no lost time when it becomes empty."

"Well," said Nate", it looks like you have a winner here, so what can I do to help?"

"Nothing, just help me with the wheel if you have time. The boys and I will do the rest. I will start the wheel next Monday," said Ben. With Nate's approval, he would send the money and place the order next Friday when Henry went to town.

Two crews were into fencing, and that was going well. Two crews were cutting and rolling hay, which was being delivered to the three corrals. Barley and oats were being cut and thrashed at the thrashing house. The straw from these grains had to be picked up and stored outside. The grain was tossed up and down on a sheet of cloth while the Indians waved large pieces of canvas to blow off the shell and straw stems. The grain was then sacked and stored in the grain house. Most of these grains were used for feed. When Ben got the mill up and working, they would be blended with corn and bone meal to make good cattle and horse feed.

Running Paw came one afternoon with sacks he had painted with "O&S Farms, Big Blue River" in red and blue. He was so happy to show them off. Ben liked the idea so well he asked if the side of the canvas on three wagons could be painted just like a teepee and Running Paw said, "Yes!" After all, they would be taking a lot of corn to town and it had to be kept dry. That way more people could see where the corn was coming from, and the more they would want to buy!

Henry came in with the biggest decision of the year. Thanksgiving was going to be the day, the year 1818, and he had been able to get three women to agree that the weddings would be held on Sunday after Thanksgiving.

"My God," the girls said. "We now have a date!" They could now start to plan. Nate would make six new beds and 12 chairs. That should be enough to get everyone by with what they had. He would build two more tables that could be pushed together. This was one fun place to live. Everyone had something to do and knew how to do it. Yes sir, the days were full!

It was already late September, and hog killing time would start off the first weekend of October. That was always a big event and this year, because of the in-town sales, the wedding, and giving a few hams to the Indians before their long journey south and west, Ben thought they had better kill 35. Doing ten a day would mean three to four days at the job. The girls wanted to have it all done before the wedding.

This Friday, Henry had been asked to take two wagons to town and bring back all the 20 foot or longer oak 2x6's he could haul, 100 pounds of 10 penny nails and all the 3/8 inch, 3 inch long bolts he could get. Ben would start the mill house. After all, April 1819 would be here before he knew it, and those big stones would be ready to start the last leg of their journey.

My God! There were so many things to be done at hog killing time, with lots of work for the women rendering fat from the skins and other fat parts of the pigs, preparing the hams and ribs for smoking, preparing bacon to be salted, and making sausage. There are a lot of pork chops coming from 35 head of hogs. There were also pickled hog's feet, ears, and headcheese. All this was real work, and it took all the women and a few men to get the job done. There were also three smokehouses to be prepared for smoking.

Still, with all the tasks at hand, the girls planned the weddings, so church services would be held on Sunday morning, and after church they would have dinner, and the weddings would start at 3 in the afternoon. After the weddings, they would serve cake and coffee. Those that wanted to could stay all night. So that meant the preacher and Bill would arrive on Friday sometime and stay until Monday. Tom and Barbara Ann would stay at Ben's. Joe and Alice Marie, along with the preacher and his wife, would bunk at Doc and Sarah's. Henry and Mary Ann would stay at Nate and Helen's place. Jim and Ben Jr. were asked to stay at the bunkhouse for a few days, until everything returned to normal.

Along with picking up the lumber, Henry was asked to convey information to several people in town. He was asked to ride over to Fort Henry and ask the Captain if there had been any information from the Sharp brothers. He was to return Sunday night, as always, and report the news.

Yes, the Captain had good news from the Sharp people! They would take the 500 gun order, and would forward two guns to be reviewed by the Army before the contract was signed. The guns would be delivered over a three year period. It looked like they were going to do the deal at this time. Ben could not be happier!

The two wagons loaded with lumber were moved down by the river and Ben picked his crew to start the mill house. Two Indians were selected - Running Paw and Little Bear. Henry would be the driving force, with Ben riding shot gun. All the others were pulling corn and bringing it to the cribs. Doc and Tom were in charge of all that. They had planted 200 acres this year, with 50 of it in new ground. The old ground had been receiving its yearly dose of fertilizer from the corral, and the ground was rich. Some of the stalks had three ears on them! Maybe they could do better than 40 bushels to the acre. They would just have to wait to see.

Bill had suggested putting some seats in a covered wagon so all three couples could go out together. That seemed to please everyone. The preacher had made arrangements to have a deacon cover Sunday services, and Bill said he was going to close up for two days and put a sign on the door, "Going to a Wedding. Be back Tuesday."

The wagon pulled up at Doc's place at 5 p.m., and everyone ran over to meet the visitors and see what everyone looked like. It was a good time for all. They would eat, and drink tea, milk, and coffee. Right now, they wanted to put the animals to rest with food and drink. It had been a long seven-hour ride.

Bill and the preacher could not believe their eyes at how well the place was kept, and how large it was! Bill thought he was a big shot buying grain, and soon to be flour and meal, from the largest grain company west of the Mississippi - and they were right at his back door!

The women were beside themselves, marrying off their girls to nice men like this. My God, any woman would give her right arm to land a man like Henry Wilson or Joe Martin and to move onto a big farm like the O&S! This was a storybook tale, but here they were, ready to take the vows and go forth and multiply. The Lord had blessed them all!

While the men made a tour of the place, the girls were busy getting acquainted and talking girl talk about who would go first and wear what, and where they would sleep for the first night. My God, there was more to talk about than they had time for. Little Flower was having trouble understanding all this, but being a girl it did not take her long to figure it out.

The Indian men could not see what all the fuss was about, but after working with the white men for over a year, they knew them to be smart. The white man's way of life was not bad. They had plenty of food to eat and clothes to wear. He paid them a dollar per day, which they could spend and buy things with.

It was time to eat! The bell was rung, and everyone gathered around three long tables which Helen and Elisabeth had set up. Sarah had fixed a table for the Indian men, and the preacher was asked to say a few words and bless the food. The room went quiet as everyone bowed their heads. His words were clear: *"Oh dear God, whom we love with all our heart, but do not understand the way you lead us sometimes, we say thank you for bringing us to this place, and we ask, oh God, that you bless the food that has been prepared for our bodies. Most of all, dear God, bless and keep safe the young people that will take vows on Sunday. Bless their children, and may they love you and follow in your ways, as we have tried to do. Amen."*

After that, the room became full of life and it was eating time. The fall night was cool as the sun began to set, and everyone gathered on the front porch to have cake and drink, and to watch a perfect day on the prairie come to a close. Tomorrow, everyone would tour the place and have some fun!

There were still chickens to be fed, cows to milk, smokehouses to tend, and things that make a farm work. The boys would show the girls around while they did their work and give them one last chance to change their minds. They didn't think they were going to have any takers, but it was the right thing to do. They needed to see where they would spend the rest of their lives. The girls picked out the places where they wanted their houses to be built, and before you knew it, the day was over.

Sunday it was a big breakfast and off to church, which was going to be conducted at Nate and Helen's place as close to sunrise as they could get it. Chairs had been set up in Nate's backyard, and the back porch would be used as a pulpit. The preacher had chosen to talk about when God called upon Moses to go to Egypt and free his people and how Moses had said to God, "No, I cannot do that, I'm too weak", and God said, "That is all right, I'm sending your brother Aaron with you." He tied the story to Ben and Nate and how they had led their people to the Promised Land here in the prairie, where they would love and grow. What a beautiful way to start the day! Then they sang songs, and were happy to be in each other's care.

Things had changed a bit on eating lunch, and the rest of the morning was spent preparing for the weddings at 3 p.m. They would eat a big meal when that was over. It was November 30th, 1818, and three young men were about to take new wives. It would be a day in their lives that could never be forgotten. Everything that could be done was going to be done to make this the best day of their lives. It was decided that the oldest would be first and that put Henry in the lead; then came Joe, and last Tom.

Everyone gathered at Nate's at 2:30 p.m. dressed in their best. They sang songs, and the preacher had more words to say. Then the preacher started the wedding by saying, "As we are gathered here today as friends and family, and as God is our witness, do you Henry Wilson, take this woman Mary Ann Hammersmith, to be your lawful wedded wife; to love and cherish in sickness and in health, for all the days of your life?"

"I do!" exclaimed Henry.

"Do you Mary Ann Hammersmith, take this man Henry Wilson to be your lawful wedded husband to love and cherish, and bear his children for all the days of your life?" asked the preacher.

"I do!" exclaimed Mary Ann.

"Then before these witnesses and the eyes of God, I pronounce you man and wife!" stated the preacher.

The same was completed for Joe and Tom. With that, a long prayer was offered and it was time to eat!

They now had three more people in their lives, and how they would fit into the everyday life of the farm was anyone's guess. Would they be good wives and take care of their men? Would they pick up their share of the daily work? It would be hard for the first year, until the men got their houses built and the furnishings to make it a home. The new brides would want to bring things from their old homes that their mothers wanted them to have. Joe and Henry would have to take a wagon to town every time they went, in order to bring back things the girls would want for their lives. Mr. and Mrs. Hammersmith were very generous and wanted to supply clothing, special foods, and things you cannot raise on a farm. There would be a big adjustment period for everyone!

With the crops in and hog killing time over, it was time to put the tools in the shed and get ready for winter. With the building of the mill house and three new homes, most of the winter would be spent building - weather permitting. Ben needed timbers for the mill, and they needed logs for the new homes. So crews were sent into the woods to cut and debark logs.

With the new corn crop in the cribs, one crew was used to shell corn most of the winter. That way there would be lots ready for the grinder come spring, when the stones were due to arrive.

Building would go fast with full crews working 10 hours per day. They hoped to have one home done by the New Year and be well on their way with the other two by plowing time. The Indians had decided to spend the winter at the farm and did not want to give up their warm bunkhouse for a teepee.

Henry came back from town in March saying the stones were due to arrive by the next weekend. Of course, Ben wanted to be there to supervise their off loading and to make sure everything they needed to set them in place would be brought back from town. The mill house was pretty well done, and the water wheel was finished and lifted into place. About the only thing left were the stones.

By April 1, 1819, the grinder was ready, and all the men took a little time off to watch Ben grind the first cornmeal. God, this thing was fast! The hopper held four bushels and it was in sacks in minutes. At this rate, it would not take long to go through 6,000 bushels of corn. All Ben could say was, "Bill, get ready for your first load of meal. It will be on your back dock by Friday, and every two days thereafter!"

Bill Hammersmith took a look at the first load in the new O&S Grain Company sacks and said, "I will not have any problems getting rid of this. Just as soon as the people find out it is in town, they will line up to buy. I should be able to get a good price and get rid of it as fast as you bring it to town!"

"Well, I don't know about all that. The mill seems to turn it out pretty fast. We may have two loads a day before long," said Henry.

"I don't care if you have three loads a day! You have got the only grinder in the country, and people have to eat. Just as soon as word gets out, you will have to figure a way to get product upriver to Sarasota. They will want meal also," stated Bill.

"We plan to grind wheat for white flour and mix corn, barley, rye, and bone meal to make a good animal feed," said Henry.

"If you get all that done, your mill is going to be overloaded with work very soon," stated Bill.

"Well, all I can say is Ben Sharp seems to know where he is going and how he plans to get there!" declared Henry.

The days were going well, but there was never enough time to talk to his old friend. He missed the days when he could walk down the hill and spend an hour on Nate's front porch. So today he was going to turn the mill over to Tom and go over to the shop and spend some time with him.

As he walked up to the shop, Nate was busy making a rim for the hay cutter. He looked up from his work and asked, "And what can I do for you, sir? What are you doing here in the middle of the day? Is there anything wrong?"

"Yes sir, there sure is! I miss you! I never get to see you anymore except at the nightly meeting and a while on Sunday, and to tell the truth - I just miss talking to you!" said Ben.

"Well, in that case, sir, come into my parlor and sit a spell - and don't forget to wipe your feet!" stated Nate.

"Nate, you are good at what you do. There is no way in God's name O&S could be where it is today without the machines you have made. No, you are the best, Nate Owens, and God has given you much, but I didn't come over here to tell you how great you are. It might give you the big head," said Ben.

"Shut up, and tell me what is on your mind," insisted Nate.

"Well, I have been thinking", began Ben.

Then Nate interrupted, "I didn't think you were sick, so that means you are normal. What have you been thinking about?"

"Nate, they have begun to use the steam engine down South in the cotton business and in boats. What if we could get our hands on one? We could make another mill when we overwork the stones; but most of all, I'm thinking we are putting lots more wheat, barley, and rye in the ground, and to thrash the way we are doing it will take forever. If we had a steam engine, you could build a big round basket with some beater bars that as the basket turned the grain would be beat out of its shells, while another basket could be mounted on the side to blow out the straw. The grain would then roll over the top edge through a screen into a sack. We could thrash one hundred times more grain, and do it faster and cleaner. We could use the engine for a saw mill, and anything else we can think up," said Ben.

"I thought you said you came down here because you missed me! I don't need all that extra work, but you are right! Where would we get an engine, and what kind should we look for? I know nothing about steam engines," said Nate.

"I don't either, but we can learn," stated Ben.

"Well, I will talk to Bill and see what he knows. I guess now that you have got all that off your mind, you are not lonely any-more!" exclaimed Nate.

"What else would I talk to you about? We don't fish or hunt together," said Ben.

"I don't care what you talk to me about. It is always good to hear your views. You're always telling me how great the O&S Grain Company is that they have Nate Owens to build things. What about Ben Sharp and his mill? The fact is that we are here, and it was your leadership that brought us here. We are a team and I love you. God knows that," declared Nate.

"With that kind of talk, I had better get my tail back over to help Tom. I will see you tonight," said Ben.

Tom and Running Paw were doing fine, and really didn't need Ben's help. He looked around, and there were over 150 sacks on the mill floor. Then he said, "Tom, why don't you go over to the barn and bring us a wagon. We have one here now, but it is not enough. That way, we can load them up ready to go to town to-morrow morning. As a matter of fact, I will drive one of them. I need to talk to Bill Hammersmith, anyway."

It was dark when they finished loading and headed over to the shop for their nightly meeting. There were still 3,000 bush-els of corn in the cribs. At 20 cents per pound, they would de-liver $1,600 worth of meal to Mr. Hammersmith tomorrow. The wheat, barley, and rye were still awaiting the stones. It looked like they would have another outstanding year, and Ben would report that tonight!

After loading the wagons, it was time to make their way over to the shop. It was time to go over the past days' work and talk about what to do tomorrow. Ben was feeling very good after talking to Nate this afternoon. He had lots of information to share with the men. Everyone was already on hand when Tom, Running Paw, and Ben walked up. Joe and Sam had been planting corn all day, and it looked like they would get 250 acres in this spring. Tom and Doc had been busy trying to keep the mill in corn all day, and it seemed as fast as Doc could get it shelled and bagged, Tom and Running Paw were grinding and bagging it. After everyone had given their report on the day and got their duty for the next day, Ben took charge of the meeting.

He said, "Men, I have got two things on my mind tonight I thought I would talk to you about - maybe three things. Nate is working on a sickle mower that can be pulled by a team, and that one man can ride on and cut hay. It looks like he will be finished with it just in time when the grass and hay is ready to cut. Let's wish him luck, and hope it works as well as he has planned. Next, I want to thank all of you that helped get the mill and mill house ready for service. The whole system could not be better! From what we have been able to figure out, it should bring in over $6,000 this year without any problems, and I really figure that is a low number. I have not put cattle sales or white flour in that amount. With the increased acreage Jim and Sam have planned for next year, we should have very good years back to back, and that brings up my next subject. I would like to call a business meeting tonight after we have all eaten and washed up. The meeting will be at my house at 7 p.m. I would like everyone to be there except the hired hands. I will try and get you all in bed by 9:30 or 10 p.m. That is all I'm going to tell you now. You will have to be there to hear the rest."

Then Ben continued, "Tom gave me a few minutes off this afternoon, and I went over and talked to Nate about a steam engine. Maybe you are thinking, 'What are we going to do with a steam engine?' Well, I have got some plans in the back of my

head. Number one - we need more wheat. Now I don't like growing wheat, because it is a winter crop. In other words, we have to
get it in the ground right after we get done with corn. In order for
it to do well, it should be planted in corn ground. The next thing
I don't like about the crop is that it is ready for harvest in June
and July. That makes the heads heavy with grain, and bad winds
and weather lay it down, making it hard to cut and heavy with
water. However, we have to have it to make bread; we need it to
blend with our feed we will sell. With that said, we have to thrash
the darn stuff and that is a lot of work. With a steam engine, I
believe our machine builder, Mr. Owens, can build a thrashing
machine that would be as good as any on the market and cost us
less. With these two machines, we can thrash for other farmers in
the area for a price. If we get a steam engine tractor, we can build
a grinder and saw mill to go with it. Times are changing fast. The
railroad is here and expanding every day. We can bring that kind
of equipment into the farm by train, and have it shipped from
almost any place in the country. I need to know what you fellows
think about these ideas."

Tom spoke up, saying, "Dad, you have not been wrong so far,
and I vote to give it a try.

Nate asked, "How long do you think it would take us to get
one?" Ben replied, "I don't know, but if I had to guess I would
say a year, maybe two".

"Well, that is good. It gives me more time to plan and build
a thrashing machine," stated Nate.

"Is there anyone here with a no vote?" asked Ben. No one
said anything. "Well, with that I will go to town tomorrow with
the load of meal, and talk to Bill about it. I will see you at 7
o'clock," declared Ben.

At 7 p.m. on April 29, 1818, nine men sat in Ben Sharp's living room across from the fireplace and prepared to listen to what
he had to say. He began, "I have called you here tonight to talk
to you about our farms, and about the business they have grown
to be. I have not talked to Nate, Doc, or anyone else regarding

this. Therefore, what I have to say tonight is from my thoughts, and we may have to have another meeting after this one to make sure we are all on the same path. Men, I believe our farms have grown too big to not have more organization about them. I propose tonight that we form a corporation around O&S and that it be called whatever we wish: the O&S Corporation, or the O&S Grain Corporation, or whatever we vote to call it. With that said, I vote that we divide the corporation into 5 parts. There would be four owners of the Corporation, plus the Corporation would also become an owner."

After a slight pause Ben continued, "The owners would be Nate, Doc, Henry, and myself. The fifth owner would be the Corporation. It would work like this: we would name Sarah as our bookkeeper and secretary; and Henry's wife, Mary Ann, as backup, since she has got some business experience at the trading post. All moneys received and paid out for the year, would be recorded by the secretary during the year. On December 31st of each year, the books would be closed for that year, and the profit so noted. Whatever profit left would then be divided into five equal parts. A check would be made out to each of the four Owners. The Corporation share would remain with the Corporation, but would not be carried forward as profit for the New Year. In other words, the Corporation has a right to make a profit the same as the other four Owners. Now, along with the Owners getting a check on January 1st of each year, and every year thereafter - if there are any profits for their share, I also propose as of January 1st of this year, that each one of us working for the Corporation would receive a weekly wage of $2.00 per day, due to be paid weekly and not to include Sunday."

Then Ben said, "Now, this money is your personal money, and you may do with it as you wish. The only thing that I would like to ask is that your shares of the Corporation stay in your family. Do not sell or transfer those shares to any outsider. In other words, Nate's shares belong to him and his family, and the same thing with Doc, Henry, and myself. Again, the Corporation would own the farms, its lands, buildings, equipment, live-stock, and crops - whatever that is worth. It would be divided into five parts as a net worth to each of you. If the Corporation was ever to be dissolved, whatever holdings it owned would be divided into four parts. Not only will you get a check yearly for the profits the Corporation has made, but you also will own, on paper, one quarter of all the assets owned by the Corporation. Now with that, I will shut up and open the floor for questions. If you have none, Nate and I will go to town and have papers made up showing all of this in writing."

Henry spoke up and said, "I don't feel like I'm part of the family, and maybe should not be included".

Ben said, "No! Henry, you have been here with us from day one, and you have every right to a share."

"Well, in that case Mr. Sharp, why don't we go to bed and think about all this, and have another meeting after you write up the papers? We can see that what you have said is the same as what has been written down. Then we can change the writings, and sign the papers," suggested Henry.

"Henry, you have good ideas and I agree. It has been a long day!" said Ben. With that, everyone said their goodnights and went home to their own beds.

Next day, they had two wagon loads of meal to go to town. It was agreed that Nate and Ben would make the trip. Loaded wagons take a little longer, so it was decided that they would stay all night, take care of business the next day, and then return home. Bill Owens, Nate's son, was now 20 years old and was normally Nate's daily helper. For the next two days, he would be in charge of the shop.

They arrived around 5 pm and went over to see Bill Hammersmith about a place to sleep and see if he wanted to unload the wagons tonight or wait until morning. He said, "Back them up to my new warehouse door, and we will unload in the morning"

Nate said, "God, man you sure know how to make a man happy!"

Bill said, "By the way, have you fellows had anything to eat all day?"

Ben replied, "Not much".

"Well, in that case, let's go up to the house and see what the wife has in the pot", offered Mr. Hammersmith.

Nate spoke up and asked, "Do you have any bunks left in the bunkhouse?"

Bill's reply was, "For you fellows - always! If not, we will make a place for you."

"Good! We will take you up on everything!" said Nate.

Then Ben asked, "Bill, do you have any time tomorrow to talk about business, or can we talk about it tonight?"

"What is on your mind?" asked Mr. Hammersmith.

Nate exclaimed, "This crazy man wants to buy a tractor steam engine!"

"Sure, let's talk about it at supper, and we will get that behind us. That way we can unload the wagons first thing in the morning, and you boys can do your shopping and head on home," replied Bill.

Later that evening Mr. Hammersmith inquired, "Now, what is this tractor steam engine all about?"

"Bill, we have heard where the steam engine is being used for many things such as in the cotton business, and boats, etc. We have heard now that Mr. Robert Fulton has made a tractor steam engine. A machine like that could do a lot of jobs around the O&S Grain Company. One of our bigger problems is that we believe that within a few years, we will have more grain to grind than our stone can keep up with. We would like to build a grinder that could be run off of the steam engine. The machine could be used as a saw mill, and Nate has got some ideas about building a thrashing machine that could be powered by the machine. There are all kinds of work we would like to have it do. So, we have decided to look into buying one," explained Ben.

"Fellows, I'm a trading post operator, and I know just as much about a steam engine as a hog does about Sunday!" exclaimed Mr. Hammersmith.

Then Ben asked, "Where do you think we should go to get information about such a thing?"

"Well, I would start with the boat Captain," suggested Bill.

"Why the boat Captain?" inquired Nate.

"Because his boat is powered by a steam engine built by Mr. Fulton. He should have an address on the company that made it," explained Bill.

Ben spoke up saying, "I knew I would find out something by asking you! You should put up a sign in the trading post saying, 'Information for Sale - $1.00.'"

"You can go down to the dock tomorrow and see what the Captain has to say," suggested Bill.

Nate said, "We have another question. Will you charge us another dollar for that information also?"

"I might as well, since I don't make that much on cornmeal!" said Bill.

"Another question - do you have any lawyers in town?" asked Ben.

"Well, as a matter of fact we do. Since we got a new sheriff last year, we now have a lawyer. I think he does business out of his home on River Road, but I don't know which house," replied Bill.

"Well, we will find it," said Ben.

"Now that we have got all that out of the way and you are feeling better after a good meal, we would like to know how our daughter and son-in-law are doing," asked Bill.

"Well, it's too early to tell, but we think you are about to become a grandpa," said Ben.

"You are kidding me!" exclaimed Bill.

"No! Henry has been talking about it the last week, and I think the girls know more than they want to say," said Ben.

"How nice, I'm so happy! Does she need anything?"

"Not that I know of."

"Please tell them you let the news leak, and that we are as happy as can be!" exclaimed Bill.

"Well, why don't you wait a few weeks? Then you can take the buckboard out of storage and come out to see us. You should come out on Saturday, stay all night, and come home Sunday," suggested Ben.

"We just might do that!" declared Bill.

With all of that out of the way, Nate said, "I think it is my bedtime."

Bill spoke up saying, "Take the Grey and Roan out of the corral tomorrow morning and ride down to River Road to see the lawyer. I don't know how far it is."

"Thank you Bill, that is very nice of you!"

Next morning they were up early, saddled the horses, and went to find some breakfast. They found a small restaurant down by the river and ordered some ham and eggs. They could see the boat down by the dock and people beginning to stir. After breakfast, Ben walked up onto the boat and asked where he might find the Captain. In a few minutes, a big man smoking a pipe walked up and said, "I'm Captain Easton. How can I help you?"

"Sir, we understand you run the boat with a steam engine," stated Ben.

"Yes sir! We sure do," said the Captain.

"How do you like it?" inquired Ben.

"We are very happy with it," stated the Captain.

"What do you use to fire the boiler?" Nate wanted to know.

"We use coal, but we can fire on wood if we run out of coal," explained the Captain.

"Does it use much?" questioned Ben.

"Well, if the river is high and we are carrying a big load, we use one ton per day," replied Captain Easton.

"Is that all?" asked Ben.

"Yes, that is pretty much the story," stated the Captain.

"Well, Captain, who made this steam engine?" Ben wanted to know.

"Mr. Robert Fulton! His company pretty well makes most all of the steam engines running the boats," declared Captain Easton.

"Do you have an address for him?" asked Ben.

"Yes sir! He has given us a parts book and instructions on how we should take care of the engine," said the Captain.

"Would you be kind enough to give us that address?" requested Ben, and then continued, "We are thinking about buying a steam tractor from him".

"I would be glad to," stated the Captain. In a few minutes, he came back with a sheet of paper with an address and everything they needed. Ben thanked him, and he and Nate headed back up to the horses tied off at the restaurant.

They had no idea where they were going as they rode down River Road. It was not long before Nate pulled up next to a man walking along the road and asked him if there was a lawyer living along this road. The man said, "Yes sir! He lives in the house with the two big apple trees in the front yard, about four houses down."

"Thank you, Sir," said Nate. They tied the horses off at the rail and walked up on the porch to knock on the door.

The man who opened the door was in his mid-thirties and very well groomed. Nate said, "Sir, we are looking for a lawyer".

The man stuck out his hand and said, "You just found one. My name in Mike Bradshaw. How can I help you?"

"Well Sir, we would like to draw up papers on a new Corporation. Can you help us?"

"Well, that is how I make my living. I hope I can! Come on in and tell me about it", invited Mr. Bradshaw.

They walked in and sat down at a table in the middle of the room. A few minutes later, a young woman came into the room and asked if she could get them some coffee. "No, ma'am! Thank you, we just had breakfast," said Ben.

Mr. Bradshaw inquired, "Tell me about the Corporation".

Ben filled him in on the details and said, "That is pretty much what we want to do."

Mr. Bradshaw said, "Here is what we have to do. First, I want to tell you since Nebraska is not a state, the Corporation Charter will have to be written under Territory laws. They are pretty vague at this time, and I can pretty well draw your Corporation bylaws any way you so direct me."

Then he explained, "This is what I need. You need to write down the names of each person named as officers and how you want the Corporation to work. The Charter will have to be drawn in six copies; one for each of the Officers, one for my files, and one for the Territory Office. You should write it up the way you want it, and then I will write it up according to Territory law and give you a draft copy for all Officers to review. After you have all agreed on what you want, return the Charter to me, and I will write it into the final six-copy form and return it to you for signatures."

"Very well, Mr. Bradshaw," agreed Ben, then added "Sir, one of our partners is Mr. Henry Wilson. He will be dropping the papers off in a week, or sooner."

"Very well, I look forward to working with you," said Mr. Bradshaw.

Ben and Nate talked about business all the way home. Ben said, "If the boys get 250 acres of corn in this year, we could have 8 to 10 thousand bushels on hand this fall. That would be more than the Trading Post could buy, and more would have to be sold to the Army. We will ask Henry to stop by the Fort and see how much the Captain wants. Now I have got a question - if he wants to buy cornmeal and white flour from us, what do we tell him?"

"Well, let's ask Bill what he wants to do. If it is all right by him, then we will sell to them; if not, the Army will have to go through Bill."

"Now what do you want to do about this feed we are getting ready to make this fall? Do you just want to sell to Bill, and let everyone go through him? Or, do you want to sell to the Army?" asked Ben.

"I say in our area, that we sell to Bill. After all, he is part of the family now and he has always been good to us," replied Nate.

"That sounds good to me. If we keep on growing, we will set up another dealer," stated Ben.

"I like that. We only have one place to ship to now," agreed Nate.

Since Ben was the only one that understood the Corporation business, he had decided to write the papers up, and then have Sarah write them in print. She had a much better handwriting than he did. He would start tomorrow night after work and see if he could finish it in a week.

The letter he would send to the Fulton Boiler Maker would ask questions like how long would it take to get a tractor steam engine, and how much would it cost? He could see from the address that it was made in Ohio, but how would they get such a machine out to Nebraska? Maybe it could be shipped by train. There was word that the railroad would be in Lincoln by this fall, and that surveyors had been working not more than a quarter mile from the O & S Farms. Maybe it would pass right by their front door. He would have Henry ask the railroad boss in Lincoln what the plan was. If the railroad did come close to their farms, Henry would ask if they could build a switch track or siding, so they could ship corn and feed without going to Omaha. My! My, times are changing. My God, a train going by our front door - who would have ever thought that in 1803,

The letter went out with Henry on the next trip to town, and Ben gave his address as the O & S Grain Company, Big Blue

River, General Delivery, Lincoln, Nebraska. He thought that within a month he should hear from the Fulton people. Well, he was right and wrong. It took three weeks. He was beside himself as to what they had to say!

11:

A man by the name of Joe Fulton had answered his letter. Ben did not know if he was a brother or son to the Fulton people. They wanted $3,000 for the tractor steam engine, and it could be delivered next spring. Ben did not know if he wanted it that soon, or if the railroad did come through, if it would be at his front door by then. He thought he had better get some more information before he told them, "Yes". He would also talk to the rest of the Owners before he said, "Yes".

The Corporation Charter had two more nights and he thought Sarah would be done with it. He had already had the final meeting with the Owners, and would be ready to give everything to Mr. Bradshaw by next week. He and Sarah both had been very busy and had not been able to work on the Charter as they had wanted to.

Besides everything else going on in Sarah and Doc's household, they had been told there were to be two more weddings! It seemed Sam and Little Flower were in love and wanted to know what Doc and Sarah thought about it. The news caught Doc and Sarah by surprise; however, after watching them for over two years, it was thought something like this could happen.

Doc said, "I don't see anything wrong with it. After all, she is half French. What do you think the Chief is going to say about it?"

Sarah said, "There is one way to find out. That is to have her ask for a powwow, and have Sam ask the Chief for his daughter's hand. I think he is going to want gifts. I don't know how much, but I'm sure he will want something."

Sam said he would do that, and get back to them just as soon as a meeting could be arranged.

At the same time this was going on at Doc's, Ben and Elisabeth were hearing the same message from Ben Jr. at their house. It seems everyone wanted to get married! It was hard to believe, but after 16 years on the prairie Ben Jr. and Sue Marie were now 24 years old. Everyone was happy with the news.

Elisabeth asked, "When do you want to do this?"

Ben Jr. replied, "I don't know. We have not set the date - we just thought we should tell you."

Elisabeth spoke up saying, "If you do get married in the fall, why don't you stay with us? We have more than enough room now that Tom has his own place."

"It is all right with me. I will ask Barbara Ann what she wants to do," replied Tom.

In the meantime Sam reported that Little Flower had talked with her father Chief White Head and he had agreed. He wanted a great deal for his daughter and said that Sam must come to see him with the gifts. He also said Chief White Head did not like giving his daughter to a white man but since he had taken "a white woman", it was only fair that he give back what he had taken. The meeting was set for Sam to appear before the Chief in three days. The gifts he wanted were five horses, three young cows and a bull, twenty chickens and three hams. The chief had grown to love the O&H ham very much and wanted to get a good supply for the winter.

On the day of the meeting Sam and Little Flower would ride in one wagon with the hams, chickens and two horses tied to back

224

of the wagon. Two of the Indian workers would bring the other three horses and the cows and bull. The trip was started early in the morning so they could arrive around mid-day. When they arrived everyone was ready for the caravan to arrive. As the wagon and animals' went through the teepee rows everyone cheered.

The guard directed them to the Chief's teepee. He was ready for them, all dressed out in his ceremonial dress, smoking his pipe. There were some pots hanging over the fire and two women were busy doing things around the teepee. Little Flower told Sam the younger woman was her sister and the older woman was the chief wife that he had taken after her mother's death. The chief got up from his blanket and shook Sam's hand. It was the first time he had met Sam. He then told them to sit down and that he was to serve buffalo stew and tea. The chief wanted to know if he was a warrior and Sam said no, he was a farmer. He then told him he was the Doctor's son whom the chief had met once before with their leader Big Ben.

They talked for a long time and enjoyed the buffalo stew. The chief wished them much happiness and to have many papoose. He was very pleased with the horses and cows. He said, "We can take the cows with us when we move camp but we cannot take care of the pigs."

He said he had learned to love the meat but could not raise the pigs. He wanted to know if he could come to the wedding. Sam and Little Flower said yes.

Sarah let Ben know the Charter was done and that Henry could take it to Mr. Bradshaw on Friday. Ben told Henry, "When you give it to him, see if you can stay around long enough to see what he thinks about it, and when he will have it done. When you get done with him, stop by the railroad office, and see what is going on there. See if you can find out when the train will pass out this way. Also, tell them we would like to get a switch and side rail installed so we can ship corn by railroad."

Henry said, "I will be glad to take care of those two matters".

Henry got into town around 4 pm and after backing up to the warehouse, saddled a horse, and went down on River Road to see Mr. Bradshaw. He knocked on the door and Mrs. Bradshaw let him in. She asked Henry to sit down, and said her husband would be with him in a minute.

Mr. Bradshaw came in and shook Henry's hand saying, "It is good to see you, Henry! I see you have some papers there."

"Yes sir", began Henry, "I think we have got everything in order, and Mr. Sharp asked me to deliver them to you. Sir, he wanted to know if you could look the Charter over and see what you think, and when you suppose you would be done with it."

"Henry, I can do that. Would you like some coffee while you wait?" asked Mr. Bradshaw.

"No sir! But I could drink a big glass of cold water," stated Henry. Within a few minutes, Mrs. Bradshaw brought in a glass and pitcher of water.

It felt good to Henry to sit and relax for a few minutes after being on that old wagon for six hours. Mr. Bradshaw came back into the room and said, "My God, Henry, you people have done an outstanding job on this Charter! I could almost use it as is. Tell Mr. Sharp that I will take it over to the newspaper office and see if they can set, type, and run me off six copies. Tell him I will have it ready in a week from today."

"Very good, sir. I thank you for the quick service and the cold water."

12:

It was now after 5 pm and Henry still had to unload the wagon and put the mules to bed. He was hungry and tired and he would let the railroad man go until tomorrow. His mother-in-law had a nice supper fixed for him and he had been given his wife's old room to spend the night in. They had some small talk about life at the farms; and yes, they would be grandparents sometime this winter. Grandma said, "Please let me know when the baby is due and I will leave Bill to batch for a week, and I will come out and take care of them".

Henry said, "That would be very nice of you, but you do not have to do that".

"I would like to be with Mary Ann those last few days," insisted Mrs. Hammersmith.

"Very well, pack your things, and when the time comes I will take you home with me," agreed Henry.

Next morning, Henry went over to the Railroad Office and took care of Ben's last request. It was 7 am when he opened the door. A man was sitting at a desk drinking coffee. Henry said, "Good morning", and introduced himself saying he was from O & S Farms out on Big Blue River.

The man got up from behind the desk and said, "Yes sir! I have heard about you fellows. My name is Arthur Hill. I oversee the building of the railroad out here. What can I do for you?"

"Sir", began Henry, "we at the O & S Grain Company would like to know if the railroad is going to come close to our farms; and if so, how close."

"Well, that is a good question, and yes, it is. Let's look at the map here on the wall, and I can give you a pretty good idea. Let's see, your spread is down here by the river and my markings show us coming within 2,000 feet or so of your property lines," said Mr. Hill.

"Well, you see, sir, we are planning on shipping a lot of corn and animal feed in the years to come, and we would like to know if we could get a rail spire leading off the main track somewhere along that route?" asked Henry.

"Yes Sir! You sure can! We would be glad to have you as a customer. As a matter of fact, you are about 35 miles from here and that would be a good place to have a siding.

"Here is the deal", began Mr. Hill. "You folks cut the ties for the siding and spire, and the railroad will build the bed and track. I think we should build a loading spire, plus a side track."

"What do you mean by that?" asked Henry.

Mr. Hill explained, "That means you would have a place to load and unload cars, and when they were loaded you could move them to the siding, and the train will pick them up and drop off new cars."

"Sir that would be far better than we had hoped for. Mr. Sharp will be on Cloud 9!" exclaimed Henry.

"Well, it's nice doing business with you. We need freight to haul," stated Mr. Hill.

"When do you think this would be done, Mr. Hill?" asked Henry.

"Well, if I can keep men on the track, I would say by next July we should have it done," replied Mr. Hill.

"How many ties do we need?" questioned Henry.

"That depends on how far you want to be away from the main rail system. You fellows lay it out, and we will build it. You will have to be five feet apart on the ties," stated Mr. Hill.

"How long do you want the ties?" inquired Henry?

"They need to be 8 feet, but you should have 8 to 10 each 12 foot long for the switch ties," replied Mr. Hill.

"We thank you very much, Mr. Hill, and we will have the ties ready," promised Henry.

"Thanks for dropping by, and stop by any time you have a question," offered Mr. Hill.

Henry had a good day and was ready to head for home. He could not wait to tell the other Owners what he had just learned. It was far more than they had ever expected. As he drove the wagon home, his thoughts turned to all that had happened to him since the first day he met Nate Owens and Ben Sharp and what he had learned about Almighty God. Why had God chosen him to meet with these two men? He thought now would be a good time to offer God a prayer and say thanks for all his blessings.

"Almighty God, I thank you for leading me to these two men. I'm sorry for the 20 years I was lost and not following your teachings, but I'm now in your house and I vow to stay there until you pull the last hair on my head. Since I have followed your teaching, I have a life and means never before thought of. Thank you for loaning me my wonderful wife, and our new baby soon to arrive. Please keep them well and strong, and may we always follow in your teachings. Amen."

It was dark when Henry pulled onto the farm grounds, and he was tired. He thought he would put the mules in the barn and go to bed. He would bring Ben up-to-date in the morning and leave it up to him to tell the rest about all that had happened.

He met with Ben right after breakfast the next morning and told him about everything.

"Henry, you mean to tell me that the railroad is going to be that close to our farms?" asked Ben.

"Yes sir!" replied Henry. "That is what he told me"

"Henry, do you know what this means? It means that we here at O & S Grain Company are years ahead of anyone that wants to grind feed and bread supplies. We now can build a business that will outlast your kids and children. What a break this is! You, Doc, and I will walk up there this morning and see if we can spot any surveyor markings. If so, we will step off the siding and loading dock. That way I can put some men to work on the ties this fall," stated Ben.

Henry went down to the corncrib to find Doc and told him Ben needed to see him. Doc walked with him up to the barn where Ben was, and the three of them headed out to the suspected train siding. Ben told Doc all about Henry's meeting with the railroad, and what they were about to do. Doc had the same feeling as Ben and said, "Fellows, this is better than fresh butter, and we don't have to do a lot of churning to get it!"

As they walked around to see if they could find some surveyor markings, Ben spoke up, saying, "Fellows, keep your heads down and watch for snakes. We have not cut the grass in this area, and you may come upon a buzz tail."

After about ten minutes, Doc called out, saying he thought he had something. Sure enough, there was a wooden peg with a number on top. After a little more searching the men found more stakes, and they seemed to run in a straight line. Ben said to Henry, "Go down to the barn and see if you can find two of Nate's snake forks. We will stick them in the ground and make our own surveyor markings."

"Good idea!" agreed Henry.

After looking around, they decided the train would pass about 2,000 yards from their land. They stepped off where the siding should go, and it looked like it would be about 500 feet from the main track for the siding and the loading dock, and they would run parallel with each other. That would mean about 200 eight foot ties and 10 each 12 foot units.

The problem was the siding was going to be on O & S land. This meant the railroad had never said anything to them about the track crossing O & S land. Ben thought he would speak to them about it. It looked to him that the railroad would use up about 25 acres. At 25 cents per acre it was not worth worrying about; however, he needed paperwork showing the land had been leased to the railroad. Besides that, the road was going through the new 1,280 acres he had just bought from the U.S. Government, and he needed the right to cross the tracks, or they would be land-locked for a big part of the 1,280 acres. Agreements were going to be needed. That night Ben brought the rest of the Owners and men up-to-date. He said he would start letters to the tractor people right away.

His letter went out to Mr. Futon the next day. He told Mr. Fulton that yes; he wanted the tractor, but in order to ship it he had to wait on the railroad being done and getting a siding to the farms. He informed Mr. Fulton that the railroad had said they would be ready by July 1820 and that he would like to take delivery of the tractor as close to that date as he could. In the meantime, he would like to get all the information which could be supplied on how the tractor works, and he would like to know if a down payment was required on the tractor in order to build it and ship it on or about that date.

Before you knew it, another season had come and gone. The kids had gotten married in November, as the other boys had done, and moved in with Ben and Elisabeth and Doc and Sarah. They had outstanding years on their corn. Nate and Bill had finished the sickle cutter, and were well along on their way to building a thrashing machine. More plows had been made, and Ben had hired more of the Indians for the work. The railroad crews were moving west and the O & S Siding was done. However, there was still work to be done on building loading docks for the rail cars. Nate had finally gotten his church and schoolhouse, and a three thousand gallon water tank had been built with a windmill to pump water from the river for fires. The Indians had painted the O & S Grain Company, Big Blue River, Nebraska on the side.

Everything was growing everywhere. People were coming and going, feed was now being ground and sold to the trading post, and more cattle were being raised than the Army could buy. Another buyer would have to be found, or they would have to cut back on the breeding. In order to keep up with it all, Ben had fixed up a room in the blacksmith shop where he could be close to Nate, and he used that for an office.

Ben Jr. had taken over hauling the corn and feed to town, and they were now running three wagons a day. On one of these days, Ben Jr. had brought back a letter from the Fulton tractor people. The tractor would be shipped on July 1, 1820, so that meant the docks had to be done in order to offload the unit. Ben had talked to the railroad and asked if he could get a boxcar set on the siding, and if he could ship cornmeal and feed to town instead of the wagons going daily, or every other day. That way, he would only have to go to town once a week to deal with banking and other business.

It was May 15, 1820, when they started the docks besides the siding. Ben had figured it would take a good month to build, and he wanted to make sure they were ready when the tractor came. His plan was to build a ramp at the end of the siding where the track stopped, 50 inches high and five feet wider than the track siding. That way, anything coming to O & S could be pulled off the railcar down the ramp to the ground. In the case of the tractor, it could be driven off. Another ramp would be built parallel with the siding, 20 feet longer than a rail car with ramps on both ends. That way, a wagon could be pulled up alongside the car to load or unload.

Shipping the products by railcar meant they had to be handled four times before they reached the end user. However, it was a lot better than driving three wagons 35 miles every day or so and staying overnight. Besides, Bill Hammersmith was going to pop the buttons off his shirt with his chest stuck out so far from telling people he was waiting on a railcar load of feed and flour any day. He needed more meal, flour, and feed daily, but O &

S was making more and faster than he could keep up with. You could not believe the people coming and going everyday: railroad workers, boat people, and people going west and north. It was unbelievable!

Captain Kelly had been over at the bank on some business. He told the banker that if he saw Ben Sharp to ask him to stop by the Fort. Ben could not figure out what he wanted, and rode over to see him on Monday when he got his banking business done. He tied his horse out front and went in. The Captain was talking with two soldiers and an Indian when he walked in. Captain Kelly pointed to a bench on the side of the room, and Ben sat down and waited until he was done.

When the men left, the Captain got up and went over to Ben and shook his hand. He said, "Mr. Sharp, I have some bad news. We have received orders from Washington that we will have to move the Fort North about 75 miles. It seems there are so many people moving west that the city of Omaha and all the people west and south need us more there than they do here. The Government wants us to move to a new Fort up there. Now, the Fort is to be much larger - I think maybe 100 to 150 men. Here we only house 50 to 75 soldiers and some wives. I'm thinking the Fort will need a hundred head of cattle a year. Can you get that far north with the cattle?" the Captain asked.

Ben replied, "Let me talk to the men, but yes, I think so".

Then the Captain continued, "Also, I will need a lot more feed, meal, flour, and horses."

"When are you going to make this move?" inquired Ben.

"It will be sometime next spring, if the new Fort is done," responded Captain Kelly.

"Well, that gives me some time to think about it! I will have to get together with the rest of the boys and see what they think. I will let you know next time I'm in town," answered Ben.

"That is good enough for me. What else is going on out at O & S?" asked the Captain.

"Well, we have a new church, a new water tank, a new rail siding, and a new steam tractor coming in a week or so. Watch the railroad, and you may see it come through town," replied Ben.

"Sounds like you boys have been busy!" exclaimed Captain Kelly.

"Yes, we get up early and go to bed late. I will have some answers for you the next time I'm in town," promised Ben. With that, Ben headed for home.

Ben had stopped by the Post Office and there was a letter from Mr. Fulton which read that the tractor had been shipped on the 25th of June, and that with good luck it could be there in three weeks. It was already May 28, and that meant the tractor could arrive in two weeks. What a time that was going to be! He thought he might as well give everyone the day off to watch this big machine come to life.

Around 5 pm Ben arrived home and went down to see Nate. The evening meeting was just getting started. After the work reports were all in, Ben gave his news about the tractor and the Fort. He said he would like to talk to Nate and get back to them later about the Fort moving north. When the meeting was over he asked Nate if he wanted to meet after supper or wait and go over things in the morning.

Nate said, "Let's make it in the morning; I'm tired tonight".

"Me too; my bed will feel good after all that riding today," agreed Ben.

Next morning Ben met Nate at the shop and they had their talk. "Nate, Captain Kelly wants us to move 100 head of cattle, some mules, and horses; if we have any, 75 miles north next year. Can we do it?" asked Ben.

"Well, yes we can. We would have to make a Texas cattle drive," responded Nate.

"We would need a point rider, two side riders, two rear riders, and a chuck or food wagon. One of these six men would have to be in charge. I would think it would take about one and a half weeks to make the trip," stated Ben.

Nate suggested, "Let's find out who would like to make a cattle drive, and we will get ready."

"I will tell the Captain that it will take about a week and a half to make the trip, and we will need a corral to run the stock into when we get there. Now on the feed and flour, why don't we ship by train?" proposed Ben.

"See what the Captain thinks about that. If we can do that, we have opened our first market north!" exclaimed Nate.

"Nate, it looks like the tractor will be here in a week, or so. I would like to get a load of wood up by the siding ready to fire the boiler. I would also like for you and Bill to be in charge of driving the tractor off the car. The two of you have more experience around machinery than the rest of us. I do not know if the braking system of the tractor is enough to hold it back as you drive it down the ramp. We will have to see. I think we should rig a couple of blocks and tackles and let it down slowly," said Ben.

Nate replied, "I agree. I sure don't want to drive that big thing down that ramp and have it get away."

"How are you doing with the thrashing machine? Will it be ready for this year's crop?" asked Ben.

"I don't know. I think I may need about three more weeks to get done."

"Well, don't lose any sleep over it. If you don't get done, I will have the men cut and tie some bundles so that we can test it later," offered Ben.

"Sounds good to me!" agreed Nate.

Two weeks later, as Nate was coming out of the shop, he heard the train up at the siding. He looked that way to see the biggest machine he had ever seen in his life! The big silver thing sitting upon the flatcar made it look like it came out of the heavens. He stared at the thing for a few seconds, and then rushed back into the shop to alert Ben and Bill.

Ben took one look and said, "My God! What have we got here? Let's ring the bell and let everyone know the big machine is here."

In a few minutes, everyone arrived at the rail siding to have a closer look. The back wheels were taller than a man. There was a little roof over the drivers' seat that made it look bigger than it was. God, it was big!

Bill walked up the ramp and got onboard the car where he could walk around the thing. It was pretty silver with not a spot on it anywhere. There were two large wheels. They were about 24 inches in diameter and 8 inches wide. The back wheels were a good 6 feet tall and 14 inches wide. They had big cleats across them in a "V" shape. Just under the seat, which was way up high, was a platform. Just in front of the platform was the firebox door. The platform was large enough to hold a large amount of wood and allow a man to move around. On the right side were two large cans for water. There was a ladder that went up to the seat. Bill climbed into the seat and sat down.

Never had he seen the things he was looking at, and he did not understand what he saw. There was a round gauge with numbers on it. The numbers went from 0 to 100, and everything from 80 to 100 was in red. On the left side was a pipe coming from the tank, or engine, as he called it. Six inches from the tank was a lever. The pipe got bigger after it left the lever. Then there was one more lever. The pipe turned upward with a large tank on top of it with a lid and two latches. Down in front of him were three more levers, one on the left, and one on the right. Another lever was located in the center. He sat there for a while trying to understand what he was looking at. After a while, he climbed down and finished his walk around.

By this time, Nate wanted to take a look. When he was done he went to Ben and Bill and said, "What we need to do is take the book tonight and read everything and compare what we have just seen. There is no need for us to try and unload this thing tonight. Bill, I'm going to give you the rest of the day off, and you can study the book. By the time I get done tonight, I will have a good look at it and tomorrow morning we will compare what we have read, and what we have seen. We will then start to unload this monster."

Everybody stood around and talked for awhile, and Ben took his tour. They agreed to meet in the morning and start their work.

They couldn't wait! The men were out of bed at 5 am and down at the shop, where they sat down at a table in Ben's office and asked, "What did you find out?"

Ben spoke up, saying, "Fellows, I feel I have taken unfair advantage of you, because I have read the book many times when I was trying to make the decision to buy the tractor. I will tell what I saw and read, and you can take it from there.

"On the back where you saw the platform is the place to store wood. The two cans on the right side are for extra water. Now, the can on top is where we fill the boiler or tank. The reason for the two levers on the tank is that we cannot add water to the boiler when it is under pressure. We fill the can with the front lever closed, and then we close the back lever. With the back lever and lid closed, we now can open the front lever and let the water in. If it is not enough to bring the boiler to the full mark, it will have to be redone.

"The three levers in front next to the driving wheel do the following: the one in the middle makes the tractor go forward, the one on the right makes the wheels turn to the right, the one on the left makes the wheels turn to the left, the thing with the rope is a whistle, the other thing in the middle of the boiler is a pop-off valve and allows the steam to escape if it goes too far above 80 PSI.

Nate spoke up and said, "Well, you got pretty much the same as I did, but I think you explained it better. What do you think, Bill?"

"I think you are right, and the rest we will just have to learn," responded Bill.

Ben said, "I think you two should take charge of this tractor."

Nate exclaimed, "If I'm going to be in charge of it, then let's get water into it and get a fire started!"

"Very well, Mr. Owens, let's do it!" exclaimed Bill.

Then Ben suggested, "By the way, the tube on the right side holds a rake or poker to stir the firebox with. We should use good, clean water and we can use river water if we strain it. We should also make a big tank and catch rain water later. It will make the boiler last longer."

With that done, they headed out the door to start the show. Nate said to Bill, "You get two of the Indians, some drums, and a wagon. I would try and use as much spring water as you can get. It will be nice and clean and we will put a rag over the fill can as we pour it into the boiler. Ben and I will start to get the firewood ready, and the block and tackles on the back."

Within two hours, Bill had eight barrels of water and two buckets. They started to fill the boiler. The two Indians dipped and handed Bill water. By this time, Ben and Nate had the tie down cut loose and the firebox loaded. They were ready to light a fire. It took a while to get the fire to burn well, but soon it started to get hot. Nate kept stirring it, and after a half hour the gauge began to show a number. After another 30 minutes, the pressure was up to 80 PSI. Bill was going to be the driver. He first pushed the lever on the right side open just a little. The wheel on the right side of the tractor started to move. He pushed it open a little bit more, and the wheel turned faster. It was learned this wheel would run a belt which would run the saw mill or thrashing machine. When he pulled the lever back, the wheel began to slow down. He then tried the lever on the left and the same thing happened.

Bill then asked Nate if they were ready. Nate said, "Yes, we hope so!"

He had set the block so that there were 12 inches of slack in the ropes. This would allow them to see how well the tractor moved forward. Bill pulled the middle lever back to him slowly. At first the tractor did not move, but as he pulled it back a little bit more, the tractor moved under its own power forward. He pushed the lever forward and it stopped. This time, Nate let out about two feet of slack in the rope, and again Bill pulled the lever back and the tractor moved forward. This action was kept up until the tractor was on the ground. Everyone was so happy they were jumping around like kids. "It works! It works!"

By now, some of the women had come up to see the excitement.

With the unloading, the pressure had dropped down to 60 PSI, so they raked the firebox and checked the water. It was ok, and in a few minutes the pressure was back to 80 and Nate said, "Let's take it home".

With that, Bill got back up onto the seat and pulled the lever back, and off they went. It did not go very fast and it was hard to steer, but Bill was young and strong, and he did well. He drove the tractor down to the shop and parked it alongside their shop. Ben wanted to drive a little bit, and Nate wanted to drive. After everyone had a turn, they let it cool down.

It was now up to Nate and Bill to get the thrashing machine done. Right on time Nate said, "We think we have a thrashing machine ready. We had a little trouble trying to see how long we wanted the belt that runs from the tractor to the thrasher, but we have got it figured out after cutting it off twice. What we have found is that by opening the steam valve that runs the wheel, we can control the speed of the thrashing machine. We also have the same control on the blower wheel, and have discovered that we can run almost one hour without the steam pressure going below 60 PSI, and the thrasher still runs pretty fast. I can tell you this much, we have got a winner here!

"As the grain is fed into the front end of the thrasher, the beater bars break the straw away from the grain head. The blower then blows the straw into the canvas ducking we have made that directs it to a pile. The grain keeps tumbling around in the beater cage, thus blowing out more straw and grain shells. As the cage becomes full, the beater bars push the grain over the edge of the cage into a sack. We may not have the cleanest grain, but it is a lot faster than what we have been doing. I'm sure we will find a way to get it a little cleaner before we grind it into flour. We may not have to clean the grain we grind into feed."

"Well, you have made it on time. Jim and Sam are going to cut wheat next week, weather permitting. If you fellows are happy with it, let's move it down there in the pasture with the big double gate. Let's locate it so we have lots of room to get wagons in and out and use the straw pile for feed later," said Ben.

"Good idea Ben. We will block it up and get the belts ready. We will get clean water and wood on hand, and we will be ready for Jim and Sam," responded Nate

Ben said, "I can't wait to see this thing in action!"

Monday came and Jim and Sam were in the field before sunrise. They had taken four of the Indian workers with them to rake behind the sickle cutter and load the wagons. Tom, Bill, Nate, and Ben had gotten the boiler on the tractor ready to go, with pressure at the 80 mark. The first wagonload of wheat pulled up to the front of the machine at 7 am. Bill climbed up and started the machine and blowers. He set the speed at half to see how things would work out. The first pitchfork full of wheat went into the thrasher and the machine changed sounds just a little. They could not believe how fast it got rid of each fork full that was fed to the machine. Within five minutes, they had wheat ready to be sacked.

Doc walked up about then and said, "I will sew the sacks for you, if somebody will load them."

Ben was jumping around like a kid getting to go fishing for the first time. He said, "Nate, I just cannot believe your skills. You and Bill are the best in the land! Besides, when these farmers around here find out what this thing will do, they will want us to thrash for them. We can do that providing we do not have to take the tractor too far and the road is fair. Rather than charge them money, let's do it for two percent of the crop and our meals for the crew each day. That way, we will have more grain and feed to sell."

Nate responded, "You may think we are the greatest machine builders, but you sure don't miss much when it comes to making money!"

"Just remember, Mr. Owens, we are a team. Let's keep training people like Tom, Henry, Bill, and all the others on the things we do, because we are not getting any younger," stated Ben.

"You are right. I don't hit as many blows with my hammer as I used to," agreed Nate.

By noon they had finished almost half of the 60 acres, and it looked like they were getting about 30 bushels per acre. They had over 90 sacks done.

Ben said, "I just cannot believe it. This machine is going to change the way we grow grain."

There was so much excitement going on: the kids were playing in the straw, one of the workers was bagging the grain, Doc was sewing the sacks up, and Ben was throwing them onto the wagon. Bill was firing the boiler, directing the straw blower, and making sure everything was working well.

Henry's wife and Elisabeth came out to the work area and said, "Since you fellows cannot hear the bell, it's time to eat some lunch." The men started to slow things down so they could quit for a while.

After lunch they went back to the work at hand. Their thoughts were to finish the 60 acres by dark and start on the rye the next day. While all this excitement was going on, a rider would stop now and then to get a closer look at what was happening. It would not be long until other farmers would want their crops thrashed. Ben did not think there would be any callers this year because it was so late, but next year was another story.

The mill was running 10 hours every day. Most of the corn was done for this year, except for what Ben held back - 1,000 bushels to blend with rye and bone meal for feed. He needed to get the first load of feed to the trading post and see what people thought about it. He had some sacks painted with "O & S Grain Co. FEED" written on them. The first load was due to go out on the next train Friday. That way, it should arrive at the trading post on Monday.

When Bill Hammersmith slid open the railcar door and saw the feed sacks, he couldn't wait to open one. When he looked inside he said, "My God, this will be great as chicken feed or animal feed. Let me get Captain Kelly over here and see if he will take some of this for the Fort."

He unloaded the car and around three pm Captain Kelly rode up. They went into the warehouse to look at the feed. After inspecting the bags, the Captain said, "What is Ben Sharp trying to do, set the world on fire? I will take ten bags and let you know in a week what we have here."

"Very good," said Mr. Hammersmith. "I won't even put it on your bill for two weeks."

In the meantime, Bill sold five bags to the local stable owner. He was hoping Ben would ship another car load Friday.

Captain Kelly came back in the store on Friday and said, "It is very good stuff. My animals can't get enough of it, and the chickens are laying more and bigger eggs. So you tell Ben if he ever thinks about shutting that mill down, that I will send the Army out there!"

Everything seemed to fall into place: thrashing machine, sickle cutter, big plows, corn Sheller, flour, meal, and now animal feed. Business was good for the O & S Grain Co. and the days flew by like lightning!

13:

It did not seem like any time had gone by before Ben was told the Fort had moved. He thought he had better take one of the boys and ride north to check things out and see what was going on. He asked Doc if he wanted to go along. Doc said he would like to see that part of the country. After all, that was originally going to be his first choice for a home, and he would like to see what was up there.

Monday morning they saddled their horses, got some food, water, and sleeping bags, and off they went. Ben did not know where he was going. He thought the trip would take the better part of a week - two days up, two days back, and a day or so for business. It had to be at least 75 miles up there. On day two, they arrived in Omaha around 3 pm.

Now they thought Lincoln was a growing town, but it was nothing like what they were seeing here. People were everywhere, and Ben thought this must be all the people in the world. They did not have any idea where the Fort was, so they stopped in front of a stable to ask a man if he knew anything about Fort Henry. The man said it was 15 miles north near the Platte River.

Ben asked Doc, "What do you want to do? Should we stay here tonight and take care of business tomorrow and the ride out there; or ride out tonight, do our business at the Fort, and then come back?"

Doc said, "No! Let's stay here and nose around a bit, find a place to stay, and get something to eat. Tomorrow we can ride north, take care of the Fort, and then head home."

Ben said, "I like that."

With that, they started the horses at a slow walk down Main Street. It was just not real what they were looking at. There were leather shops, gun shops, saloons, barber shops, hotels, and anything you needed - wagons and people everywhere!

Ben said, "Let's ride down to the river where we came across, and see what has changed". They kept going down Main Street and after five minutes the river came up, but they were lost. It did not look like the same place they came to 15 years ago! The ferry had been replaced by a steamboat. It was flat like the ferry, but it was powered by a steam engine and a water wheel. It carried far more people, wagons, and teams. After twenty minutes of standing around watching, they headed back to town.

After a short distance, a restaurant and hotel came into view that looked good. Ben got down and went in. The man at the desk said he had rooms and they were 50 cents and you could eat next door at the restaurant, and they had a stable out back. Ben took two rooms and paid the man.

Doc asked, "Do you have a place where a man can get a good bath?"

"Yes sir! Over at the barbershop you can get a haircut, shave, and a bath."

Ben said, "I might take them up on all of it."

Doc said, "Me too. When we get home, our wives won't know us."

The man at the desk gave them keys for rooms 7 and 9 just across the hall from one another. Ben wanted to check out his room before he put the horses away. The room was nice and it had a window, and a vanity with a wash bowl and pitcher. A peg was on the back of the door to hang your hat and gun. Ben stepped across the hall and asked how Doc's room was, and he said it was fine with him.

It was now 5 pm, so Doc said, "Let's get cleaned up and then eat".

They went out the door and down the street to the barber shop. There was one man in the chair and two sitting along the wall. Ben asked if they could get a bath and the barber motioned toward a door on the left of the room. Doc pushed it open and went in. There was a man at the counter and Doc asked him how much a bath would cost. The man said, "25 cents for the bath and towels, and a washcloth is another 10 cents."

Doc said, "We will take two."

When they went back out into the barber shop the three men were gone. Ben asked if they could get a shave and a haircut and the barber said, "Yes sir! You sure can. You will be my last two customers for the day. That will be 25 cents for a shave and hair cut."

Ben suggested, "Doc, since this was your idea you can go first. I want to see what you are going to look like. We just rode in this afternoon and we are looking for a feed store or a trading post."

The barber responded, "We have two. There is a big one up on Oak Street, and then we have another on Indian Ridge not too far from the cattle pens."

It took about 45 minutes for the two of them to get done.

It was 6.30 pm when they went into the restaurant. The place was pretty crowded. They found a table and sat down. In a few minutes, a young woman came over and asked them what they would like to eat. Ben said he would like a steak, potatoes, and corn on the cob. Doc said, "Make it two".

The young woman returned in a few minutes with everything they had asked for, plus a little gravy for the potatoes. The two men enjoyed their meal and sat there talking about the great job the thrasher had done, and how the machine would change farming.

"You know Ben; I started out to be a doctor. Now I'm a farmer and a doctor, and Sarah and I could not be more pleased. I thank God every day for running into you on that wagon trail. Thank you, Ben Sharp, for all you have done," said Doc.

Ben stated "Doc, you, and Sarah have paid your dues and you are still paying. No thanks are needed."

With that, Ben pushed his chair back a little and started to get up from the table. As he did so, a young cowboy with too much to drink stumbled into him.

Ben pulled the chair back and said, "I'm sorry, sir, I did not see you."

The cowboy said, "You God damn city slickers! You are all the same, always trying to push us working men around!"

Ben said, "No sir! I'm not a city slicker. I'm a farmer in town for a little business, and I'm not looking for a fight."

"You are wearing a gun, you sweet smelling son of a bitch. Do you know how to use it?" inquired the cowboy.

Ben said once more, "Sir! I'm not looking for trouble."

"Come on outside, you son of a bitch, and we will see how good you are!"

Ben took his time putting the chair back under the table. Slowly, he made his way to the door. As he opened the door to step out, the young cowboy was leaning against the hitching rail. "Here comes that yellow belly son of a bitch!" said the cowboy.

Ben did not say a word. Doc quickly stepped out the door and moved to Ben's left side. Ben walked straight up to the young man, and as he got within a foot of him he brought the broad side of his right hand up and slapped the man across the side of his face. He hit him so hard his head went back and his hat went flying off into the dirt. The young man's right hand went down for his pistol, and as he did Ben pressed him against the rail with his body and with his right hand he caught his arm.

Ben's left hand removed the pistol from its holster. He brought the pistol around in front; he opened the cylinder and dumped the shells onto the ground. He then cocked the pistol with the hammer back, turning the pistol upside down. With a hard blow he then struck the hammer against the rail post. The hammer snapped and the trigger fell to the ground. Placing the gun back into its holster, he then grabbed the young man by his shirt and pulled him over to the watering trough, dunking his head into the water. He picked up the man's hat, put it on his head, kicked him in the butt, and said, "Now go sleep off that whiskey before you get into trouble!"

Ben slowly walked back to the sidewalk, as Doc moved down the walk and joined him.

A few more steps and they entered the hotel. He said to Doc as they went up the stairs, "The last thing we need is a gun fight. That man could not have been much older than Tom or Henry."

"Well, I think you did a good job. Let's hope we can get out of town without any trouble."

Next morning they got a bite to eat and rode over to Oak Street to check on the trading post. The barber was right. It was big, and it looked like the place could pay its bills. Ben went in and asked if the owner was around. A boy behind the counter stuck his head around the door and said, "Mr. Miller, there is a man out here to see you."

In just a minute a tall man, Ben-sized, stepped out from the backroom, and said, "How can I help you?"

"I'm Ben Sharp, and this is Doc Martin. We own a grain company down on the Big Blue River, and we have cattle and chicken feed for sale. We also grind our own flour and cornmeal. Would you be interested in buying any of this?" asked Ben.

"Lord God, yes, man! Tell me a little bit about your operation," responded Mr. Miller.

"We have been down there 15, maybe 17 years, have a big grinding mill, and we have been selling to Bill Hammersmith at the trading post in Lincoln for close to ten years", began Ben.

"Yes, I have heard of Bill. I have never met him, but I understand he runs a fine store" interjected Mr. Miller.

"Yes sir! He pays his bills on time, and he has been a good customer. We have also been selling to the Army, but they have moved up here on us and that is why we are here. We will be talking to Captain Kelly tomorrow to see if he still needs our service," continued Ben.

Mr. Miller asked, "How would you get your products up here?

"Well sir, the railroad just put us in a siding last year, and we have been shipping by train. I think the train runs from Omaha up to Lincoln now. If it does, I can ship once a week, or once a month - whatever you want" answered Ben.

"Well, Mr. Sharp, we sure could use all the products you have just described. When do you want to start?" asked Mr. Miller.

"Well, we came up here to see Captain Kelly and his new Fort. We need to find out what he needs, and then we can make a better decision."

"Could I get your name and address, how you would like the bill made out, and where you want it shipped to?" asked Ben.

Very good Sir, we can do that," said Ben. Then Doc asked the young man behind the counter for a piece of paper and a pencil. He wrote down O & S Grain Company, General Delivery, Big Blue River, Omaha, Nebraska, and handed it to Mr. Miller. Mr. Miller then gave him his shipping address.

Ben said, "I will send you a letter as soon as I get back and let you know what Captain Kelly had to say, and when we could ship".

"Thank God you fellows stopped by. I need your products badly!" exclaimed Mr. Miller.

"By the way, Mr. Miller, do you know where the new Fort is located?" asked Ben.

"I have heard it is close to the mouth of Shell Creek and the Platte River. That is the best I can do for you. It will be a hard day's ride," replied Mr. Miller.

"Thank you Sir, you will be hearing from us," promised Ben.

As they mounted for the ride out to the Fort, Doc said, "We have had a good morning. Let's get out of town before that young cowboy gets his gun fixed."

"Not a bad idea," Ben replied, adding, "We sure don't need a gun fight!" They were as happy as could be that they had found a new customer, but Ben was beginning to worry that there was not enough product to supply everyone if Captain Kelly wanted a lot. They might not have enough to fill all the orders.

It was a nice day and with a long ride in front of them, they heeled the horses to a trot and headed northwest. They knew pretty much where they were going since they had come this way 17 years ago, but things had changed. There was a farm every few miles and the land looked different. Ben thought he would ride to the Platte and stay on the north side of the Platte until they came to the mouth of Shell Creek, or the Fort - whichever came first.

It was close to 6 pm when they spotted the Fort about a half mile up front of them, and about a mile north of the Platte. There was a big sign across the top of the gate that read, "WELCOME TO FORT HENRY". Riding up to a big building marked "Headquarters"; Ben dismounted and went up the steps. A guard at the top said in a firm voice, "State your business!"

"My name is Ben Sharp, and I would like to speak to Captain Kelly," stated Ben.

The guard said, "Sir, we do not have a Captain Kelly. We have a Major Kelly, but he is in Quarters."

"Please tell him that Ben Sharp is here to see him," requested Ben.

"Yes sir, will do!" replied the guard. With that, the guard was off the porch and heading for the building marked "OQ". Ben was watching as he knocked on the door. A woman opened the door and the guard said something to her he could not hear. A few minutes later, Major Kelly came to the door and seeing Ben on the porch made a gesture for him to come on over to the house.

Ben and Doc left their horses tied at the rail and walked over to the house. Ben stuck out his hand and said, "Congratulations on that Major rank!"

"Thank you, sir! The Army thought that since I had more people to take care of, they would raise my pay!" responded Major Kelly.

"Sir, I'm sorry to be so late, but we rode in from Omaha this morning. We had a little business to take care of and we got a late start," said Ben.

"Not a problem, Mr. Sharp, you are always welcome, day or night," replied Major Kelly.

"Major Kelly, I would like for you meet Doctor Martin. Doc is our partner, and also our doctor. Doc Martin, his wife Sarah and two sons are part owners of the O & S Grain Company, and we are darn glad to have them," stated Ben.

"Glad to meet you Sir, and if you ever want to leave the farm, we can always use a good doctor here at the Fort," said Major Kelly.

"Well, thank you Major, but I'm as happy as I could be down there with my people," replied Doc.

"Have you fellows had anything to eat?" asked the Major.

"Not since this morning," Ben replied.

"Well, let me get my boots on, and we will go over to the Mess Hall and see if the cook has got anything left," suggested Major Kelly.

They sat down at a table and the cook asked, "What would you fellows like?"

Doc spoke up, saying, "We are not picky, and we will take what is left over".

The cook replied, "Two leftovers coming up!"

In a few minutes, the cook brought over a tray with two plates full of stew, potatoes, peas, and two big briskets, and two big glasses of milk.

Ben said, "My God man, I cannot go to bed on all of this. I will have to go back to work!"

They all sat down at the table and Ben asked, "How do you like your new home?"

The Major said, "Its fine, but it is a lot more work than Omaha was. We have 150 men here, and Washington tells me they would like to bring that to 200 men by next summer. I guess they feel the country is growing and it needs more protection."

Ben inquired, "Sir, we rode up to see what you might need."

"We are just about out of everything", replied the Major, and then continued, "I need mules, horses, cornmeal, feed, and flour. When can you get me a few things?"

Ben answered, "Major, things have changed some since you left. I cannot bring you any livestock before the summer calving season is over, and it will take me three days to get here. Do you have a place to put them?"

"Yes sir! We have a big pasture out back that should graze a hundred head for two months," responded the Major.

"In that case, I will start a drive just as soon as I can get men out of the fields and calving is over. As to the other supplies, we are now shipping by train. Can you receive a railcar load and unload it?" inquired Ben.

"For now, the car can come to Omaha, and we will have to bring our supplies by wagon to the Fort. The government has promised us a rail siding by next fall. I'm sure we can take care of it until then," advised the Major.

"Major Kelly, I will take care of this first cattle drive. Sir, is there any way after this first drive you could send some men to make the next drive? I will feed and provide a place for them to sleep until the drive starts. I will also refill the chuck wagon. Major, I just don't have five or six men that I can pull out of the fields for 10 days to make the drive," stated Ben.

"Don't you worry about it, Ben, I have got some cowboys here as soldiers that would love to go on a 10 day TDY cattle drive. We can take care of that little problem!" declared the Major.

With dinner finished, Major Kelly said to one of the soldiers, "Go tell the Officer of the Day to meet me here in the Mess Hall".

"Yes Sir, will do!" said the soldier. In a little bit a Lieutenant Jones reported and asked the Major what he could do for him.

"Lieutenant, I would like for you to take these two men over to the bunkhouse and get them a bed, and see that their horses get rubbed down and fed."

"Will do, Sir!" replied the Lieutenant.

The Major said, "I will see you in the morning. What time do you plan on leaving?"

Ben said, "As early as we can, sir. It is a good two days' ride back home."

"I understand, and I will meet you here in the morning at 6 Am.," stated the Major.

"That will be fine, sir. We will be here," agreed Ben and Doc.

Next morning they all met once again at the Mess Hall where they were provided a big breakfast with all the trimmings.

Ben said, "Major, Doc, and I thank you for the business."

The Major responded, "Ben, it is you fellows I need to thank. I have 150 men here to feed, and you fellows are the men for the job. Plus, I know I can trust you, and I know the kind of products you deliver."

"Well, we just want you to know we are grateful," said Ben.

"Well, you are very welcome, and I wish you a good trip home," declared the Major.

With that, they all headed for the door as the Major said, "I have had your horses saddled and ready to go".

Ben said "Thank you sir and I will write just as soon as I get a better idea on how many cattle I can ship, and when the train will leave with your first shipment."

The sun was already in full view as Ben and Doc rode out the front gate. Doc said to Ben, "You know, if we can cover 5 miles every hour, we could be home by 8 pm."

"But Doc, that will make us ride an unbroken trail for two hours in the dark. I think we should quit about 5 pm. and do the rest tomorrow. Let's wait and see what five o'clock brings us," suggested Ben.

"You are right Ben, five o'clock it is," agreed Doc.

With that, they heeled their mounts into an easy trot and headed southwest.

In three hours they came upon a nice clear creek and decided to stop and let their horses drink and rest a bit. Ben pulled out some jerky and got his canteen out as they sat down on a big rock. It was mid-September 1820, and the men would be pulling corn in another month. By now, most of the new calves should be on the ground and he could get a good count on the amount of cattle he would be able to send north next spring. They had stopped growing rye, and had planted 150 acres of oats this last winter so they would have plenty of grain to grind.

Doc said, "We had better hit the trail again. We are not going to get home sitting here."

"You are right Doc, I just keep thinking about so many things that are going on" said Ben.

Doc advised, "You had better be thinking about the rain-storm that is building there in the west".

"Again, I think you are right. We will ride on for a while, keeping our eyes on a place to take shelter," said Ben.

After an hour or so, Ben spotted some thick brush a hundred yards off the trail and said to Doc, "Did you bring your rain gear?"

"I sure did, thanks to Sarah," replied Doc.

"Well, let's pull up over there by the brush, hobble the horses, and make a camp," advised Ben.

Ben had a small hand ax in his saddlebags, so he cut down a few of the brush and piled them on top of some other brush. They laid the saddle blankets on the ground under the roof. Doc cut some stakes and they laid their rain gear over the stakes. They placed their saddles under the shelter, and unrolled their bedrolls.

It was not raining hard, but it looked like it was going to. They could not build a fire, but they had jerky and water, and that was all they needed. The roof Ben had made out of brush was keeping most of the rain off of them, so they were looking forward to a good night of rest.

Next morning, the rain had stopped and they were up and ready before the sun. With a little luck and a hard day's ride, they would sleep in a real bed tonight, after a good meal. It was 5 pm when they rode across the railroad and headed for the barn. Nate had just finished the nightly meeting, and everyone was glad to see them back. While they were all together, Ben gave a short briefing on the trip, leaving out the drunken cowboy. Of course, old big-mouth Doc had to tell the story and everyone wanted all the details. With all of that to laugh about, it was off to supper and bed.

14:

Things had been going great. With eight plows working, they were farming 700 acres and had been for years. They would like to do 1,000 acres, but the tools and equipment would not let them. The Army had been taking 150 head of cattle every year since Doc and Ben went up to see the Fort in 1820.

By this time, Henry had five children: three boys and two girls. Tom and his wife had four kids: two boys and two girls. Joe had three boys and one girl. Sam and Little Flower had five children and Ben Jr. had two. Doc had really turned into a baby doctor, as he had delivered all 20 without a problem, and he was proud of all of them! He had doctored them when they acquired the mumps and measles and set all their broken bones. The kids had gone to school in their schoolhouse, and to the church they had built. Now, most of the older ones were going to school in Omaha and Lincoln.

The farm Nate sold when they left Ohio had been paid off for years, and he had the bank account moved from Ohio to Lincoln. Ben's house was still in his and Elisabeth's name, but was getting old by now. The gun business back in Ohio was still going well, and the brothers had been putting money in his account for 40 years.

The O&S Grain Company had made more money than the five owners knew what to do with; the Corporation was worth more than anyone could believe. It had been a good life for all of them. They were all getting older: Ben was now 78 years old, and Nate was 77. They were happy there were a lot of young people to keep O & S going for years and years. They had grandkids, and were about to start a new crop of great-grandkids to take care of things long after their passing.

Doc and Sarah were the youngest of the old ones, except for Henry. Both were going strong, and Doc was hoping he could deliver many more babies. All of the women for years had worn three hats: Sarah was Doc's nurse and the Company bookkeeper, while Elisabeth was the schoolteacher, and Helen was the Sunday school teacher and the Youth Group Supervisor. The men were proud of how these women had helped build the family and the Company. This was the early 1800s and everyone had the same chance as these people did, but they had succeeded where others had failed. This would be a head start for the younger people and the 1900s coming up. God had blessed these people and all their work.

Nate sat across from Ben as he fumbled with some papers he had on his desk. He thought, my God, he had known this man for over 50 years. He was more than a friend, and better than a brother, which he did not have. He thought about the time back in Ohio when they first planned to go west. How excited he was to build a gun that had now made history; but most of all, how he had led these people to so much success without getting mad, but with a strong hand and a gentle touch. No, Ben Sharp was not an average man - he was a godsend! He wondered if he wouldn't still be back in Ohio fixing wagons and shoeing horses if it had not been for this man. He also thought about the times Ben had saved his life when the Indians took his kids, and how he had come in contact with the first Indians on the Prairies, and how he had so skillfully avoided a confrontation. If it had not been for Ben, he might have let fright overcome him and run for his life. Not Ben Sharp! His action saved Nate's own life, and maybe the life of the whole train. He wished as he watched him that their lives could once again return to the ages of 26 and 25 but they had sons and grandsons, and life would go on.

It was the fall of 1854, and Elisabeth Sharp had just fed her husband a light breakfast. He had not been feeling well and was short of breath. She was sending him over to see Doc Martin about the problem and see what he had to say. As he came around the corner from the kitchen, he fell against the fireplace wall. Elisabeth saw him stagger and went to his side. She placed her head under his armpit and helped him back to the bedroom. She got him into bed and took off his shoes. Then she went out the door to get Doc Martin.

Doc and Sarah were having breakfast when she bolted through the door.

"Doc please come and look at Ben! He is sick!" pleaded Elisabeth.

"What is wrong with him?" asked Doc.

"I don't know" sobbed Elisabeth, adding, "He fell against the fireplace wall after breakfast".

"Let me get my bag, and I will be right with you," said Doc.

Sarah asked, "Do you want me to go with you?"

Doc replied, "No, not at this time!"

Doc hurried across the lot to the house, where he found Ben still on the bed as Elisabeth had left him. Doc opened his shirt to check his chest. His heart was uneven and was running at 90 to 120 beats per minute. Not good at all. "How much breakfast did he have?" asked Doc.

"Not much," replied Elisabeth.

"Well, let's prop him up so he can breathe a little better," suggested Doc. Then he took out some pills from his bag, and placed one under Ben's tongue.

"Can you get a glass of cold water?" asked Doc. Elisabeth was back in a minute and Doc said, "I think he has had a heart attack. I'm going to stay with him for a while. You go on and get out of here."

Elisabeth left the room and went over to tell Nate and Helen. She then asked Nate if he would find the boys, Tom and Ben Jr., and tell them about their father.

Nate said, "I sure will, and I will be over there just as soon as I find them".

Nate located Tom down by the barn taking care of the mules. Ben Jr. was coming out of his house. Tom threw up his hands and said, "Oh God, please be kind!"

All three men returned to the house where Doc greeted them with, "I have a sick man in there, and he doesn't need the three of you right now, so get out of here. I will keep you informed if anything changes."

With that, they all went into the front room and sat down.

By this time, Helen and Sarah showed up and they gathered around the kitchen table. Time lagged on. None of the O & S men used tobacco or drink, so a big pot of coffee was brewed up. Everyone had a cup, and the other O & S people began to show up to find out what was going on. The three men moved outside on the porch to cut down on the noise as they tried to answer their questions. Henry came in from the fields and said that farming would have to wait; he was going to stay here until he knew Ben was better.

Morning turned into noon, and noon turned into night. After all this time, Doc came out of the room and said, "Yes, Ben has had a bad heart attack. His heart has slowed down a great deal and he is resting well, and his breathing is slowly coming back to normal."

Nate asked, "Is he going to be all right, Doc?"

"I don't know. We will have to see through the night, and pray that a brighter day will come with the sunrise," replied Doc.

Tom asked, "Can we do anything?"

"No just pray, and we have to give him time to try and fight back," stated Doc.

Nate asked Doc, "Are you going to stay with him all night?"

Doc replied, "I will lie down in Tom's room."

Nate said, "In that case, I will sit with him. If I need you, I will wake you up."

Nate took up a chair next to Ben's bed where he could watch his chest rise and fall. He watched his face, and it seemed to be at peace. He sat there until well after midnight, then he got up from his chair and knelt by his bed, folded his hands, and looked west. *He prayed, "Oh merciful God who is greater than us, all I ask, Oh God, is for you to spare our brother, friend, and your servant. I know you just loaned him to us, but we love him and need him. Please restore his life and his good health. I ask God, as the morning comes to a new day, as the sun comes up, please God, and bring with it our old friend. I ask this, Oh God, as my father, that you grant me this prayer. Amen."*

The night wore on, and as far as he could tell there was little change in his breathing. Nate leaned over and said to him, "Rest well, my friend. You need to get your strength back. If you need to pee raise your finger, and I will get you up." Ben nodded his head very slowly that he understood.

Elisabeth came into the room with a big cup of coffee and asked Nate, "What would you like to eat?"

Nate answered, "Nothing right now; coffee is fine. Ben has rested well all night, and has been awake now and then, but only stares at the ceiling. All the people that come by to check on him this morning tell them that he is resting well, but there is no change as far as we can see."

"Nate, don't you want to lie down? You have been up all night," asked Elisabeth.

"No! I'm fine. This coffee will pick me right up" replied Nate.

Helen came in to check on her husband, but knew she could not get him out of that room once Doc had let him in. She was not going to plead with him.

Doc came in and did his check, and said, "His heart is almost normal, but we need to try and get some nutrients into him if we can". Then he said to Nate, "I'm worried because I do not know if the heart is recovering, or if it is getting weaker. I'm also afraid that if I give him something, it could make his weak heart work harder, and I do not want that."

With that, he went out to see what Elisabeth could cook up. Shortly, she came back with a cup of warm chicken soup.

Doc turned to Elisabeth and said, "Can you bring me a tea-spoon and a clean towel?"

She said, "Yes!"

Nate lifted Ben's head and shoulders just a little bit and placed a pillow under him. Doc dropped a drop of the soup onto the back of his hand because the soup had to be almost the same temperature as the body. Doc then filled the spoon half full, and pressed it against Ben's lips.

Ben was awake, but did not speak. You could see in his face and eyes that he knew they were there and trying to help him. Doc gave him three teaspoonfuls and then wiped the spoon off. Then he gave him two spoons of water. They then removed the pillow and checked his heart rate once more. The rate seemed to be normal, maybe two or three beats higher than before the soup. He would check again in a few minutes.

The morning wore on and Doc checked the heart rate every 10 to 15 minutes. Around noon he told Nate he did not like it. It seemed to him that Ben's skin was losing its color and seemed to be turning gray. This told Doc the heart was not delivering blood to the body as it needed. All they could do was wait.

At 4 o'clock Doc checked once more, and turned to Nate and said, "I'm afraid we are losing our friend. His heart rate has dropped to 46 and his skin is getting worse. I'm going to leave him in your and God's hands. I have done all I can do".

With that, he left the room and found Elisabeth and the three children there in the kitchen. He took Elisabeth into his arms and said to her, "I think we are going to lose him. He is very weak and his skin is losing its color, which means the heart is getting weaker. I have done all I can do".

"I know that, Doc!" exclaimed Elisabeth. With that, she broke into tears as Tom took her into his arms. She asked, "Can I see him?"

Doc said, "Nate is still with him, and yes, I don't see why not".

Elisabeth went into the room and said to Nate, "I need to be with him for a while."

Nate picked up his chair and moved it over by the window, where he looked out into the night sky, but he did not leave the room.

Elisabeth knelt down by Ben's bedside and placed her right arm over his body. She cried softly and put her lips by his ear. She whispered into his ear, "Ben, please don't leave me! I need you so much, and I love you as much as I love God. I have begged God all day not to take you. Please Ben, don't go!" She lay there with her arm across his body. It seemed she could tell he knew she was there and felt at peace.

She stayed there for a long time, until Tom came to the doorway and asked, "Mother, are you all right?"

With that, she got up and went to his arms as he walked her back to the kitchen. Nate returned to Ben's bedside as Helen came in. She said, "Nate, you need to get some rest and something to eat. You have been here two days."

"No! I will not leave my friend. He is on his way to God's kingdom and I will walk with him to the gates. No! I will not leave until the Lord takes his hand."

She knew there was no use arguing with her husband at this time and left the room.

Nate sat with him until midnight. When he knew he was about to draw his last breath, he got up and went to his side. He picked up his hand and said, "Ben, my friend, I love you with all my heart. I will turn you over to God Almighty. Please save me a place."

With that he bent down and kissed him on the forehead. Benjamin Joseph Sharp was gone. God rest his soul!

THE END

ABOUT THE AUTHOR

The author has been married 62 years. He and his wife Elisabeth now live high over the Missouri River, just a short distance from the Daniel Boone Home Site, in Missouri rich wine Country. They have traveled the world over and lived many years abroad. Norman is strong in Environmental Engineering and Research, and has now etched his name in the invention and writing world.

TO FIND OUT ALL YOU WANT TO KNOW
ABOUT THE NATION CONVERTING TO THE
CFL LIGHT BULB BY 2012: PLEASE CLICK THIS
SITE: NSPSAFETY.COM. Remember environment
safety is not an idea, but a must! In order for all
nations and its people to live safely on the same planet.